Praise for

Sorry, B

"Here, since Explore Armenia was so central to the plot, Voskuni fills the book with details about food, history, dances, songs, etiquette, stereotypes, politics, and even artistic motifs. . . . The overall effect is celebratory and defiant, and it pairs beautifully with Nar's journey to fully accept who she is."

—*The New York Times Book Review*

"Underneath the humor is such an important story of love between two women and the journey to rediscovering Armenian culture and heritage."

—Jesse Q. Sutanto, bestselling author of
The Good, the Bad, and the Aunties

"A beautiful love letter to Armenian culture wrapped up in a warm and witty romance that absolutely sizzles with chemistry. Like heroine Nareh, Voskuni is forging a remarkable path, and I will gladly follow wherever it leads!"

—Dahlia Adler, author of *Going Bicoastal*

"*Sorry, Bro* is one of my new favorite romances! Sharp, funny, and full of heart, it's a love letter to Armenian culture and a thoughtful exploration of the ways our roots define us, all wrapped up in the most delightful romance. I couldn't put it down!"

—Jenny L. Howe, author of *On the Plus Side*

"Taleen Voskuni expertly braids romance with jaw-dropping atmosphere and swift hits of knowledge and strength. She pours her heart onto the page with power and beauty in a way that makes readers feel seen and cared for. . . . *Sorry, Bro* is as indulgent as it is profound, breathtaking as it is healing, and in one word: EXQUISITE."

—Courtney Kae, author of *In the Case of Heartbreak*

"The most heartwarming tale of family, heritage, loving bravely, and loving yourself, with a humor that adds a light touch to the poignant themes and a vivid San Francisco setting that brings the whole story to life. *Sorry, Bro* made me laugh and touched me deeply in equal measures."

—Kyla Zhao, author of *Valley Verified*

"Voskuni debuts with a bighearted queer rom-com uniquely inflected with Armenian American culture. . . . This is a treat."

—*Publishers Weekly*

"With this radiantly ravishing debut, Voskuni beautifully illustrates the courage it can take to be your own true self and risk everything for love." —*Booklist* (starred review)

"Voskuni's debut is equal parts comic, heartfelt, and profoundly rooted in Armenian culture, with a lead you'll want to befriend and a romance you'll want to cheer on in equal measure. A sparkling story about love, family, and identity."

—*Kirkus Reviews* (starred review)

Berkley titles by Taleen Voskuni

Sorry, Bro

Lavash at First Sight

Lavash at First Sight

TALEEN VOSKUNI

Berkley Romance

NEW YORK

BERKLEY ROMANCE
Published by Berkley
An imprint of Penguin Random House LLC
penguinrandomhouse.com

Library of Congress Cataloging-in-Publication Data

Names: Voskuni, Taleen, author.
Title: Lavash at first sight / Taleen Voskuni.
Description: First edition. | New York: Berkley Romance, 2024.
Identifiers: LCCN 2023048579 (print) | LCCN 2023048580 (ebook) |
ISBN 9780593547328 (trade paperback) | ISBN 9780593547335 (epub)
Subjects: LCGFT: Romance fiction. | Lesbian fiction. | Novels.
Classification: LCC PS3622.O84 L38 2024 (print) |
LCC PS3622.O84 (ebook) | DDC 813/.6—dc23/eng/20231017
LC record available at https://lccn.loc.gov/2023048579
LC ebook record available at https://lccn.loc.gov/2023048580

First Edition: May 2024

Printed in the United States of America
1st Printing

Book design by Diahann Sturge-Campbell

For queer Armenians everywhere

Chapter One

$\mathcal{J}$ open the conference room door, balancing my laptop (Air, for efficiency) and water bottle (navy blue, for subliminal "I'm not a girlie girl" vibes), and am happily surprised to find my boyfriend, Kyle, sitting in a swivel chair, concentrating on his screen.

"Early for my meeting? I'm honored," I say, sliding next to him. *My good luck charm*, I think, right before the biggest presentation of my career.

God, he's hot. I never thought I'd be with a guy like this, the tennis player look: tall with thin, toned limbs and thick, almost-wavy, almost-blond hair. He looks perilously handsome in his blue oxford button-down. I idolized men like this back in high school and none of them would ever look at me. Me, the perfectly average in every way, swarthy Armenian girl. But guess what, thick eyebrows and big butts are in now, and I bagged my dream guy; he's mine.

I rest my hand on his knee, and he instantly sloughs it off. Ugh, his stupid rules, I forgot. But we're in the room without any windows facing the office, with an opaque door. Seemed safe to me.

"Not at work, Ellie," he chides.

Our dating is a secret even though we're in lateral positions, so it's technically allowed—we don't even report to the same boss! Kyle goes to such great lengths to hide our relationship at work and outside work that sometimes I worry he's lost interest in me. Since he's not from the Bay Area and moved out here for this job, most of his buddies are his coworkers, so when he's out with them, I'm not allowed. But then he'll text me Friday late evening and come over, and he'll grab my waist and lift me up to kiss me like we're the only two people in the world.

The thought of it stirs me, and I whisper into his ear, "Right, I'll have to wait until after work to give you the present I've been working on."

He pushes his swivel chair away and, damn it, looks like I've gone too far. I'll have to be in damage control mode. "I'm sorry, I'm sorry," I say before he speaks.

Then he does. "I'm not sure we should keep doing this."

He's serious. The way he looks at me isn't with any of his Friday night desire—it's the way he looks at one of our coworkers when he's rejected their idea for being "too out of scope."

The blue of his eyes that had me thinking of him as my secret ocean-eyed boyfriend now feels empty and vast. The sharpness of his features, which I'd always imagined gently pricking me in the most enticing ways, morphs into ice picks.

"I can be more subtle, I promise. I lost myself there, that wasn't me."

I need this, I need him. It's only been a few months, but he's the one for me. I could see us working our way up the ranks, a power couple now at Abilify and then beyond. Two Fortune 500 CEOs, married. Think of the Bloomberg profiles. Hell, he's so hot we might even make *Vanity Fair*.

His voice is almost even, except for a hint of disgust in it. "I've been wanting to tell you. This isn't working. I feel like I'm living two lives; I hate it."

He hates it. He hates being with me. He hates *me*. The logic is simple, sound, and I'm not talking myself out of it. He's doing it, he's breaking up with me now, in the goddamn Wallaby conference room (all of the rooms are named after Australian creatures because of the origins of Jack, Abilify's cofounder), four minutes before the chairs fill up with our company's most important directors and VPs.

I need this account. I'd practiced my slides over twenty times and got feedback from all my direct reports. It was supposed to be perfect. Now I can't even remember the title.

Instead, images from the weekend fill my head, of curling up beside him under his tartan duvet, the hour far too late, abandoned glasses of scotch on the nightstand.

"We were getting so close. I thought we were going to start"— I'm almost too embarrassed to say it— "dating. For real, and be your actual girlfriend. You told me all those things about your brother—"

"Stop. It's done. I'm sorry I had to do it here, but I've been holding it in for days."

The shock of him wanting to break up with me for days

is interrupted by the Tremendous Trio—the three women I manage—pushing open the conference door. The first of them, Nina, stops short when she spots Kyle and me. "We can . . . come back?"

They know. Kyle and I are supposed to be a secret, but it's what he wanted, not what I wanted, so I couldn't help but tell my crew anyway. Not like it came as a surprise; Abby was all over it with her intuition and had been dropping hints for weeks. I felt slightly uncomfortable sharing about my love life with my direct reports, but I tried to keep it as vague and professional as possible. No comments about a certain penchant for reverse cowgirl, for instance.

I wave her off. "Meeting's starting in a few, come in." I am doing my best impression of a normal, happy person. I rush over to their side of the conference table. Kyle loses himself in his computer.

"You all feeling ready with your sections?" I ask them.

"Entirely. I committed it to memory and have written out and answered in my head all possible questions that may be fielded." That's Jasmine, the quant star of the group.

"Are . . . you ready?" Abby asks me, voice uneasy.

Never show weakness as the leader. I need to turn these feelings to anger and then channel it into dominating this presentation and landing Operation Wolf for my team. Screw Kyle and his sneaking around with me. He thinks he's better than me? He's a nobody from some Nowheresville town. Which, admittedly, is pretty cool that he made the journey all the way out here on his own. No! He's the worst.

"Totally," I tell her as bile rises in my throat.

It's then that the CEO, Reid Erikson, pushes in. He is one of the only people in the company who scare the shit out of me, with his bald head and missile eyes, his targeted commands, and his whole lack-of-smiling thing. The man always wears a Patagonia vest, without fail, daily, except on the one or two hundred-degree days where he removes it, revealing a Patagonia-branded T-shirt underneath.

I didn't know he would be attending this meeting. He was not on the invite list, but Operation Wolf is a big deal. The cold of the conference room settles over me, like he brought the Nordic winds in with him.

He's trailed by the cofounder and president, Jack, who plants himself in a corner and says in his Australian accent, "Y'all mind if I do some squats in here?" No one minds, and Jack begins bending his ass toward the window, up and down.

Then rush in the VPs and directors, including my boss, Jamie, the marketing VP. Jamie's . . . okay. I don't feel like she's necessarily rooting for my success, but her insistence on perfection, especially with presentation slides, has pushed my abilities to the next level. She's an odd one. Always has her nails perfectly manicured and sports curated minimalist jewelry but also is really buff, loves hiking and skiing, and never eats. Well, not true—she seems to subsist on Oreo snack packs stashed in her purse. I nod to her briefly—Jamie likes brief—and she acknowledges me with a blink.

The whole reason we're here is that we're in the process of wooing Abilify's potentially biggest client, Zarek's, the world's largest international coffee chain, whose logo is a wolf, to join our performance management platform.

That's right, we do performance review software. Keeping track of how good or crappy your employees are. Not exactly the most inspiring product of all time, but it's a solid group of people, and we're growing fast. They call us a unicorn in Silicon Valley, meaning we're already worth a billion dollars. The founders (including the terrifying Reid) took a chance on me when I was no one, and now look where I am: senior product marketing manager. Just one tiny hop step away from director, which is practically in smelling distance. All I need to do is land Operation Wolf.

I peer at Kyle, who has not looked up, and is angry-typing, which at this company is a show of deep focus, and revered by all. Don't bother someone who is angry-typing.

I step to the front of the room, and flawlessly transfer my slides to the conference room's screen. Which is saying something, because every room transfers differently, and all of them are multi-stepped and often buggy, but I made it my mission when we got the new tech installed to never be that person who can't figure out how to get her slides up on the screen, and have to ask for . . . ugh . . . *help*.

But when I scan the room, the morning light breaking through the fog, even Reid's presence doesn't bother me as much as seeing Kyle, who still hasn't looked up from his damn computer. Last week we changed up our routine, and instead of hiding at one of our houses, we went out to Emerald Eyes, a club full of young twentysomethings, which I took as a sign that things were going well. When I realized on the way out that I lost my phone, he ran back in and made a huge point of searching the dance floor, finding the manager, and yelling at unhelpful employees. That was it, I thought, he obviously cares about me. Now I'm wondering if he's just a power-tripping sadist.

I keep vacillating between hatred toward him and self-pity toward myself. I want to jump onto the table and point at Kyle and yell, "We were together, I was falling in love with him, and he broke my heart five fucking minutes ago," and then kneel down and burst into tears. Those imaginary tears feel very tempting, and a little too real, like they could actually happen.

Jamie clears her throat, breaking my reverie. I read the title slide in my head: *Operation Wolf: Taming the Beast / Customized Portal for Prospective Client*. But I cannot speak. Something is happening to my eyes; they're getting hot, wet. My throat swells, and I know if I say one word, it's all going to come spilling out, fountains of tears and choked cries.

But everyone would think it's because I'm nervous about this presentation, which is not the case. So I let out a couple of closed-mouth coughs bordering on chokes, put up a finger, and crease my eyes into seriousness, as if there's an involuntary physical battle being waged inside me (which there is), and then, to a bevy of stunned and concerned faces, I step out of the conference room, run up two flights of stairs until I get away from the Abilify offices, fly into the bathroom, and let everything out. Then I pray I haven't ruined it all.

* * *

I REALLY DON'T deserve my team. In my stead, Nina stepped up and began presenting my slides as well as hers, and she, Abby, and Jasmine switched off until I walked back in four minutes later as if nothing had happened. As I've learned from watching leaders, I simply said, "Excuse me. Thanks for taking over, team," and then jumped in where they left off. I resolved not to look anywhere near Kyle, and that tactic seemed to work.

Jamie had seen the presentation but still took notes in her immaculate handwriting in her millennial-pink notebook (even though she's a Gen Xer). She swears by writing everything down by hand and has gotten me in the habit of it, too. She made a couple of new points she'd never brought up before, so I had to gracefully concede to them, but it didn't bother me too much.

Reid asked a couple of questions that weren't difficult to answer—if you understand a CEO's mindset, which I made a point to do—and I gave concise, confident replies to them. He nodded shortly and settled back in his seat. Normally he'd put his feet up on the table, but there are too many people in the conference room for that.

And on the final slide and some brief discussion, the magic words come from Jamie. "It sounds like we're all in agreement here. Ellie, your team can proceed with this portal vision. Please stay in close sync with tech and sales as you build it out. We'll need it done in two weeks."

I should feel elated, getting this validation and green light to move forward, but I don't. I feel dry, unwanted, like Jamie ripped a page out of her notebook, crumpled it up, and tossed it.

"Thank you," I say, a lot more coolly than I would have if my heart hadn't been recently trampled over. I wonder if that makes me more of a boss, not showing excitement. Then I wonder if that's really who I want to be, and immediately shove that thought away. Of course it is.

Chapter Two

*A*t my desk, after a congratulatory huddle with the Tremendous Trio, I tell them we're all going out to a celebratory lunch at Zorba's, on me. They deserve so much more, too, but I will be sure, as always, to make it clear in their performance reviews. I check my phone. A missed call from my mom plus a text.

> How are you Nazeli jan? Give me call to say hi

My family refuses to call me by Ellie, my nickname, and sticks to my real name, Nazeli. It sounds beautiful in Armenian but awful translated into English, like a portmanteau of nauseating and mausoleum-y. So professionally, I go by Ellie. Mom called minutes after Kyle dumped me (a lump rises in my throat thinking those words). The woman has a sixth sense, though she never knew Kyle and I were dating. I knew she'd lament yet another white boyfriend, so I was keeping him hidden unless things started to progress. Which, of course . . . I guess my instinct was right.

I hole up in the phone booth Abilify has purchased—not like a red British phone booth, but a sleek modern one, sort of like a sexy coffin with a window, plunked down in the corner of the office. There's a decent view of all the desks, including Kyle's, though he's not here yet—he's probably in some other meeting, probably completely over me.

The phone booth still smells new, that freshly manufactured plastic scent that hits hard as soon as the door shuts. I dial my mom and she picks up after several rings.

"Nazig jan," (the diminutive of Nazeli) she starts. "You haven't called. Are you okay?"

We didn't talk for one day, which is enough for an Armenian parent to file a missing person report. I'm twenty-seven, unmarried, and live away from home, which is a cardinal sin, and believe me, the tears and stomps were aplenty when I announced, at twenty-five, that I was moving out to an apartment in the city, with a *roommate*. They're over it now, though.

"I'm fine," I say.

"You don't sound very happy. Are you eating okay?"

"Oh yeah."

I haven't been. Cooking is usually one of my most favorite things to do—especially with my parents, anything from prepping a big Armenian Christmas feast to a casual Sunday dinner, which we used to do all the time—but with all the planning for Operation Wolf, plus my weekend nights being devoted to Kyle, I haven't spent much time in the kitchen, with or without my parents. Takeout and the Whole Foods hot bar when I'm too hungry to wait. What I wouldn't give for a sini kufte right now, the ultimate comfort food, a meat-on-meat pie spiced with cumin and pine nuts. Kneading the meat side by side with my mom sounds like the most relaxing thing in the world right about now.

"You are lying, but that's okay. I make you harisseh and bring to you tonight."

"No, Mom, it's okay. I'm fine. It's a half-hour drive."

"It's no problem. Rima makes every meal for her son; he has not cooked once since he left the home. Did you hear . . ." she says, then launches into a five-minute monologue about Rima's son, which I have to interrupt, otherwise I'll be sitting in this phone booth all day listening to stories about people I hardly know.

"How's the business going?" I ask, even though I know it's going just fine, same as always. My parents own Hagop's Fine Armenian Foods, a packaged food company that makes lavash, falafel packs, manti, and dolmas, and that used to make hummus until the market got too crowded. They mostly sell in Middle Eastern stores throughout California and two local San Francisco grocery co-ops.

"Is going okay, we are preparing for the Chicago conference. You know Ned Richardson is going to be there and Bab was able to set up a meeting with him. If it's successful, we can be in True Food Grocers chain, can you believe?"

Huh. That would be a huge deal, major growth for the company. Before I can respond, she goes on. "You would be very good at that meeting. You know all the business talk and how to be around these people. Bab and I . . ." Here she hesitates a moment. "We want you to come to Chicago, help us. We are getting old now. This year, is harder for us to carry all the tables and food everywhere. You know Bab's knee, not getting any better. And I am afraid what the Chicago trees will do to my allergies. I don't know those trees."

The conference is next week, and with Operation Wolf, there's no way. Plus, my parents are notorious for naysaying any business help I offer them. Their branding isn't up-to-date; it looks so old-school. The name alone is a bit of a mouthful and gives off a nineties vibe. I've tried to get them to update their design a million times, but they haven't listened. We've gone through this song and dance of "please we need your help but don't change a single thing we're doing" so often that I've soured a bit on their business. If they'd let me in, just a little, they'd see how much we could change things together. But I know they won't budge on a thing when it comes to Hagop's Fine Armenian Foods. I do feel for them lugging all their stuff around, but I tell my mom, "I can't just take off work like that."

She is undeterred. "Only three days of work to take off. Wednesday, Thursday, Friday. Then the Saturday Sunday you don't have to take off. You telling me you can't take three days?"

Outside the booth, twenty feet away or so, Kyle is returning to his desk. He glances in my direction, probably feeling my gaze, then, face utterly blank, turns away. The phone booth seems to contract, the air sucked out, the sound a pure void. I'm convinced the door isn't going to open, that I'm going to die in here.

"Hold on, Bab wants to say hi."

My father's sonorous voice booms, shaking me from my

claustrophobia. "Nazeli? Listen, today I learn that there are approximately, wait for me, I will say the whole thing: 100,000,000,000,000,000,000,000 stars in the universe. And the scientists think there are more planets than stars, if you believe this. But!" he shouts. "We are the only planet we know of with life. This is God's miracle," he says, reverent.

"That's pretty amazing," I say.

"This is why you must come to Chicago with us."

Oh my God, these two. They are unbearable in how well they team up.

"We have one beautiful life, and we want you to come spend it with family, help us."

"Why can't Edmond go?"

My much younger brother is still in college, but it's summer break now, so I don't see why he can't join, especially since it seems the primary need is brawn.

"He is beginning his summer training, didn't we tell you? He's going to Pebble Beach for almost a month."

The pride in my father's voice is clear. Baby bro happens to be a gifted golfer, and got into Stanford on a golf scholarship. I'll still never forgive him for besting me in the ranking of schools, since I'm supposed to be the brainy one, but at least I know I got into Berkeley on a Regents' scholarship, which will forever be a point of pride.

"Okay, okay, I'll think about it," I say, knowing there's no way I'm going to go.

We hang up shortly afterward, and before I can make it back

to my desk, I'm ambushed by Jamie, who looks more serious than usual. Probably wants to talk about some Operation Wolf details.

"Have a minute? I booked Dingo for us." She motions toward a nearby glass conference room.

"Of course," I say, wondering if I'm going to get any work done today.

We sit on the same side of the table, facing each other. She clicks a pink fingernail against the table.

"Listen," she says, and a part of me irrationally flares up, fearing I'm about to get fired. "I'm trying so hard with you."

Oh no, am I? But my performance reviews are excellent—mostly excellent—though Jamie always manages to find plenty of room for growth. Still, Abilify policy states that an employee needs to be on a performance improvement plan (aka you're about to get canned, so shape up) before they can fire you for cause. And I'm certainly not on a performance improvement plan. I give this place my all. At least, I thought I did.

"The beginning of that presentation, you walking out? That was unacceptable."

"I had a medical—"

"No, you were nervous, I could tell. Listen, we all get nervous, I bet even Reid gets nervous. But when he has to deliver bad news to the board, do you think he walks out of the room and throws up, then comes back?"

"I wasn't—"

"Whatever feeling you were having, you need to murder it on

the spot, and move on. If you can't kill it completely, lock it in a box to come back to later. Therapy's great for that. I have the number of a fantastic lady who does therapy for corporate leaders."

"Oh, thanks. That'd be great." There is no way that therapist takes insurance.

Jamie leans back in her chair, as if gabbing with a girlfriend. "You're so close to being perfect, but there are things like that that make me question whether or not you are upper-management material."

"Things?"

She straightens. "There's something else I've been meaning to talk to you about."

Oh God, I honestly have no clue what she is about to say. Wait, maybe she knows about Kyle. Should I preempt this? Jump in and say it's over? No, never admit to wrongdoing. Not that hooking up with Kyle is wrong, because neither of us is each other's report or in the same growth chain, but lateral office relationships are still looked down upon.

"I've got an unbeatable deal to sign up at Equinox that includes ten private trainer sessions for only—brace yourself because this number is nuts—seven hundred dollars. Can you believe that?"

I am staring deerlike because I'm not sure if she wants me to agree this number is wildly high (my take) or wildly low. I give a "wow" that I hope can be interpreted either way.

"I'll forward you the details. I get a little discount off my membership, too, so everyone wins."

So she doesn't know about Kyle and me, she's just MLMing

about her gym membership. Wait. That's not all it is. She prefaced this by saying this is part of what's preventing me from being upper-management material. My body is?

I mean, it's true that I've gained a little weight recently, but I thought that it suited me. Love weight, I called it, from being with Kyle. Ugh.

She flexes her bicep. "Gotta keep up with all the macho BS in this office, be one of them. No better way to do that than muscle tone. Got it?"

I am mentally gluing my mouth shut, otherwise it would plummet to the ground. Forget the hundreds of dollars a month that a gym costs, plus the personal training sessions—I'm still trying to wrap my head around my boss telling me to get in shape in order to be considered for a promotion. Is that real?

I would talk to HR about this, but I know what happens to people who talk to HR. Fired. Not right away, but eventually. You're labeled "a problem person," and they find a way. Besides, Melissa, the head of HR, is Jamie's best work friend. So I nod along.

"Totally," I say.

When Jamie opens her mouth, I wonder what fresh hell is coming for me. "Hiking is fantastic, too. We're so lucky to live in a place where we're surrounded by breathtaking trails," she continues, and I'm wondering when this conversation is going to end.

You know what, on top of her delirious overstepping in this conversation, I hate exercise. Nothing about it ever has, or ever will, appeal to me. I don't mind casual strolls; I can walk for hours through the city if there are interesting things to look at, places to go. But being yelled at by a perfectly toned fitness instructor with fake lashes to "embrace the burn" is not my idea of a good time. Armenians, as a whole, aren't big exercisers. My parents don't work out, my cousins don't, my grandparents didn't, and my great-grandparents were marched by Ottoman Turks through the Syrian desert with no food or water and left to die, so yeah, the survivors didn't go on fucking hikes after that.

Mercifully, Jamie ends the conversation shortly thereafter.

I walk back to my desk and stare blankly at the screen in front of me.

Kyle, a couple of rows ahead, stands up and goes to another meeting without looking my way.

My phone buzzes with a text, a group chat with my parents.

We are so happy you are coming to Chicago!

And I decide, yes, screw this place, I am going to Chicago.

Chapter Three

It's 6:30 a.m. when I step off the El train—that seems to be what they call their subway here—and into the station, just a block from my hotel. I stifle a yawn as I pull my carry-on onto the escalator. I have to say, so far the public transit tour of Chicago I've gotten has been impressive. The train car didn't fill me with the need to play a "what's that smell" guessing game. The stations have been nondescript in the best way, neither sparkling clean nor dirty, just there, and everything was on time, which I value.

I pulled an all-nighter on the four-hour flight, cramming in all the work I would have to get done for today, shooting off emails like well-oiled cannons, one after the other. It was the only way I could convince Jamie to let me go on this trip without her completely freaking out.

"I'll be available twenty-four seven," I told her. "Operation Wolf won't slip through the cracks; it'll be my top priority."

Jamie's anxiety manifests in rapid-fire questions, and she asked me why I was going on this trip, how essential it truly was, what my working hours would be specifically, any times I would absolutely not be available, and how I was going to use the two-hour time zone difference to my advantage.

After my constant reassurance, she gave me a grim look and said, "Fine, I trust you."

Outside, the weather hits me first. It's June, which in San Francisco is a cold month. I'm still in my airplane puffer jacket, and I rip it off. How the hell is it this warm outside before 7:00 a.m.? I . . . I love it.

There are some people out, purposefully walking to their jobs, and I wish my carry-on didn't grind against the street so loudly, because I hate to be the center of attention this way. Not because I feel unsafe. No, I feel a strange sense of safety on this early morning street—these surroundings, the weather, are subconsciously relaxing me. The buildings are tall, which I like, but not crammed together. These streets are sparkling clean for a city, and oh, I can see one of the famous black towers; not the Sears, the other one. I look it up on my phone—the Hancock Tower. It feels reassuring, knowing the buildings you've seen in photos and movies truly exist.

In the short block I'm walking, I pass by an immense cream-stone church with a striking floral-patterned stained glass, and I wonder if I'm in a special area or if every church here has such attention to detail. Unlike my parents, I'm not particularly religious, but there is an undeniable cultural importance of the Armenian Apostolic Church to Armenians. The first nation to declare Christianity its official religion, Armenia was the "land of a thousand churches" at one point in history. Almost to a fault. My classmate in Armenian school Lara had said, "If only it had been 'land of a thousand armies,' maybe we'd still have all our homeland."

I seamlessly check into my room at the hotel, which is on the thirty-sixth floor, a lucky high number. I set down my bags and fling open the sheer window curtains, which reveal an absolutely jaw-dropping view of downtown Chicago. The Sears Tower, and a mishmash of architecture in different styles. Modern blue-green glass on one, cement on another, art deco with gold-leaf accents. Okay, Chicago, you are all right in my book.

I have to admit, I wasn't that pumped to visit this city. I was born and raised in the San Francisco Bay Area, and spending the last several years in the city proper can give one a sense of snobbery. Visiting Illinois? In the middle of the country? Did they even have a Bloomingdale's here? Was it a real city?

It is. It's bigger and more impressive than San Francisco so far. Everyone gushes about San Francisco's beauty, and I guess from some objective point of view I see it, but even when looking out at some vista, the Golden Gate in the background, the city doesn't ever feel welcoming to me. Not comfortable. And not in a cool way, like in Manhattan. New York preens its feathers for you and tempts you into it, even while being constantly out of reach. San Francisco looks at you and says, "Eh."

I call my parents.

My mom picks up on the fifth ring. "Nazeli? You made it?"

Her voice is thick with sleep. I thought that maybe this conference would be an exception to my parents' unspoken rule of "sleep as late as possible and risk being late every single day," but I suppose nothing can curb their need to snooze uninterrupted.

I stifle a yawn. "You should see my view. The whole downtown, it's gorgeous. Can you see it from there?"

Now her voice fills with anguish, which combines with the sleep to make it sound like she's lamenting my actual death. "I still can't believe you didn't stay with us and you chose all the way up there."

Not staying in their hotel was a whole deal that I had to muck through. But there is no way I was flying across the country to a brand-new city for five days just to stay in a charmless hotel across the street from a convention center. No matter how many times my parents propped up the benefits of the bridge between the hotel and the center. That's actually a con for me, I told them, meaning I would never breathe in actual Chicago air, and instead be channeled from one soulless place to another.

I start unpacking while speaking to her, setting up my electric toothbrush and charger in the bathroom, lining up bottles of serums and toners. There's a giant tub in here that seems like such a waste; no way am I going to have time to take a long, warm soak. I hang up the couple of nicer dresses and tops I brought, stifling near-constant yawns, secretly jealous of my parents lying in bed. I reassure them I'll be over soon. On my phone, I look up spots to grab a coffee, and with a cheer in my heart, I realize I can get it iced—how refreshing that would feel on my trip down to McCormick Place in this humid warmth. I think I'm going to like it here.

It's DAY ONE of the Food and Beverage Packagers of America Conference—aka PakCon—and you can tell by the energy here, everyone seems optimistic and lit by sparks as they make their way to talks or to the main convention hall. The conference is well underway, we're still at the entrance, and our booth is not set up because we were hours late.

My parents went back to sleep immediately after my call—not strictly true, as my father hadn't even woken up; he could sleep through a fire alarm. So when I knocked on their hotel room door, my mother answered it bleary-eyed, hair in curlers. We both spent ten minutes pushing and pulling and cajoling my father out of bed, which feels like waking a sleeping giant. He's not a huge man, but not small, either, and his deadweight is impressive. I spent the next hour on my laptop giving directives to the designer, who woke up early and answered my red-eye emails, and I wondered all the while if Jamie would be impressed that I'd have a deliverable to her so early during my trip. Then I thought about Kyle.

While waiting for my parents in their hotel room, I witnessed an argument between them about whether or not my father should wear white pants (him: for, her: against), then stole away to my texts. I read the last exchange Kyle and I had:

Friday May 26,
8:03 p.m.

Kyle: Uber's ETA is 27 minutes

Me: I love that preciseness. It's like foreplay

Kyle: Good. Get ready.

Sunday May 28,
9:01 a.m.

Me: Up for brunch? Mission City's madagascar vanilla waffles are calling me

Sunday May 28,
10:57 a.m.

Kyle: Sorry, just woke up

Me: That's okay. Do you still want to go?

Kyle: Nah, got too much to prepare for this week

Me: Gotcha, no worries! I should prepare too

Monday May 29,
8:40 p.m.

Me: Want to check out my final preso for Operation Wolf?

Tuesday May 30,
10:13 a.m.

Kyle: Sure, send it to me

> **Me:** Thank you so much! You always have the best insights

He had simply replied to my Operation Wolf email with **Looks good. You seem ready.** And that's when I should have known. He'd always been a little arm's length with me, but his coldness after our intimate Friday night was the first red flag, and then the actual siren was that he had nothing of substance to say about my presentation. Usually he reveled in picking apart the weak areas and coming up with suggestions for how to improve. Honestly, it was helpful, since he and Jamie seem to think alike, and he'd often fix up the exact sections she'd say were her favorite parts. In my hubris I took his email as a major compliment and puffed myself up that this projected real growth in my career, but the only projection it showed was that singlehood was in my future.

Listening to my parents' squabbles in the background, I hear the words float into my mind: *Everything is negotiable.* There is no way that this is really *over* over. Kyle has never been the type to express any strong emotions, so I was surprised when he opened up to me Friday night about the cruel ways his older brother bullied him. He must have panicked and felt he'd overshared and shut this down. But I need to show him that it doesn't make me see him differently. I text him.

> **Me:** I respect your decision but want to let you know I miss you

It's still 6:30 a.m. on the West Coast, so I don't expect a reply, even though I know he'll be waking up shortly. Still, it feels safer this way, texting when he's sleeping.

Two hours later, it's 10:00 in the morning in Chicago, 8:00 a.m. on the West Coast, but still no answer. Whatever, I tell myself. It's still early. Who texts *that* early in the morning?

I've hauled the bulk of my parents' booth supplies across the hotel bridge while Bab protested the entire time. "You are babying the man who won the Lebanese Ironman in 1974!" When I asked if they really had the Ironman competition back then, he blushed and said it was an equivalent but that our people were made to lift—shorter and squatter, mountainous peasant folk.

The supplies—banners, food samples in a cooler, brochures, swag of many forms, and three folding chairs—are propped on the floor while my parents strategize how best to get to their booth spot, and whether they should set up the booth now and sit, or try to attend a few panels and schmooze instead.

"How have you guys not decided this already?" I ask, not disguising the annoyance in my voice.

Sometimes I think it's a miracle they're able to run their own business at all. This lack of preparation would not fly at Abilify. It's a terrible thought but one that crosses my mind at times like this.

I do know why they stay in business, though, and that's because the product is unmatched. Both sides of my family have been hugely into cooking for generations, have passed down secrets and tricks to make recipes shine, and my parents pour centuries of tradition and love into their food. They found a way to make it shelf-stable, too. Mostly, though, their food goes bad quicker than your average packaged product because my parents won't add any unnatural preservatives to it. Hagop's Fine Armenian Foods, from what I can tell, has a cult following, but even the best product needs to be marketed properly.

Last year, I drew up a plan for them detailing how quickly they could update their geriatric-looking logo (of course, I didn't call it that, being the soul of professionalism). But both of them, Bab especially, kept shaking their heads and muttering throughout my pitch. My advice was cut off at the quick, as if my expert recommendations were some child's whimsy. They really are fortunate the food is so good.

Everything at the convention center is earsplitting. The floors are linoleum, and the ceilings are so high that everyone's conversations and footsteps echo. There's shouting and laughing, the noise of roller luggage pinging off my ears, mingling with my parents' argument. But there's another voice above it all, a sharp one, that draws me in.

I turn, and some hundred feet away, a woman about my age is having a conversation—that's generous, more like an argument— with a mustachioed man in a cheap suit, standing in front of a door. She's shoved her phone into his face.

". . . right here in the email. Here's Terry Hobart's talk, and here's my name, on the list."

Before I realize it, I'm walking toward her, getting a better look. She has shoulder-length curly hair that's sandy brown but sort of blondish at the ends and appears natural. She's sporting a nineties-looking ribbed mock-turtleneck crop top in stripes of autumn tones over rust-colored jeans. There's a hint of a tattoo on her arm peeking out from her sleeve. She has wide, mournful eyes, with a tilt upward that suggests shrewdness, maybe mischievousness. I wonder if she's from my part of the world— her face shape looks familiar, like the Armenians I grew up with.

The man gives off a "no can do" huff. "Ma'am, I can only accept printed tickets, not email confirmations. Like I said, you can get your tickets reprinted at the front desk."

She's openly angry, not bothering to hide the fire in her eyes. She feels so real, the way she's boldly expressing herself. Not the kind of subdued emotions I'm used to and revere at work, but there is something about her rage that is so honest.

"What does 'accept' mean? You're the only gatekeeper here, there's no scanner, so it's only you and your best judgment. I'm showing you I'm allowed at this event."

"We only accept printed tickets for these special events."

I hate this man already. This is the type of immovable attitude that people at Abilify cannot stand. That nothing is your problem, that rules have to be followed exactly to the letter. That's what drew me to tech, the responsibility and the trust to make decisions using critical assessment, not following someone else's written code. This woman clearly purchased tickets and should be allowed in. Then I wonder if she ever printed the ticket, or if she lost it. Is she the type to be obsessive about her possessions, or is she a touch careless? Something in her energy makes me feel like it could be the latter. I picture her hotel room like it's one of those "the suitcase exploded in the bedroom" situations, and wonder what corner of the mess those tickets could be tucked away in. And what other cute clothes she's brought with her, strewn over chairs and lamps. Then I tell myself to stop.

She draws in a breath like she's holding herself back. "The line is around the building. By the time I get my *printed* ticket, this talk will be over. Come on, dude."

It's the "dude" that sends me over the edge. She is feeling like home, reminding me of California. But it's also more than that.

I step up behind the man and tap him on the shoulder. "Excuse me, sir. I'm having the hardest time trying to figure out where convention room 70C is. Hold on—I've got my map."

I flap the folded paper open, tenting his vision. The woman's hands are on her hips, and she is fuming, ready to say something to me no doubt, until we make eye contact, and unbeknownst to mustache man, I discreetly wave her into the conference room. There's a flicker of recognition in her eyes, and she darts in, light on her feet. She turns once briefly, hands in a prayer pose, and mouths, "Thank you." The smile on her face is one I know will stay etched in my mind.

I only wish I could have run in after her.

Chapter Four

I return to my parents, who have come to a decision about what to do next (set up the booth). They seem in good spirits, whirling their heads around the convention hall, squinting at people's badges to see if they recognize any brand names. With an armful of chairs, I use my free hand to wheel the luggage full of supplies toward the main convention hall. Before we enter, a massive cardboard sign with a football catches my eye. Catches everyone's, I'm certain; it's large enough, and the words are not only easy to parse, but very enticing.

ENTER THE PAKCON SUPERSTARS CHALLENGE!
WIN *YOUR* PRODUCT PLACEMENT DURING OUR
1-MINUTE SUPER BOWL AD!

"Mom, Bab," I say, turning around. "Have you heard about this? Is it a raffle or something?"

I read the slightly smaller print and am skimming the phrase *series of challenges* when vexation catches in Mom's voice. "That has nothing to do with us."

"You know about it?"

She waves away the cardboard sign as if it's a pesky gnat. "They do every year, it's not for brands like us. It's for big brands, lots of people at the company."

My dad seems similarly unfazed. "We see the brands that always win. Hera is right, is not for us. Just as Luke said, in the Bible, not to want more than your fair share."

I'm looking from one to the other, ready to plop down on the chair and refuse to move until they revise their answers.

"What you looking at?" asks my mom, not getting the hint.

Reluctantly, I say, "Have some judges taste your food, and they'll send you right to the top."

"They don't like our food," my father says, with a hint of bitterness.

I wish my parents would feel they could try something new, take risks. I was hoping my presence here could push them toward that (instead of my simply being their lackey). I could have hired someone to help them if that's all they need from me. It's frustrating, but mostly I'm annoyed that an opportunity is right there for the taking and they have no desire to try. It makes me feel extra justified that I never joined the family business. Part of it would have been so sweet, prepping and chopping and rolling food all day long with the people and the foods I grew up with, but I didn't want my future to be confined to my parents' business. I'd feel too boxed in, like I never made anything of myself on my own. Meanwhile, tech was there—shiny, glamorous, full of openings—and anyone at Cal who was interested in making money in their career (which was not everyone!) was headed that way, so I went, too. Plus, the Abilify recruiter at the career fair table was smoking hot, so I literally walked in that direction.

I remember then an Armenian folktale. It's fuzzy in my mind, but I start to narrate out loud the pieces that come to me. There's definitely a man who declares that he's leaving home on a quest to find his pakht, or "luck." Along the way he runs into situations and people who he helps, and they try to give him rewards of gold and marriage (because, you know, women equaled property back then), but he refuses it all, saying he's too busy and needs to find his pakht. Then he somehow gets eaten by a lion because of his refusal to see the luck right before him. My parents are being like that man, and I tell them as much.

My mother dutifully listens to my clumsy retelling of the folktale. She pats my shoulder. "Maybe next year we do," she says. "This year we're not prepared. And . . . please no tell anyone else that story until you have reread it. I find the Armenian children's version for you."

I twist my mouth and pull the luggage with more force than necessary, pushing into the hall.

We've set up the booth, our banner advertising Hagop's Fine Armenian Foods, and a delectable-looking table full of handmade delicacies.

It's hour two out here, and I am salivating. From the cooler,

I sneak a dolma and take a bite. My mom slaps my hand. "Vai, those are for the customers."

"It was a messed-up one, bursting at the end." A lie.

My father chimes in, "Impossible, all our dolma is perfect."

I smile and shove the rest in my mouth.

I've been splitting my time coaxing people to our booth and hiding like a child, beneath the table with my laptop, getting work done. Jamie has wanted a say in every step of Operation Wolf and is now asking to be cc'ed on all my emails. I tell the Tremendous Trio we need to start cc'ing Jamie, and Nina pings me a private message with an annoyed emoji face. I send her back a "yep" and a wink.

As for the customers, I'm not sure how useful having a booth here actually is. Everyone simply seems to want the free food, and while they comment on how delicious it is, most of the people's badges show they're from other packaged food companies. No buyers or distributors. Being friendly with the competition is nice, but isn't going to grow the brand.

Then, my back pocket buzzes, and I pull out my phone. A text from Kyle. Holy shit. The convention hall noise disappears as I lock eyes on my phone, anticipating what it'll say.

> **Kyle:** Where are you? Didn't see you around then saw the OOO calendar had your name on it through the rest of the week

Curious, huh? This is a good sign. If he really didn't care, he wouldn't bother to ask me, and the fact that he went hunting for more information in the shared office calendar? Only positive. Dumb jerk realizes he misses me, too.

> **Me:** In Chicago at a food convention, helping out my parents. I'll be back Monday

A minute later—because him answering instantly would be too much to ask—he texts back.

> **Kyle:** Well, have fun.

My eyebrows pinch. The hall's din is raucous once again. *Well?* I can't stand him. I am not going back to him, I tell myself. I don't need to deal with this push and pull of "do you like me or not?"; these cryptic texts would require teams of advanced linguists to parse. "But what is his intention," I hear a graduate student asking. No, I am done.

The conversation and the tease of dolma have made me suddenly ravenous. With our own food off-limits, I offer to venture out and find some for all of us while my parents hold down the fort.

On the map I find a café within the convention center and worry that the food might be mediocre, which would be a bummer, but what choice do I have other than going around the hall sampling everyone's food like I'm at Costco?

As I trek through the high-ceilinged halls, I catch myself scanning faces, hoping to find the one I'm looking for—the angry girl. No, I think, *angry* isn't the right descriptor. The girl with that mischievous smile. But there must be ten thousand people here. I'm not going to see her again.

After I order some sad-looking sandwiches, I wait for my number to be called and slump over my phone, seeing what new challenges have arisen at Abilify.

Then there's an insistent tap on my shoulder. I whirl around, assuming my order is being hand delivered for some reason, but no, what I see is much better than a convention club sandwich. It's her. The woman who didn't have her tickets printed. Before I know it, I am smiling huge.

She's leaning against the counter at her hip, staring straight into my eyes. "Didn't think I'd get a chance to thank you in person. My knight in shining armor."

Her voice drips with honey, so much different than when she was arguing with that awful guy. I want to bathe in it.

"I've never heard you speak at normal volume," I reply before I have a chance to edit my inner thoughts to temper them for weirdness.

I cringe in horror and am on the verge of apologizing when she laughs out loud, a surprise laugh, like she doesn't get surprised often and is impressed by me.

She raises an eyebrow. "And what's the verdict? Acceptable? Bizarre?"

"Mellifluous," I say, not worried anymore about censoring myself.

Her smile again. Makes this drab convention hall feel like

the Garden of Eden. "Million-dollar word, I like it." She cocks her head. "Want to take your airplane food to go, and grab a beer with me? We can get the bard to sing of your many selfless acts."

I'm caught off guard. Whatever I'm doing, it's working for her. But there's no way I can get even the slightest buzz while I'm on the clock. I made the mistake of drinking a beer at lunch one time at work, and the rest of the day was a wash for me. No clue how Don Draper and his crew used to handle the two-martini lunch. And my parents still need their cardboard sandwiches.

"Trust me, I'd love nothing more, but I have to get back to the booth." Her smile shrinks slightly, like she's working hard to rein in her disappointment. I add, "Are you free tonight? We could grab a drink then, maybe more than one."

Her eyes, which are mostly cedar brown like mine, have a green glint at the edges. "You speak my language."

I vaguely hear someone call, "Twenty-three," which is my number, but I ignore it.

I pull out my phone. I hope it's not too forward, but how else are we supposed to meet up again? "I can give you my number, or you can give me yours, whatever you're comfortable with."

She grabs my phone from my hands, and our fingers graze momentarily. Hers are cool to the touch. "I'm comfortable with a whole lot."

She types rapidly and returns my phone. It reads Vanya cute convention girl at the top, and I can't help but laugh. Vanya—what a beautiful name, like melting snow.

"Seven?" she asks, smirking.

"Seven," I say, almost a whisper.

She turns and slips into a crowd of people, disappearing from sight entirely. I text her.

This is Ellie, your knight in shining armor.

Chapter Five

$\mathcal{V}$anya suggests meeting at the bar of the hotel, the same one my parents are staying at across from McCormick Place, and while I'd rather explore the city, the convenience of it works out for now. I'm in my parents' room, organizing some of the supplies from the booth we took back with us. Luckily we're able to leave all the bulky items back in the convention hall so I don't have to be a porter every single day.

Bab lies reclined on the bed while Mom touches up her makeup in the bathroom. She shouts in Armenian, "Hagop, don't you dare fall asleep."

"I am resting my knee," he calls back, indignant.

I inch into the bathroom. "Uh, Mom, can I borrow some of your makeup?"

She gestures for me to dive in. "You're coming with us to the meet greet?"

Her makeup bag is a mess, and made up purely of Lancôme products, both ones she's purchased and free gifts. Those free gifts are like currency in my family, and when Lancôme has a good one, my mom and aunts and cousins (and I) will go on a pilgrimage like we're visiting the Holy Land, strategizing how to spend the minimum amount and get the gifts and swap out the samples each of us likes best.

I pull out an eyeliner and touch up my winged tips. "I'm actually meeting someone."

She stops mid–mascara stroke. "A date? You didn't tell me you know anyone in Chicago."

Concentrating on creating a smooth line, I say, "It's not a date, I just met them."

My mom slams down the mascara. "Nazeli, you can't go out with strange men in a new city, that is very dangerous."

"Very dangerous," my father echoes from the bed. I guess he didn't fall asleep.

"We're going to the hotel bar downstairs, totally safe, lots of people," I say. Then, gathering up my courage, I say, "And it's not a guy, it's a girl."

My mom's mouth tightens into a little O, and she is keeping from looking surprised and disappointed. "Oh, I see. That's better, not so dangerous."

I came out to my parents, extremely awkwardly, six years ago. I came out to my little brother before then, and his only response was "Ew. Whatever, I don't care." He was fourteen—a very immature fourteen.

The only reason I said anything was that I fell for this girl during my senior year of college, and it turned out she liked me, too. Katie was white, fully out to her parents since she was twelve, and they were all understanding and supportive; they baked her a "we love our daughter" cake and showered her with rainbow confetti that same night. So after dating for two months—a very intense two months where I was convinced I'd met the love of my life—she encouraged me to tell my parents. We couldn't keep it a secret forever, and again, I was hearing not-officially-sanctioned-by-the-state wedding bells in our near future (this was 2011, and gay marriage wasn't legal yet). If it wasn't for this deep conviction that Katie was The One, I probably never would've said anything to them.

So one cold Saturday afternoon when I was home for the weekend and we were gathered in the family room deciding what lazy-day movie to watch, I told them. I said, "I'm dating a girl. I like girls and boys but I'm dating a girl. I wanted you to know."

After some clarifying questions that cemented that *yes*, I was indeed telling them the thing they were afraid I was telling them, there was yelling, crossing themselves, tears, misquoting the Bible (I had prepared for the Bible references and scoured the internet for all references to homosexuality and specifically lesbians to come armed to this discussion), and ultimately—by some stroke of luck—emotional vulnerability that led my parents to the conclusion that they weren't happy with this but I'm still their daughter no matter what, and they love me and will support me. It might take some time, but they'd get there.

When I told them Katie dumped me for another woman (a yoga-teaching free spirit named Cassie, whom I still hate a teeny bit) and left my heart in shreds, they consoled me, and I could feel their hidden smiles as they hugged me.

I haven't dated a woman since then, so that's where we're at.

Reluctant acceptance. And bless them, they're trying so hard to be modern, when I swear sometimes I feel like my parents are stuck in 1965.

I open a tube of lipstick, a particular shade of red pink that would do nothing to flatter me, and put it back. "She seems nice, but if it isn't going well, I'll come join you guys?"

I rifle through the makeup bag and check out two more shades before selecting one that ends up looking only okay. There's concern in my mother's eyes, and all her movements are slower now, like she is afraid of breaking some set of invisible fragile objects all around her. "Yes, please text, let us know how you are. I worry."

She looks sad suddenly, which makes me feel awful, like I'm doing something to make her upset. But if it's the fact that I'm getting a drink with a woman, then sorry, Mom, I can't help who I am. Still, I lean in to hug her. "I'll be careful, and text you."

Not long after, she and Bab leave, and I purposefully let them go first so they don't stalk me at the bar.

I take one last look at myself, wishing I had time to change my outfit, but decide it's fine. This shows how nonchalant I am. Didn't even bother with new clothes. So jeans and flowy white top that ties at the end it is. A daytime look if there ever was one. Maybe now I know what all those magazines were talking about when they said that every woman in her late twenties needs to own a blazer that converts her outfit seamlessly from day to night. I'm still twenty-seven, though, which isn't firmly into the late twenties yet.

Well, this is what I'm going with. I open the door and head down to the bar.

Chapter Six

$\mathcal{J}$'m on time practically to the second, and surprised to see that Vanya's already there, sipping a beer. Maybe my little daydream of her as being perpetually late and forgetful was off base. And she definitely got an opportunity to change, as she is now wearing a plum-colored linen crop top over black jeans with a few layered necklaces. Her tattoo is visible now, but from here I can't tell what it is; a person perhaps.

She's shining like a precious stone, something unusual and arzhekavor—that Armenian word meaning "valuable," but with more pizzazz, pops into my mind. Being around my parents always unearths my Armenian vocabulary.

It's not that the bar is bad, no, it's trying to be good, or rather trying to be nothing you want to notice. Dark granite countertop, striped-back bar chairs with brown leather seats, a series of lamps hanging that are unremarkable to the point of being invisible. There are people from the conference all over, lanyards with their badges hanging around their necks. Lots of pantsuits. But Vanya's sitting here making everything around her glow.

As I approach, she cocks her head my way and then, recognizing me, turns on that smile, and I feel myself shooting one back. I scoot into the firm leather chair next to her.

"Purple really suits you," I say, and then, like a homing device, my consciousness zeroes in on her tattoo, and recognition dawns. I know exactly what it is. I blurt out, "Is that Mother Armenia? Are you Armenian?"

God, I hope she's Armenian and not some white person who thought the Soviet-era statue looked cool. But no, her eyes— she has to be from Armenia, Lebanon, Iran, Palestine, somewhere.

And Vanya? She looks delighted, like running into a long-lost friend.

"I am. It's my Armenian-detect-o-meter. Any Armenian knows her, and to everyone else, it's a badass tattoo."

She is a badass, sculpted in sixties Soviet style, her posture rigid, holding a sword horizontally across her body, ready to defend herself, the homeland.

Vanya continues, "Ellie the Armenian. Don't think I've ever met an Armenian named Ellie. Or, *Ellie*," she says with a heightened Armenian accent, drawing out the *l*'s.

"It's really Nazeli," I say. "But I go by Ellie. Easier for everyone."

"Not everyone," she corrects. "I love the name Nazeli, always did. One of our most delicate names. Like you've dipped your finger into the end of the pond and watched the ripples grow out of it."

I gawk; she is incredible. The way she's taken this name that I've always thought was "difficult" and turned it into something so beautiful. "You're a poet then?"

She waves me off. "Not quite. But we can get into that in a bit. What're you drinking?"

"Macallan, neat." Then I say, "It's on me," realizing the brand name is going to cost us. Macallan is a bit of a beginner's scotch, but since I'm not trying to impress a man tonight, I'm forgoing the Laphroaigs and Taliskers for something a little easier. Jamie's the one who taught me that. She only drinks beer and scotch, and wine when paired with food at a dinner, so I followed suit.

"Oof, scotch. I wouldn't have guessed you were actually three bros in a trench coat."

I laugh, leaning toward her. "Once you get into it, scotch can be fun, trying to suss out all the flavors."

She raises an eyebrow. "*Can* be fun, uh-huh. By the end of the night, I'm going to get you to try the girliest drink possible."

"I'm up for anything."

"I like to hear that."

With that, she catches the bartender's eye. "My esteemed friend here would like a glass of your finest Macallan."

I put my hands on the bar and quickly interject. "Nope, not your finest, please. Ten-year works for me."

The bartender nods and turns to pour my drink.

"You trying to bankrupt me, Vanya?"

She puts her hands over her mouth, contrite. "Whoops, forgot that there are levels of scotches. Not that this place would have a zillion-dollar bottle casually resting on the shelf."

It's easy, being with her. The realization comes suddenly. She makes me feel like everything I say is weighed with importance, that she accepts it all, even when she's making fun of me. I don't for a moment feel like I'm being assessed—am I funny enough? Pretty enough? It hasn't been long, but with her, right now anyway, I feel like enough.

I pick up the drink in front of me and take a sip of the familiar bite, the sugar toward the end, searching for it like a palate lifeline. Then I wonder if I really enjoy this drink at all.

Vanya turns to me, almost marveling with that tilt of her chin. "Are you one of those fabled East Coast Armenians?"

I'm touched she thinks I could be from the East Coast. And I know what she means. The East Coast Armenians seem like a fairy tale; I've only met one or two in my lifetime.

"Nope, your run-of-the-mill Californian Armenian."

"Me too!" she chimes, as if on the trail. I catch her excitement, too; we're both hot on our way to uncover how connected we really are. With there being so few Armenians in the world, there's always a high chance when meeting a new Armenian that you'll know some of the same people. Plus, I was right—that *dude* she uttered from earlier could have been nothing but Californian.

"I'm not from LA, though," she says. "That would be too easy to guess."

If she's not from Southern California, the largest Armenian

diaspora, and she's not from the Bay Area, because I would have at least heard of her, she's got to be from—

"Fresno?" I ask.

"Nope. Bay Area."

"What? That's where I'm from. How do we not know each other?"

I thought I knew everyone my age from the area. Well, maybe she's not my age; I shouldn't assume. But I went to the Armenian school, my parents are deeply plugged into the community, almost too much into it. How'd Vanya slip under the radar?

Then she says, "Saratoga," and I realize ah, that's why.

"San Francisco proper," I reply. "An hour apart on a good day." And she nods along, understanding.

That hour-long distance is enough for us not to have met. None of the Armenians in the South Bay went to the Armenian school since the drive is so long. And Saratoga . . . she must be doing well to live in a ritzy area like that.

"What's your deal with the food conference?" I ask. "Do you have a packaged brand, or are you in the grocery business, or what?"

"I was about to ask you the same. I tried peeping on your badge earlier, but it was flipped around."

I sit back in the chair and finish the scotch more quickly than I should to savor it. "My parents' brand, it's Armenian, maybe you know it. Hagop's Fine Armenian Foods? You can find it in all the Persian and Arabic stores in the Bay. Lavash, manti, dolma, things like that."

She squints. "That definitely sounds familiar."

And I have to admit I'm the tiniest bit crushed that she isn't familiar with my parents' brand. But then that furthers my resolve to push them into expansion. Even Armenians don't know about them? Come on!

"What about you?"

She finishes her beer. "Weirdly, same here. I work for my parents' brand, and it's also Armenian food, or more like, Armenian-food inspired. The Green Falafel? We're in smaller grocery chains all over the Bay Area, delis, some health cafés. I've been working with them for the past four years, and it's a pretty sweet gig."

The name flicks some bell of recognition, and then it comes to me, a memory from a few months back. I was running errands during my lunch break and didn't have time to eat, popped into the health food store next door, and grabbed a falafel, hummus, and dolma pack to go. The Green Falafel brand. And I remember it, specifically, because it wasn't very good.

"Oh my gosh, yes," I say. "I saw it recently but haven't tried it yet. Next time I'm going to."

No way I'm going to tell her that her family's food sucks. But I wonder about how similar our paths are, how in another life without my foray into tech, I could be like her, working for my parents, making their brand my own. A tiny part of me is envious of her, because I imagine to gladly work for your parents, there has to be a level of trust and respect there, which my parents refuse to give me when it comes to Hagop's Fine Armenian Foods.

There's pride in her smile, and then she says, "I wonder if our parents know each other. Their generation is more likely to."

"I'll ask them. What's your last name? We're the Gregorians."

"Simonian. Damn, we have a lot in common."

"Oh, the only thing is that I don't work for my parents. I'm here helping them out with the booth this weekend."

And to escape having to see my ex in the office for the next few days, and not have to deal with my demanding boss. I wonder then if this is my quarter-life crisis. I do the math— that'd mean I'd live to one hundred and eight. Yeah, that sounds about right.

"What do you do then?" she asks, brow slightly knit in confusion.

I sit up straight and deliver in one breath, "I'm a senior product marketing manager for a disruptive performance management software company." I add, beaming, "A unicorn, actually."

She nods. "I didn't understand a single word you said, but sounds cool."

I laugh and wonder if she truly didn't. I am not about to impress her with Abilify, and that makes me feel stripped of my clothing, but also . . . I don't mind if she sees? Not literally. Or maybe literally; I haven't decided yet.

She holds her empty glass and tilts it around, making water rings on the countertop. "I asked to meet here because of a combination of convenience and caution. I'm staying upstairs and wanted to make sure you weren't, you know, weird in a bad way. Since your only flaw seems to be liking scotch, how about we try somewhere else?"

"Absolutely, yes," I say.

"Hold on, let me do some quick research."

She types on her phone lightning fast for a minute or so, then looks up. "I found our place, let's go."

I follow her out, not bothering to ask where it is, knowing I'm up for it.

Chapter Seven

We're standing side by side on a rooftop bar overlooking the Chicago River, reveling in the warm breezes this high up. If Vanya's trying to impress me, she's getting an "Exceeds Expectations" in her performance review. The spot is modern, with long, sleek benches and rectangular firepits that are on but contribute more to the ambiance than the need to warm the space. It's filled with people in their late twenties to early thirties, shockingly nondescript, like they are neither overly casual (like San Francisco) nor overly dressed up (like LA or New York). It's almost as if they are extras placed here in the movie of Vanya and me, though I know, from their perspective, Vanya and I are their extras.

I'm alone for the moment, waiting for Vanya to return with the promised girlie drinks, breeze tickling my skin, and I'm filled with awe at how my first day here has been so different from what I expected. How I met someone promising who only lives an hour away from me, and is Armenian and so effortlessly cool. Carefree in a way I could never be.

Then, groaning, I check my work email because I haven't for

the last hour. But there's nothing urgent, no Jamie fire drills. Only one message I need to respond to, and I do so quickly. It's six o'clock in SF, which is the lull time at work, when people start to go home, get dinner. Work will pick up again around eight their time, which means tenish my time, so, if I want to, I can get a whole two more hours with Vanya.

I might end up being a bit tipsy, but evening work is way less stressful. I can do that with a buzz.

She returns, and I feel myself warming with joy when I catch sight of her. There is something about this person. I hope she feels it, too, and everything is telling me she does, but I still need to guard my heart, at least a little.

In her hands are two cocktail glasses with pink slushy liquid, and I wonder if she's gone and gotten us strawberry daiquiris, but there's none of the usual whipped cream, pineapple, and umbrella on top.

"Frosé," she announces, handing me one. "A frozen, slushy rosé."

I never drink rosé, the most cliché of white woman wines, but for Vanya, I'm willing to consume this pink concoction.

I sip, and the cool, smooth ice is, I hate to admit it, delicious. It feels like the ideal complement to a warm summer night like this, a sweetness in taste to match the air. And the company.

"It's okay," I say, pretending to be a snob, my face about to burst into a smile.

The smile is catching onto her face. "It's breaking you, I see it. You're already a devotee. The next thing you post on social is going to be captioned #froseallday."

I am giggling—actually giggling—at her, when two men around our age with button-down oxfords and slacks show up like shadows behind us.

"Hello, ladies, how's your evening?"

And just like that, the energy between Vanya and me is zapped, the comfort and closeness gone, and we're in "God, we have to handle this shit now" mode. Her body stiffens, and her smile is gone.

"It was going well," she tells the taller one.

He laughs. "It's like that, huh? We just wanted to make some friendly conversation. I'm Hal, and this is Ben," he says, pointing to his friend. They're both completely nice-looking, and maybe if I was out with my friends, I would have chatted with them. But tonight? Zero desire.

I'm about to say something final, when Vanya slips her arm around my waist and draws me into her. The bare skin of her arm presses against my shirt. Instinctively, I wrap my arm around her shoulders, skimming them with my fingertips, the softness of her skin and the hardness of her bones. We're really doing this, but I mean, she's only pretending, right? So why do I feel like I'm about to collapse into a wet puddle at her feet?

Vanya speaks, first harsh, then cooing at me. "You've got the wrong idea. We're *together*." She turns to me, looks directly into my eyes. "And she's the love of my life."

Are we going to kiss? It feels like we should kiss, oh my God. I move my head closer to hers, until our foreheads are touching. My entire body is flushed, one huge pulsing heartbeat. She's looking at me like she's daring me to do it, to kiss her. But I haven't asked, I don't know, we're just playing around—

Then Hal speaks. "Oh shit, okay. That's—we're happy for you. Uh, enjoy your night."

As they leave, it's like I'm snapped out of a spell. I pull my head away, averting my eyes, and my arm slides back to my side, missing the warmth of her skin.

She speaks first. "I'm sorry, was that too—?"

I shake my head vigorously. "No, no. It wasn't." And then I say, realizing how dry and practical I sound midsentence, but unable to stop myself, "Plus, it was what the situation called for, and it worked!" My tone feels light and airy, devoid of feeling.

She shakes herself, like a full-body nod. "Totally."

I change the subject quickly, asking her about what exactly she does for the Green Falafel, and hope that it isn't food testing. And she goes on to tell me how she's their sales rep, so this conference is pretty important for her to try to go bigger. Our conversation starts off a tad stilted, but soon we're back to where we started, joking, flirting around the edges.

I glance down at my phone and realize it's getting late and I need to work. Then I remember—"Oh God, I left my laptop at the hotel."

"Do you need to work right now?" she asks incredulously.

"There's this huge project I'm leading, I shouldn't have come to Chicago at all, but I—I felt obligated. And I mean, now I'm happy I did. But there's a ton to catch up on."

I tell her I'm staying in River North, which I can point to from where we are.

"You got your own place, huh? Far away from the 'rents."

I laugh. "Much to my parents' horror, believe me."

"Oh, I get it." Then she pauses, draws her hand to her mouth, and bites on the edge of a nail. Her voice is low. "That's just . . . good to know. You have your own place."

She smirks. And I do the same, because yes, yes, yes, I want to take her back to my hotel room and she seems into the idea and I wish we could right now but—

I take way too audible a breath. "It is. So, uh, back to where we started. I'll call a car."

I do, and we down the last melted sips of our sticky-sweet drinks.

Chapter Eight

*I*t's around ten o'clock when we get back to my parents' and Vanya's hotel. I'm sure Mom and Bab are back in the room, watching a British murder mystery if they could find it on the preset channels, or a TNT action flick as a backup. They stay up late but aren't the biggest schmoozers in the world, so there's no doubt they left the meet and greet as soon as their business was through.

The hotel is less crowded than the bustle of before, but there are still a good number of people milling around. The convention must have about ten thousand attendees or so, and most are staying here. I'm tracking my footsteps along a vertical brown line in the carpet.

"Charming pattern, wouldn't you say?" asks Vanya.

I smile up at her, and put on my voice. "Reminds me of a certain lovely airport Howard Johnson's. You'll have to see it sometime."

She gasps. "I know the very one! The bathroom wallpaper? Just darling."

In between laughs, I brush up against her arm, feel the stickiness of her skin from all the drinks and the humidity.

"I wish we weren't punctuating this night with a trip to my parents' hotel room," I say, a light groan to my voice.

She appears unfazed. "Naz, we're Armenian, everything has to do with our parents."

First, my skin prickles hearing her nickname for me. No one has called me Naz, and coming from her, I love it. And then, I am so relieved, comforted, that she gets it. I've tried to keep my parents as arm's length as possible when it comes to my career and personal life, because they're just *so much* sometimes with their opinions and the "right" way to do things, but then they cook up a four-course meal and hand deliver it to me when I'm having a bad day. Guaranteed Kyle's mom never did that for him. She also probably never called him thirty times in a row, leaving voicemails increasing in intensity of anger when he didn't pick up his phone one night, but . . . trade-offs.

The elevator doors appear in sight, and I don't want this night to end. I don't want to have to go all the way back to River North and spend several hours working. But also, there's a light sparking in me, a hope that this, Vanya and me, might be something.

"You want to hang out tomorrow?" I ask.

"Not even a question. Yes," she replies. She is so confident with me, and it doesn't seem to come from a place of puffing herself up to seem more chill than she is. She believes in what is happening here, too. I think. I hope.

We're standing in front of the shiny brass elevators, and

neither of us moves to push the button, a signal to the end of our night. But I hear Jamie's voice in my head asking me to prove to her that me taking time off would not affect the project, so at last I press my knuckle against it.

The strap on her loose linen tank is angled dangerously on her shoulder, threatening to drop. What if it were to slip? Couldn't have that happen.

I tell her, "Um, your shoulder strap. Could I?"

I lift my hand toward it to indicate what I mean, and she nods, looking very serious all of a sudden, like she did at the rooftop bar with our heads pressed together.

My fingers brush against her skin, the light linen hooked under my index finger, which is when I hear the most familiar voice I know call out, "Nazeli?"

I turn to see my parents, arm in arm, wobbling and flushed, and horror rushes over my body in one instant surge. I yank my arm away from Vanya and try to muster all my rational thinking to figure a way out of this puzzle. I do not want them meeting Vanya right now. Not yet, please.

But I come up with nothing. It's going to happen and I cannot escape.

I give them a wan wave. "Uh, what're you guys doing here? I thought you'd be upstairs hours ago."

"The meet greet was excellent," my mom gushes, her Armenian accent sounding thicker, which can happen on the rare occasion she drinks.

Bab puffs out his chest, equally drunk. "We made the first contact with Ned Richardson, and he wants to hear something he calls 'pitch.' We told him our very successful daughter is here and will be there. Friday. We have been favored, we are not worthy, but this could be our luck."

I'm happy for them and dying that Vanya is standing right next to me and I haven't introduced her yet. Oh God, I am the worst person. I glance toward her briefly, giving her a closed-jaw smile, and she mostly seems amused, but also partially expectant. I remember then, her words, "We're Armenian, everything has to do with our parents," and I know she won't think it's too soon to meet them, especially when forced like this.

I steady my voice. "That's fantastic. You'll have to tell me about it more later. Um, this is—this is Vanya."

Apparently, when I'm inwardly dying, my instinct is to present my date like I'm a skimpily dressed model on *The Price Is Right*, showcasing a brand-new espresso maker.

"Vanya, these are my parents, Hera and Hagop."

Vanya's smile blooms, and she graciously extends her hand, which my dad immediately grasps, but once he has it, his face begins to drop, and he releases it midshake.

"Vanya. Oh—"

That's when I notice my mother looks stricken, choked from the inside. Then she sloughs it off and puts on the fakest smile I've ever seen, even worse than the time my aunt asked her to send flyers to everyone she knew about my cousin's choir concert, because wasn't his voice angelic? In reality he sounds like a crow with a sore throat, but Mom had to agree to spare feelings.

"Is okay," she whispers to Bab, and my dad begins to look at his watch as if fascinated.

The elevator dings once, and the doors open behind Vanya and me, but none of us move to go in. What in the world is going on? I want to ask them, but questions like that are not acceptable in front of non-family members.

My mom's mouth is so stretched I'm worried it'll start bleeding. "You are Vanya . . . Simonian?"

The elevator doors shut, but Vanya ignores them and gasps with joy. "I am! Do we know each other? I'm so sorry if we met and I don't remember."

My mother waves her off. "You were a child, is nothing."

"You must know my parents then?" Vanya asks, hopeful.

But I am not feeling optimistic. I know something is up. My parents know her and do *not* like her for some reason.

My dad releases a "hmph" sound, then goes on tinkering with the miniature dials on his watch.

Out of sheer embarrassment, I say, "Watch giving you trouble again, Bab? We should look into a new one."

My mom's mouth barely moves as she speaks, trying to keep the smile intact. She responds to Vanya. "We do. We knew Nora and Toros long ago. But it's been many years. So, we will not keep you any more. Very late now, it was nice seeing you."

Bab twitches at the mention of Vanya's parents' names. And Vanya seems to be catching on now, her smile dropping slightly, but she maintains her politeness. "You, too, hope to see you around."

What the hell was that about? Now I can't wait to usher them upstairs so I can grill them about their rudeness and get to the bottom of this. I wonder vaguely if Vanya's been in some scandal, but then I remember how my mother said Vanya's parents' names like touching broken glass, how my father flinched.

"What a coincidence." I laugh uneasily. "See," I tell Vanya, "we figured they would know each other."

My mom squeezes her eyes, shifting her fake smile into an uncomfortable one and mashes the elevator button twice with her thumb.

The elevator is long gone, leaving in its wake the four of us, shifting around. Vanya scratches her arm near her tattoo. My father glances up at the elevator, fruitlessly searching for more information about what's taking so long.

We are saved by a voice, or so it seems. "Anoushigus, eench guness gor—? Amah."

In the hallway mere feet away is a pretty blond woman around my mom's age, rather made up with spider lashes and visible bronzer, who was smiling at Vanya and is now clutching her chest. She's fit and seems muscular, which, as I mentioned with the exercise thing, is rare for older Armenians. The man with her dons a T-shirt with a few rhinestones and a Gucci belt over tight dark jeans. He is similarly toned, and as he draws nearer, it seems he's sporting hair plugs. I catch his brief surprise, which morphs into toughness.

By the way Vanya is blushing and my mother seems rigid as a tombstone, I am guessing these are her parents. Whoa. Not the artistic hippies I would have imagined birthed Vanya with her Mayr Hayastan tattoo, but I should know better. My parents and I look nothing alike. They're dressed formally, conservatively, like it's the eighties, but without the shoulder pads and loud prints. My mom's hairstyle makes her look older than she is, and my dad has embraced the gray. I'm not the trendiest person alive, but I like to think I am somewhat modern.

"Hera, Hagop, what a surprise," says the woman I believe must be Nora. She has an accent similar to my parents', which makes me think she must have come to the US around the same time. Not a surprise, as most Lebanese Armenians in the Bay Area immigrated here during the Lebanese Civil War in the seventies. My father was "lucky" and had a work visa in the US, but he had to leave the rest of his family behind. My mother escaped with her family during a quiet night without shelling. I feel instantly guilty thinking about all they went through, all they sacrificed to give me a life where I could rent my own apartment and work the job I want.

Then the guilt is replaced with a stomach-churning anxiousness when I see my mom's closed-off expression.

"Not too much surprise," says Mom in a stunning contradiction. She has never told a friend or acquaintance they're wrong, and is usually polite to a fault. "We are both in food business after all."

Nora laughs a short, fake laugh. "Yes, yes. And you are all together, Vanya, hm?"

She peers into Vanya's eyes, demanding answers as to what's going on. Bab and the man I assume is Toros are giving each other a death stare. I get the sense that Nora is perhaps similarly hostile to my parents.

Vanya's usual veneer of coolness has a couple of chips in it. "Nazeli and I just met. We didn't know you all . . . knew each other so well. That's nice, right?"

The elevator dings, saving us all from this awkwardness.

"It's so late, we should probably head up," I say, nodding toward the elevator.

Toros speaks, and his voice isn't as deep as my dad's, for being a more imposing figure than him. "We've got a big day tomorrow."

One by one we're squeezing into the elevator, which doesn't handle six people all that comfortably. Vanya and I are wedged in the back, and I give her a "WTF" look that she returns. My dad hits the button for the twelfth floor but doesn't ask any of the Simonians which floor they're on.

"Twelve, please," Vanya asks, then says, "Oh," when she sees it's already pressed. My eyes get huge. Same floor. Naturally.

"Tomorrow is first day of the Super Bowl competition," Nora says, seeming to put on airs. In this trapped cage, I'm smelling all the mingled perfumes and colognes of four Armenian boomers, and it's overpowering. We've got cool watery scents mingled with powdery florals and tangy fruits. I cough once, covering my mouth.

My mom raises an eyebrow. "You are doing Super Bowl competition?"

Toros scoffs. "Of course, who wouldn't try?"

Bab clears his throat and speaks at a louder-than-normal volume, voice echoing off all the metal in this box. "It would be a great chance wasted, that's what Hera and I have been saying. We are entering PakCon Superstars—that is its official name—as any rational member of this conference would do so."

I can't hide the look of disgusted shock on my face, because *this* is what gets them to do the right thing? Keeping up with the Simonians? Then again, a bit of friendly competition in business is sometimes exactly what people need to spark innovation. I shouldn't feel so slighted. This could be my chance to help my parents step up their brand.

The elevator slows, and the doors slide open to our floor.

"We'll be seeing you around, it sounds like," Toros says.

Bab simply gives a "hmph" and begins strutting toward our room, a walk I haven't before had the misfortune to see. Mom squeezes her eyes at the Simonians in something that could be loosely considered a smile before following him.

To my horror, the Simonians follow, and judging by their fierce glances at each other, I'm not the only one feeling this. How close are the damn rooms? I'm suddenly aware of how sharply sober I feel. The loose buzz from earlier has vanished.

I walk with them, in step with Vanya, waiting to get our answer, and then we do. Four doors away.

It could have been worse, I inwardly console myself. And then I see Vanya has her own room, a mere three doors down from my parents.

Toros's farewell seems more prescient than ever.

We're at Vanya's door, she and I, and our sets of parents are making their way into their rooms. Vanya's parents go in without a second glance. My parents, though, linger. Finally, my mom isn't able to keep up her shuffling and phone checking at the doorway much longer, and she disappears.

Vanya and I turn to face each other, and I speak first. "I'm going to immediately find out what the hell is going on."

"I think I got frostbite in that elevator. Holy passive aggressiveness. I almost don't want to know, but—"

I understand what she means. All we had to focus on was us and what a lovely night we had, but now it's inevitable—the parents made it clear there's *a thing* here, and we can't avoid it.

"Will I see you tomorrow?" I ask.

Vanya laughs. "Seems like it'll be hard not to. You ready to sling some kebabs or whatever they're going to have us do?"

I shake myself. "What?"

She answers, head slightly cocked, "The first challenge, no one knows what it is except we have to bring our food to the ballroom."

"Oh," I respond, remembering that as far as she knows, we've always been signed up for the PakCon Superstars challenge. "Right. Mostly."

"Get some sleep, and good luck out there. I'll text you. Not just saying that."

With those last words, she smirks, and my entire body instantly warms from it.

I slowly make to hug her, and she seems receptive, so we embrace, and it feels so freeing, getting to do this after fantasizing about it all evening, after getting that taste of a side hug in front of the bros. This is the real deal, her curls tickling my nose, picking up on the apricot scent of her hair, the press of her arms against my back. As I pull away, our cheeks skim each other, and I feel myself going beet red.

"Good night, Vanya." It comes out a whisper.

Chapter Nine

I storm into the room after my mom opens the door.

"Can someone please tell me—" I begin, but the voices are all coming at once.

"Vanya Simonian of all people!"

"That son of a gun Toros!"

I raise my voice and wave my hands. "Wait, wait. They'll be able to hear us."

Mom raises her nose in the air. "I don't care if they do, they deserve to hear."

I take a deep breath. "Could you let me know what happened with them, exactly? Who are they?"

"Snakes," my father replies.

I nod, trying so hard to keep my composure, though I want to shout at them that they're being unhelpful and, frankly, a little immature.

"They are very stuck up," says my mom. "From the city. Not like us Anjartsis."

By "the city" she means Beirut, I assume. Anjar is a small town in the east of Lebanon, majority Armenian, and Mom and Bab have always been proud to tell me about this region made up of hearty, salt-of-the-earth-type people compared to the snobbery that could be found in Beirut and the Armenians who went to French Armenian schools. But whatever that was with Vanya's parents was more than a city-country dispute. And my dad called them snakes? What?

"So you don't like them because they're from Beirut," I say, trying to temper the sarcasm in my tone, and failing. And then I'm wondering why the Simonians wouldn't like my parents—is it simply city snobbery, stemming from literally thirty to fifty years ago?

Bab waves me off. "They are not even worth our breath."

"Shad jeesht uhseer, Hagop," my mother agrees.

"We shall show them who has the superior food product," my father declares.

My mother nods fervently. "Theirs is like dry cracker in your mouth."

"They think they're too above us all to put their foods in the Arab stores, eh!" My father's face reddens, and I worry he's working himself up into a frenzy.

I barge into their show of bravado. "Speaking of the competition, are we really doing this? The Super Bowl ad challenge?"

"PakCon Superstars. Anshousht," Bab says, confirming with confidence. "Can't let those scoundrels represent our nation with their dog food. If competition is like them, we may win the top prize after all."

I'm alarmed at how much they seem to despise Vanya's parents but also amused at this fire lit under my parents when it comes to their business.

"Will you please let me help you with it? This kind of thing is my lifeblood at work. I know how to market us to the people who run PakCon. I can do it."

Mom rushes to my side and pats my arm. "Yes, you are our smart, accomplished daughter. We want you to help."

I'm beginning to glow at the praise, when she continues, "A big difference from that Vanya. I saw on her arm, she has . . . tattoo?!"

I pull away from her. "Mom, don't be so old-school. A tattoo doesn't take away your ability to be accomplished."

"We have been very modern with you dating girls, Nazeli jan," she begins. And I'm about to interrupt and tell her to please stop patting herself on the back for barely accepting my sexuality, but then she stares at me with urgency, and I'm drawn to her eyes, the terror in them. "But this is not that. Promise me," she says, tears beginning to fill her eyes. "You will not date her. Anyone but her."

My first reaction is to find Bab, hoping he'll somehow contradict her, or support me in some way, but there is resigned agreement in his downward gaze. My shirt feels itchy all of a sudden, and I scratch at my shoulder mercilessly.

"You can't ask me to do that," I say, somewhere between dazed and powerless. The guilt is too strong—with all they've done for me my whole life, I hate letting them down. As much as they drive me nuts, I love my family more than anything.

"Please," she begs, and I can see she's never meant anything more in her life.

That moment on the rooftop with Vanya, our heads bowed toward each other, the look of pure possibility in her eyes; that was something real and could bloom into an entire orchard.

So I do the thing I always fall back on with my parents, when the truth fails, when there's no other way out.

"Fine," I lie.

I'VE HAULED MY parents out of bed and gotten them to the official booth for PakCon Superstars by 9:00 a.m., aka the crack of dawn. But they have no right to complain. I got a mere five hours of sleep last night, and after pulling a long night, I feel my skin tight around my face, almost painful. My eye bags have puffed up to say hi to the world, and there's a general fuzziness coating my head.

But still, in the tunnel between the hotel and the conference center, I did not complain while my mom grumbled, "The light does not even look nice at this time of day. So sharp." Only my mom could find a way to criticize morning sunlight.

Now we're at the booth in line behind a couple of people, waiting to put our names down and enter. And pay the steep $500 entrance fee, as if the exorbitant price of PakCon wasn't enough. Once I informed them of the cost, Mom and Bab hesitated a bit and then said it'd be worth it, so I offered to pay half. They at first vehemently refused, insisting "tramuht baheh," meaning "save your money," but then gave in.

Last night in between my work—which was more stressful and took longer than anticipated because Jamie seemed to be in a contest with me as to who would write the last email response— I googled the criteria for PakCon Superstars, and the first step is registering in person.

The way it works is that each day from today—Thursday—to Saturday, there are challenges and social events each day. At the challenges, teams (i.e., brands) get cut. At the social events, there are competitions, but they are friendly and no one gets cut. However, there's a line on the website that reads "getting to know you and your brand's personality," implying you need to schmooze and you're being judged for how bubbly you are. My parents better be on their best behavior, which *can* be excellent. They're both charming when not sharing an elevator with the Simonians. My chest tightens when I remember what I "promised" my mom last night, and I wonder how cool I can play it with Vanya today.

She came through and texted me this morning.

> If I'm being honest, I'm getting through the morning waiting for the competition so we can see each other again.

And yes, she could be honest, because I love her frankness. No cryptic messages, no advanced degree needed to dissect her words. Unlike Kyle, who hasn't said a word to me.

While Mom and Bab recount *Blood on the Wisterias*, the

cheesy murder mystery movie they watched last night, I run the schedule of events in my mind again.

Today, Thursday, June 8
Mystery challenge, 1:00 p.m.

The whole competition starts off shrouded in mists of vagueness. No details on this one except for the location and to bring an array of our brand's food. I assumed it was going to be a cooking competition, but there's one coming up the following day. No idea what else it could be. Food fight? No way to prepare, which annoys me. And to add to the stress, the bottom 50 percent will be cut.

Architecture boat tour, 7:00 p.m.

The tour on the Chicago River is apparently sponsored by Big Mike's Hot Sauce. Competition TBD and participation is optional, but the website makes it seem like people who do the optional competitions will be favored for their chutzpah at the very least.

Tomorrow, Friday, June 9
Skills competition, 1:00 p.m.

Day two kicks off with a skills competition, where supposedly no brands get cut, but there is a mystery prize. Hoping it's more than a trophy, but then again we'd be lucky to get this far, so we might not even have the chance to find out.

Cooking competition, 2:00 p.m.

Immediately following is a reality show–style cooking competition. What exactly is going to be the content of the competition? It doesn't say, except to bring your brand's food again, so I'm guessing the judges will be taste testing the wares. The bottom 50 percent will be cut.

Navy Pier social, 7:00 p.m.

It says the competition will be a surprise, but the website does say it's sponsored by Lombardi's Dogs, a major Chicago institution I've heard of before, so the competition has to be hot dog related.

Saturday, June 10
Wrap-up speeches, 5:00 p.m., immediately followed by closing ceremonies, 6:00 p.m.

Apparently, in the final Super Bowl commercial, the face of the brand is going to get to say one line about their food and brand, so this competition is a precursor to it to see who has charisma and who can represent their brand well. Brand is my bread and butter, and I just hope my parents can see me as the adult I am, and trust me enough to represent them, assuming we make it to this point.

The remaining challengers will then be judged based on all the competitions they've won so far, plus that extra zhuzh they may or may not have had at the social events, and voilà, the judges will pick a winner to be announced at 6:00 p.m.

Sunday, June 11
Photos and interviews with the winner

This seems like a wrap-up where the winner gets photos and some extra press. It's the last day of PakCon, too, so this is probably an hour's worth of signing contracts and a couple of vanity pictures. Probably won't be awarded to Hagop's Fine Armenian Foods, but I know that if I can get as far as Saturday, we have a good shot.

"But how did the lady with mole on her nose know that the footprints were from corgi dog?" my mom asks Bab.

"Sorry to interrupt," I say, putting my hands on their shoulders. "But we should try to brainstorm and prepare for today's challenge."

Bab furrows his brow. "How are we supposed to when they give us no information? Guessing doesn't do any good, Nazeli jan."

He has a point. I'm so in the dark, it might be wasted energy. Or that might be my lack of sleep talking.

"What about the cooking competition tomorrow? Shouldn't we strategize?"

My dad throws up his hands good-naturedly. "What for? Hera is the best cook of anyone at the PakCon, this I guarantee you with a gold seal."

I take a breath. "Best cook of Armenian food, yes. But what if they ask us to make, I don't know, beef Stroganoff or something."

Mom waves her arm dismissively. "I can do a beef Stroganoff in my sleep."

Not the point, but I continue without getting irked. "Bad example. What if we're supposed to make, like, a Philly cheese-steak? None of us can do that."

My dad puts his arm around me. "Bezdeegus, relax. They ask us to bring our own food to the competition. No doubt they will require us to cook a meal with our own food that highlights the flavor. There is nothing to fret over."

That makes sense. It'd be most logical for brands to best showcase our food, not cook something random. Let's hope they have lebneh and dried mint back there. Certainly won't have za'atar. Well, on that point at least, we and the Simonians have an equal shot at this.

I'm curious to know what the contest organizers are like, what the general culture of the whole competition is. The sooner I can figure that out, the sooner I can understand what they're looking for and what our advantages are. One upper hand is that I'm actually thinking about this, as opposed to, say, my parents, who just want to show up the Simonians. But that drive is also pretty helpful in an event like this.

I also wonder how the Simonians will approach this entire challenge. Vanya doesn't strike me as terribly competitive, but the way she handled those guys at the bar, I don't know, I could see her getting invested and giving it her all. Her parents seem like they enjoy competition—maybe I'm wrong to assume this, but I feel like people who are extremely fit later in life usually do. Type A vibes. Plus, they have a home in swanky Saratoga, so their business must be doing well. I'm not discounting them at all, rhinestone shirts or not.

Chapter Ten

*T*he morning flies by, manning the booth and giving out samples of our food to passersby. I'm forcing my parents to be extra stingy about the samples so we have enough for the competitions. I continue to work under the table like a child with her books and try not to get stressed when Jamie says our deadline for the design deliverable has been moved a day early. I press her on why that's the case, but she says it's an upper-management decision that's out of her hands. So, cool, I guess I can sleep when I'm dead. Or fired.

My parents also fill me in on their meeting last night with Ned Richardson, the True Food grocery buyer. He seemed intrigued by my parents' earnestness about their brand—or at least, that's what I read in between the lines. Bab showed off about my mom's cooking prowess and how they captured it in their packaged food, and how Middle Eastern food in grocery stores is not authentic or flavorful enough, but how Hagop's is. All true. So Ned asked to meet them tomorrow morning in one of the conference lounge areas to hear our pitch.

I tell my parents not to worry about it, that I can own this and that I'll even create slides to share with Ned about why we stand out. And during a rare lull at work, under the table, I start on them. And fall asleep in place about half an hour later.

I wake up to my mother crouched beside me, stroking my shoulder. "Hokees, are you okay? Is time to get up now."

I adjust my neck, which feels like an iron bar is running through it, and my head is heavy with lead. Power naps have never worked for me. I only end up more tired.

"What time is it?"

"You work too hard," she chides kindly. "Always doing something. Just as important to rest."

Since I don't seem to be getting an answer, I tap the screen of my laptop and see that it's 12:45 p.m., a mere fifteen minutes until the first challenge.

"Mom!" I yell. "We can't be late. We could get cut before we even start. Come on, why didn't you wake me up sooner?"

"We make it on time," my mother retorts, not a care in the world. "You needed to sleep."

I scoot past her, bumping my head on the table as I shoot up, the dull pain jostling the already near dizziness I was feeling, and I wonder if I might simply pass out before we get a chance to leave the booth.

"Bab," I call to my dad, who is writing a note on a legal pad. "Let's all move. Can we leave this stuff here, take the cooler?"

As he's assembling his answer, I remove the cooler and the dolly from their hiding places and prep them. I usher my parents into the aisle and glance back once at the booth. Seems fine, nothing valuable left behind, though we did leave out a couple of remaining food samples. Hopefully PakCon goers will swoop by and gather them one by one. And even if not, we'll be back here after the competition.

We rush through the corridors of McCormick Place, to a chorus of *I hate being late, I hate being late* chanting in my head. I have the map in one hand and am wheeling the cooler in my other, navigating us through the intestinal labyrinth that is this conference center. My parents are striding behind, urging me to slow down, but there's no way I'm going to let us miss this. Luckily, the cooking competition room seems to be one of the largest rooms here, besides the great hall, so it's easy enough to spot as we draw near. I dare to glance at my phone, crumpling my map in the process. 12:59 p.m.

"We barely made it," I hiss at them as we open the doors.

Bab pants. "Nothing is ever on time, you didn't need to make us sprint through the hall in such an undignified fashion."

"It's called being in a rush, a very American thing that is perfectly okay."

My mom shakes her head, and she is flushed red. "I don't like it."

But then we're inside, and I cannot believe my eyes.

Chapter Eleven

*T*his space doesn't look like a conference room at all. It's been transformed into a massive, fully stocked kitchen, with rows upon rows of steel counters with sinks and ovens, and behind them seem to be endless shelves of pots and pans, six massive refrigerators, and from what I can tell, a full-on grocery store of produce and cans and oils and spices.

The room's full with about five hundred people, if I had to guess, but I remind myself that we're three to one brand, so there aren't five hundred brands to compete with, maybe more like two hundred. I don't even see the Simonians among the crowd and all the coolers they've lugged in.

But I do see several giant cameras, the kinds I've only seen on TV or in movies. Um, I didn't agree to this. Then in my mind I see the papers I signed this morning, the endless legal jargon and wait, yes I did, I literally did. There was a section in the contract that spoke vaguely about recording some of the competition, but I thought it would be a handheld camcorder type of situation, memories for the PakCon board that they'd show at their annual picnic. Maybe someone would put together a compilation in iMovie and they could post it on their website.

It all starts to make sense when I see the two people in the center of the room, away from all the contestants. There's a man, a white guy with a sturdy build who looks to be in his early forties, but he's bald, so it's hard to really tell, dressed in a blazer over a T-shirt and jeans. He has an expectant, almost manic look on his face. The woman to his right has her blond hair teased unnaturally high and seems to be wearing thick makeup, her boobs pushed up in a bustier top over jeans with sky-high heels. I smell TV people, not what I'd imagine the Food and Beverage Packagers of America Association folks look like.

"Welcome," the man says into his long black mic, "to the fifth annual PakCon Superstars event, though this year might feel a little different, for any of you who previously entered. We've given it a lot more dazzle, and set the bar higher. We are your hosts and part of the judging team. I'm Benny, and this ravishing beauty is Stephanie. You are part of an elite group . . ."

I inwardly grumble to myself that there isn't anything elite about us all except our ability to pay the entrance fee, which would be better classified as elitist. So, they jazzed it up this year. But a higher bar is a good thing. When things are hard, that's when I shine. I always did the best in classes everyone else found challenging, and sometimes slipped when they were too easy. We've so got this.

Mom and Bab are both scanning the room, obviously looking for their rivals. Mom's eyes are sharp and shrewd, while Bab looks like he's the big guy in the crew threatening to mess someone up. I'm glad he can have his illusions. I guess he *was* the Ironman back in Lebanon, but Toros looks like he can take, and throw, a punch. I inwardly shake my head, hoping their rivalry does not end up in a physical altercation.

The hosts speak, truly enjoying themselves up there, feeling very important, and I am realizing that they want this to feel like their own personal reality show. That's the culture here. Lots of flair. Drama. Not a quiet heads-down corporate event.

"Let us introduce you to the other judges," Stephanie says. And one by one she introduces them: Hugo, a French guy who owns a bouillon company we all know about; Nicholas, an Italian guy who's a representative of a huge pasta brand; another white guy, this one American, Mike, who owns the hot sauce brand sponsoring the boat event; and Melody, a white woman who owns a brand that makes diet popcorn products. Not promising. I see what Mom and Bab were saying about how these types of events aren't for people like us. This makes me scan the room, and I notice there's very little diversity in the crowd, too. I get the sense that our brand, which embraces the traditions of Western Armenian cultural cuisine, will not be at an advantage among the judges.

"So without further ado," Benny announces, staring at us with great intent, "we're going to announce our first challenge."

He pauses, scans the crowd like a magician about to produce a white bunny rabbit, then claps his hands, and a banner unfurls behind him with a snap.

I read the words as he recites them. "Challenge One: Food Styling."

There's a murmur of "oohs" among the crowd as they take in the meaning of what we're about to do next. My mouth is shut, though; it's hard to think properly with my heart clamoring in my chest, straight up to my ears. Because aesthetics? Visual beauty? Not my thing, nor my parents'. The food comes out like slop in a bowl but tastes like heaven. I'm not completely hopeless in that I can point to any two designs and tell you which is the superior one, but I could never create myself. I just don't have the eye. That's why I have such immense respect for the designers at work and let them know that I realize critiquing is a hundred times easier than creation, that I appreciate their talents. Talents I have zero of.

I remember the one time I brought a plate of cucumbers with garlic mint dip to a party and the host took a look at my platter and kindly said, "Aw, it got jostled in the car. Don't worry, we can fix it." But those disarrayed cucumbers were how I had originally plated them.

Then, a wisp of a thought pops up. Work. *Abby*. Abby, the creative one on our team, also channels her design skills into a thriving Instagram account featuring coffee, pastries, and books. She can create a flat lay that'll bring tears to your eyes. When I complimented her artistry, Abby said she learned through Pinterest. Found something similar to what she wanted to create and used it as the template.

Mom is asking, "What does this mean exactly, *food styling*?" when Benny's voice starts up again, louder to be heard among the voices.

"As you know, the winner of the entire PakCon Superstars

challenge will have their food featured in our Super Bowl TV ad. Now, the styling of your food is paramount to the ad, and we're looking for brands whose culinary delights will light up on camera—"

I whip out my phone and open the Pinterest app, which I last used to get inspiration for throw pillow colors. Then I realize I should probably set it aside for now and pay attention.

Stephanie goes on to tell us where all our cooking and food needs are located, but that we're not allowed to scout them until the timer officially starts.

Benny continues, "We'll be texting you the number of your table shortly, so please make your way over to your assigned number and bring your brand's food with you."

My phone dings with a text, and I see we're assigned one hundred and forty-nine. It's dumb but I like that number, the way it looks and feels in my head, and that gives me a sense of optimism, that not all is lost.

Mom peers over my shoulder. "Which number?" she asks, and I tell her. The crowd is already moving around us like centipede legs, so we begin to push through ourselves.

Among the throng of competitors, my shoulder is kicked back by someone who wasn't watching where they were going. I'm rubbing the offended area when I see, oh God, it's Toros.

My family stands dead still as Toros marches ahead, but Nora and Vanya stop in front of us, and we simply stare at each other, the crowd swarming on all sides.

"Hi," I say stupidly, glancing at Vanya. We were texting this morning, so I know Vanya and I are cool, but I wonder if she had to make a similar bargain with her parents about me.

"Wild, huh? Good luck out there," Vanya calls to us over the noise of shuffling feet and frantic conversation. She means it, and the honest shine in her eyes inspires a swell of tenderness in me.

In complete contrast, our mothers both give each other their variants of fake smiles, and I say, "You too," hoping to impart the same type of warmth before we move on. I glance over my shoulder once, and I see Toros doubling back, waving in our direction.

It's pandemonium in here with all the bodies racing to their tables and setting up their wares. We've reached table one forty-nine, made of steel, a chef's floating table. At my request, Bab opens the cooler and begins unloading our food onto the table. We have lavash, dolma, falafel, and manti. I think the manti would take too long to cook and style, and instead we can make a beautiful mezze plate. *Those cucumbers, though.* I shake away the memory, remembering I'll have Pinterest this time. While arranging isn't my forte, I can mimic pretty well and hope that skill extends to laying food out on a plate.

On the app, I search "Mediterranean mezze platter" and am surprised by a ton of lovely-looking results. I pick the one that looks fullest and richest, and decide this will be our beacon.

Then I start to mentally note what we'll need. They probably have olives and feta back there. That feels vaguely Italian and Mediterranean enough, that the people running this show might stock it. Hopefully some mint and pretty greens, too. Otherwise, I guess we can plate falafel with dill and bell pepper and go for more of a fusion.

And there, in the row in front of us and slightly off to the side, is where the Simonians land. They must have been headed the wrong way at first and doubled back. They don't see us, but my parents see them. I don't mind. There's fire in their eyes, and I hope it'll get them to chop like the dickens. But also evenly.

Benny's self-loving voice booms over the speakers. "Everyone, take your places now. Do not begin until you hear the buzzer. You will have twenty minutes to put together your spread." He points above him to where a digital timer is showing 20:00 in threatening red.

Thank goodness our food is all cold. The manti would need to be cooked, but we can do without it for this challenge. I wonder what foods Vanya and her family brought. Taste won't matter for this portion, so if they have skill with arranging, they should be good to go. In fact, I'm a bit worried that our dishes are too similar. The judges would probably cut one of the Middle Eastern food brands, right?

An offensive, shakes-up-your-liver buzzer rings through the room, followed by a flurry of body movement all around us. The timer reads 19:58. I lost two seconds to shock already.

I face my parents. "Mom, Bab, I was thinking we could create a mezze platter." I proffer my phone, the vaunted Pinterest photo.

Mom shakes her head. "That is too boring, everyone has seen

this before. Let us crisp some manti in the broiler and arrange on circular sini."

I was not prepared for this. I also spare a glance at the Simonians, and they are wonderfully in sync, the parents chopping while it looks like Vanya has gone off in search of produce or platters. I try for tact. "I'm not so sure about that idea. It might seem too . . . foreign to them. Plus meat and filo dough? Doesn't look as good."

"But is unique," my father adds.

"Fine, fine," I concede, noting we're already at 19:14. "Let's do both. Mom, can you do all the manti prep and Bab and I will put together the mezze?"

"Anshousht, but I might need some help at end. Hurry up with that mezze, it should be easy."

Right, super simple. I slam my phone on the table in front of Bab. "Can you cut the lavash in squares like this? I'm going to run out there to try and find—" I stare at the screen and finish, "the olives, feta, mint, radishes, parsley. But shoot, what about the lebneh? No way they'll have it back there, right?"

Bab says, "No one is tasting, so we can put on a ruse. A yogurt masquerade."

I can't help but smile. "Perfect," I say, and run off in search of the ingredients and a long wooden serving platter.

I need to fight through the crowds like pushing to the front of a concert—which I have only done once before, at the behest of my little brother, who needed to see Drake when he came to the Coliseum and, more importantly, required a chaperone to be allowed to go as a fifteen-year-old. I grab a shopping basket and dart between bodies and limbs to grab the produce needed, which makes me feel like a desperate scavenger, a feeling I don't like. I briefly wonder at myself for thinking this whole PakCon Superstars idea was a smart one. Behind a computer or in a conference room is where I'm most comfortable. I like my interactions with other humans to be a buttoned-up affair, where people throw around acronyms, not zucchini. And if they don't like something, they use a euphemism instead of elbowing strangers to get the last bunch of radishes. I was triumphant with the radishes, though. I'm similarly successful with the refrigerated products, but I do seem to be lagging. Most people are already jogging back to their tables.

The shelves with the platters have already been thoroughly picked through, and most of them are either too small or too large, or weird shapes like shells. I'm on the verge of actual panic when I see it, precisely the type of wooden platter in the photo, just the right size for an impressive display without being too huge. My hands reach the edge, when I see her. On the other side of the shelf, touching the same tray, is Vanya.

She appears apologetic, a softness to her features. "This plate's not big enough for the both of us."

I momentarily don't care about the plate; my whole mood is lifted by her levity. She's adorable, joking at a time like this, and I find myself wanting to know so much more about her. And not wanting to snatch the last good platter out of her hands.

"It's yours," I say, pushing it toward her.

"No way. I'm not taking it from you."

"Well, same here," I say, hands off the platter.

She mirrors me, lifting her hands, too. A standoff. Then we see a vulture in the form of a man in his forties eyeing our tray with a determined furrow, and we both instantly grab it again.

I say, "If neither of us takes it, someone else will. I'm sure you were here first anyway. Please, do it." Then I add, averting my eyes, "I'm sure you can find a way to pay me back later."

She's all smiles. Her teeth are small; I'd go so far as to call them cute. Never thought of someone's mouth bones being charming, but hers are.

Her voice is quieter. "I will say, I am very good at returning the favor."

Oh my God.

She grabs the plate and says, "Thank you, seriously."

And I allow myself a moment to watch her dash off—graceful pattering, like she knows I'm watching—before noticing the clock tick down to 15:02. Shoot.

This may have screwed us over into an elimination, but somehow it feels worth it. Then, the fact that I genuinely feel that way, scares me. This is not teamwork, where helping out a member of the company helps everyone. We are head-to-head, and I gave my direct competitor an advantage. Where's my fighter spirit? I need to put her out of my head for at least the next fourteen minutes and fifty-two seconds.

With military efficiency, I scan a few more rows and spot a standard white porcelain platter that's a decent size. Not the lovely rich browns of the wooden tray Vanya just took, but it's more about what's inside, right? I tell myself Abby would probably say something like that as I race back to our station, platter and groceries in hand.

The room is filling with mingling smells from frying, baking, boiling. Sweet fruit being roasted, the savory scent of garlic, as I pass station after station. Back at the table, Bab has done a decent job of cutting the lavash and laying out the dolmas and falafel, ready to be styled. Mom, though, is shaking her hands over a pungent pan of blackened manti.

"Broiler is much higher than at home, sakhat . . ."

No one has ever broiled manti before because that's not how you're supposed to do it, it'd be totally inedible, but I get it, this is all about looks. Still, I wish that instead of trying again, she could help us chop up the many vegetables I've plopped onto the workspace.

The energy in the room has become more frantic. There are fewer large movements—almost everyone is back at their tables now, plating or flash cooking, and the chatter is quieter, but the hum of it all together is like one big, nervous hive. The judges, who are all overdressed for the occasion, wend their ways through the tables, inspecting, and raising an eyebrow here and there. The cameras follow them, or wander away and home in on contestants, especially ones shouting at each other, hand waving and all.

Bab motions to where the knives are, and I pick one up and start on the radishes, when I feel my phone vibrate. Debating whether or not to lose focus here, I check it anyway. What if it's—

Jamie, via *text*, which is the scariest form of communication to receive from her, meaning she's exhausted all other options. You haven't been answering Slack or emails for the past hour. You said you were going to be available during your time away. This is a crucial moment for the team and we need you on task and communicative. Please respond ASAP.

Oh God. I can picture the ends of her baby-pink manicured nails sawed off flat, clicking against her desk as she's waiting for me to answer.

But she can wait another fifteen minutes. That's nothing in the grand scheme. But this timer ticking down, that's real. I need to refocus.

Even as I chop, I hear her words *need you on task*, and I strike the blade down harder each time. The cacophony of smells in this room becomes almost unbearable. After one particularly loud *whop* of the blade, Bab looks over.

"This is not how you cut a radish," he says gently.

He nudges me and hovers his hand over my knife, silently asking for it. I relinquish the knife, and he takes over the chopping, which, admittedly, he's better at, and it's a smart idea to keep me away from knives while I'm still seething over being chastised by my boss.

Instead, I glance toward the inspiration photo and begin arranging the ready items on our platter. Jamie's admonishment still rings red-hot in my head, and I have to keep from slamming the dolmas onto the porcelain plate. I allow myself a moment to glance toward Vanya, whose eyes have narrowed in concentration as she smooths the top of a bowl of hummus with a spoon. Their platter is already fairly well stocked with

Mediterranean-esque foods and some wild cards like roma-
nesco cauliflower, which is definitely not Armenian but goes
along with their health food vibe.

Still, looking at her is like splashing cool water over my face,
a balm for the heat of Jamie's message.

After most of the items have been arranged, I realize it's not
quite . . . it's only okay, nothing that should win a competition.
I wish I could dial Abby and get some tips, but I'd never do
that. Instead, I nudge Bab. "It needs something. It feels a little
unbalanced. What do you think?"

He inspects, like a master clockmaker attempting to detect
the slightest millimeter of a peg off course. "Is good, but it
needs—"

He begins scooting the dolmas a bit and turns over the radishes so more of the red is popping. He continues to make small
adjustments, and I start to notice the board transforming with
each one, a slow bloom from something decent to something
special. I would never have been able to do this on my own, and
I marvel at my dad's secret talent.

And . . . it's done. Holy moly, it looks fantastic. This is as
good as the Pinterest photo—better actually, since the color
variation in person pops so beautifully.

"Damn, Bab. Didn't know you had it in you."

"Please do not use the word 'damn.' But yes, I, too, am surprised. Thank you, my daughter."

Before I can smile too much about it, our attention is caught
by Mom, who is lifting a fresh, unburned batch of manti out of
the oven. They are looking prime: The filo dough is a crispy

golden brown, and the meat poking through is still sizzling but not overcooked or charred. To me, manti always looked like little kisses. The two sides of the dough pressed together like the sides of the mouth, the filling like lips. Maybe it's also because my mom is such a genius at making them, she imparts her love into each crispy piece.

But at the moment, they're all disarrayed on the baking sheet, and that's not going to win us any awards. I remember then that all the trays left over were odd shapes, and I tell my parents to hold on a second, that I'll be right back. I rush over to the trays, the only person back at this section with three minutes remaining on the clock, though there is an errant contestant or two plucking a garnish from the produce section.

I spy a tasteful heart-shaped platter (*tasteful* being the key word, because there are several of the untasteful varieties) and know this could be perfect if the three of us can pull off lining up the manti pieces.

I sprint back to my parents, lay the platter down next to the manti baking tray. Mom and Bab are waving their arms over the manti trying to cool them off.

"Let's line them up in here," I say, indicating the tray and moving my finger in straight lines across.

Bab says, "Yes, but we should do like this," using his finger to outline the tray instead.

"This is better idea," says Mom, agreeing with him. So do I, especially after seeing what Bab was able to do with the mezze platter.

Two minutes and seventeen seconds to go.

I reach for the first manti. It stings my fingers, still hot, and Mom and Bab seem to be enduring the same sensation, though their fingers have roughened over the years, so it doesn't appear to affect them as much. We work together as quickly as possible, often accidentally reaching for the same spot and then conceding it.

One outline done. One minute and thirty-nine seconds.

Yikes. But the other outlines are smaller, so we can do it.

We place one after the other, reaching a type of rhythm, my fingertips on fire to the point where I occasionally can't feel them anymore.

Fifty-one seconds.

We're in the center of the heart now, probably two or so more outlines to go. There's so little space left that I step back and let Mom and Bab fill in the details. The rest of the room feels frantic. People are shouting at one another; I feel their gestures all around me.

The last manti comes up uneven; it's too small for the space, but adding a second one wouldn't fit, either.

"What we do?" Mom asks.

"Leave it like that, is fine," Bab says.

Twenty-two seconds.

I glance at the baking pan with the rest of the unused manti pieces and spy two runts. I scoop them up and place them down in the center of the heart, side by side. I wave my hands to try to cool my fingers.

Eleven seconds.

It's not perfect yet. I adjust a couple more of the manti pieces so that everything is as even as possible, and I'm on the last few when I hear the judges chant in unison, "Five, four, three, two, one."

The buzzer goes off, loud in my chest.

"Hands up, everyone. No more adjusting. We've got cameras in here, and we will be reviewing the footage, so no cheating."

I jump back from the manti. We did it—they are perfectly even, the heart platter resting comfortably next to the mezze platter. If we ever served anything this pretty at Thanksgiving or Easter, our relatives would go wild for it, photos would be taken, compliments given, and aunties silently jealous. So if this spread isn't good enough for the judges, I'm not sure what they're looking for.

"I'm going to take a picture of this and post on Facebook," Mom says. "That Kohar, supposed grand master chef, will be red with jealousy."

One of my mom's frenemies from back when I was at Armenian school, the mom of my classmate. She posts constantly on Facebook, and I swear every meal she makes or has at a restaurant is documented there, always without a hint of modesty. Everything is "the best" or "number one." I don't blame my mom for wanting to show her up.

I'm drawn to a massive projection along one of the bare walls that reads **Styling Competition Results** and has about two hundred or so brand names on it in alphabetical order, each with an empty checkbox to its right. So that's how they're doing it? All out in the open for everyone to see who passed and who failed.

Stephanie speaks again. "Our judges will be visiting each of you to make their final decisions. Please do not speak to them unless they speak first; we have a lot of entries to get through, so we want to keep the conversation to a minimum. As soon as the judge makes their choice—pass or fail—you'll see that company's fate on the wall behind me." She waves at it with great drama, and I swear she is growing larger with the exercise of power. "Remember that about half of you today will be cut. Regardless of your outcome, excellent work, everyone, and good luck!"

Judges begin waltzing through the room with iPads, taking photos of the foods, ticking off boxes with alarming speed, and moving on. The board lights up with green check marks and red *x*'s, with an extra strike-through over the brand name to leave no doubt of who didn't make the cut. To add to the anxiousness, with each decision there's a peppy sound effect for passes and a short, sad buzzer for fails.

The judges still seem fairly far away from us, and from Vanya's family, too, and I'm not sure if I want to get it over with quickly or wait until the last moment. I want a win for Mom and Bab so badly, to show that we are good enough, that they were right to take this chance, that they could be rewarded. Even if we don't win it all—because that seems so unlikely given how many competitors there are—if we advance closer to the finals, that'd be something undeniably huge to be proud of.

As if by instinct, I glance up in the direction of the Simonians and catch Vanya staring my way, toward our table, then right at me. I can't help it. I smile at her and give her a surreptitious thumbs-up near my navel. She winks and turns around, and I swear my insides dissolve into liquid. I'm seeing her again tonight, promise to Mom or not.

She seems to be in a good mood, which means they must have finished on time, too. Her parents are blocking their display, so I can't see much of it except the edge of some lettuce. Interesting choice. Despite my parents wanting to beat the Simonians, I secretly hope we both advance to the next round. More time with Vanya. Better for my parents, too, I tell myself. They need that extra motivation, as I wonder if, without the Simonians in their face, they'd show this level of hustle again.

Looks like I'm about to find out. Melody, the health popcorn judge, approaches the Simonians' table, which is a stroke of luck since they're in the same business of creating something calorieless out of something delicious.

Then, before I can be audience to their destiny, Benny swoops next to us, and I assume he's going to judge our table, but he stops at the counter behind ours. There, a way-too-pretty, tall brunette with eyebrows that look perfected by microblading stands in front of a bowl of red-sauce spaghetti with artfully shaved Parmesan and parsley flakes. And I could swear that Benny nods toward her in an overly familiar way.

But then there's a quick jab to my ribs from Mom, and I see the Italian judge, Nicholas, presiding over our table. I am thankful we got matched with the most Mediterranean person among them, but still. Mom and Bab stand up straighter, and part of me wants to make fun of them until I realize I've done it myself.

He's a nice-looking guy, a full head of salt-and-pepper hair, in a fade to gray at his temples, but he's got a sour face, like he hasn't smiled for years. His discerning eyes examine our display. There are happy pips and whining buzzing going off all around us as the scoreboard fills. I don't dare look up to see if Vanya's advanced to the next round, though.

He points to the manti. "Never seen those." I hold my breath. *Damn it, Mom. We're going to get x-ed out for throwing some "unknown" food into the mix, despite how pleasing it looks on its tray.*

Mom takes this as an invitation to speak, and I try to grasp her hand to stop her, but she pulls it away. "Manti, a meat dumpling like my grandmother used to make in Lebanon. We have secret recipe. Only three women in my family know," she flirts.

Oh my God, Mom, I want to groan, but I keep a tight smile plastered on my face. Not going to work on this guy.

"Sounds delicious," he says, a smile—if you can call it that—beginning to twitch.

What? Is this actually working?

"Is a shame you can't taste," she replies, laying it on thick. Her eyes are shining with concern that this poor man won't get to taste her manti.

Now he breaks into a full-on smile. "I'm tempted, but better not. Maybe in the next round, though?"

With that, he takes a photo of our creation, taps his iPad screen, and walks off with a small wave. I haven't seen any other judges acknowledge a contestant as they walked away.

"Mom," I shout-whisper over the crowd. "Garzem te hagh-detzink," I tell her in Armenian. And confirming my suspicions, there's our name on the board, Hagop's Fine Armenian Foods, with a confident green check mark beside it.

It was the manti. And my mom's whole "I'm just an old country lady who wants to feed you" shtick.

"I had not one doubt in our abilities," my dad says, smiling wide at us, ready to pull us in for a hug.

Mom is still squinting at the board. "Is this correct? We advanced? Hagop, are you seeing it?"

"Hera jan, it's right there," he says in Armenian. He draws one arm over her. "We win."

And while they're scanning, I see the Green Falafel has also advanced to the next round. Vanya is hugging her parents, and while she's in an embrace with her mom, she's turned toward us, congratulating me with her eyes.

Chapter Twelve

*M*om and Bab step out of a taxi (because my parents don't trust rideshare services) and onto a platform overlooking the Chicago River. I've been hanging out here for about ten minutes waiting to meet them, and have decided this has instantly become one of my favorite places I've been. The sun's low in the sky, and though it's almost 7:00 p.m., the air's wrapped me in a warm embrace. There are skyscrapers all around us, including a huge cream art deco building with a clock tower, another that looks like a Gothic version of 30 Rock, surrounded by modern blue-, black-, and green-glassed buildings. And all the buildings wind around the Chicago River and its ripples of waves, skyscrapers following its lead and keeping it guarded. It's such an inviting mix of the past and present, and I'm hoping that we will get some architectural history on this boat tour as promised.

Bab has donned his white pants and purple-brown-green-gold-striped shirt for the occasion, which, I'll be honest, puts him ahead of Mom and me fashion-wise. Very Gucci 1991. Mom's wearing a pretty, flowy dress with some paisley arrangements on the bottom. I'm in a dress that is skirting the line between professional and sexy, semifitted and white with a daring low-cut crisscross that absolutely intentionally shows off my cleavage. But it's behind the diagonal pieces of fabric, which doesn't make the presentation so overt.

"You sure this boat is safe?" Mom asks, eyeing the water.

We're still a bit away from the crowd that's gathered for the boat, since I wanted to be able to meet them easily, but we can see our vessel.

"They do like ten tours a day," I say, not entirely sure that's true, but it feels true. "Look how big and flat they are." At least that's undeniable. It's a barge almost as wide as it is long, with plenty of seats and places to roam. The event staff plus the judges seem to already be on board. Stephanie is taking a selfie with Hugo, the French judge.

Mom wrinkles the corner of her mouth in passive agreement.

After our big win, Mom went right up to Benny and asked if he had any to-go containers. He was so taken aback he couldn't come up with a proper response other than, "No, I . . . don't know who does."

But Mom, ever persistent, wrapped all our food in lavash and popped it into the cooler, and then we celebrated by eating it picnic-style in my parents' room and recalling our various moments of worry and excitement. It was only then that I remembered Jamie's text, and the celebratory mood sloughed off me.

I hightailed it back to my hotel, where I'd been working and taking calls until I arrived here. It turns out that emergency fire drill Jamie needed me for wasn't anything significant at all; it was to weigh in on the color of the header font, between burnt orange and roasted carrot. She said I need to be there to sign off on these major changes, but I trust my team to make a call on a header color between two nearly identical shades of orange. She shouldn't be involved in the discussion at all; it's way below her pay grade. I almost suspect she butted in and made an issue out of the oranges where there wasn't one before. Jamie's always been on the tougher side, but Operation Wolf is pushing her into new, unstable territory.

In happier news, Vanya and I also texted each other mutual congratulations on our wins. She sent me a photo of their spread, and it was gorgeous, better than ours. I mean, the wooden platter helped, but Vanya said she enjoys this kind of thing. She's being modest; she definitely has a talent for aesthetics. They'd displayed their dry falafel and flat hummus with a cornucopia of fresh, salad-y foods meant to show how to make a falafel lettuce wrap. I was sure their health food judge must have loved it. We also made plans to hang out after the boat tour, spot TBD. I honestly wouldn't care if we sat on a sidewalk somewhere; I only want to spend time with her.

Now, I check out the crowd of PakCon Superstars hopefuls to spot Vanya, but she and her family don't seem to be here yet. There's still a bit of time, though. I told my parents the boat tour started at six thirty so that they would arrive before seven, and lo, here they are at a quarter to seven. It's the only way.

"Shall we?" I ask them, motioning toward the group.

"It has been a long time since I have been swimming," Mom grumbles as we approach the crowd waiting to board.

"I personally have been looking forward," Bab says. "I've read a number of articles of interest about Chicago's history of architecture. This is the Wrigley Building, for instance. The same as the gum. You remember the Doublemint commercials, of course."

Oh yes, there was a phase in my life where I wished more than anything I had a twin sister to play make-believe with, not my rough-and-tumble toddler brother who I nicknamed Randy Savage. I owed that escapism to the Wrigley's Doublemint gum commercials.

As we approach, the ropes to the boat are lifted, and contestants begin filtering on board. We're toward the back of the line, and that's when I see them—Vanya and her parents.

Toros is wearing a different rhinestone T-shirt today; Nora is in a tight dress in lime green, which is a color that suits her; and Vanya is wearing a linen jumper with a sheer pink shirt underneath paired with red platform sandals and light pink socks. I don't think I've seen anyone pull off such a look in my life.

I watch her eyes fall to the crisscross on my chest, and I know I've done well myself.

The energy takes on a hostile air then, which I quickly realize is because the parents have spotted one another. They all look away, and the best I can hope for is that the dominant theme between them this evening will be "ignoring each other's presence."

While Vanya walks away with her parents, I plot how I can steal away from mine to accidentally on purpose bump into Vanya on the boat ride.

I'm curious to see what the friendly competition on board is going to be. Hopefully they aren't planning to try to test our nerve and dare people to jump into the river. There are a few people aboard who seem like they'd be game—a couple of disheveled bros who I imagine own a disruptive energy bar company and look like they'd volunteer to star on *Jackass*.

There's an usher taking everyone to their seats, and it must be the way Vanya and I are glancing at each other, but this young man rounds up me, my parents, and the Simonians, and takes us to our seats. All next to one another. The other rows are taken or quickly filling up behind us so, stunned, we all reluctantly sit. We land in this order: Nora, Toros, Vanya, Me, Bab, Mom. This is fine. This could not possibly cause problems.

"Babe," Toros says to Nora, sounding like *beb*. "This reminds me of the Viking River Cruise we took. On the Seine . . ." He pauses and slightly glances in Bab's direction. "In France."

Bab lets out a "pff" sound and mutters, "Babam, I know where is the Seine."

Nora perks up. "Such beautiful memory, Toros. Paris will always have piece of my heart."

Mom delivers her a poison smile. "Must be so nice to have the ability to go on pleasure cruise in Europe."

Nora beams and says, "Yes, we were very lucky."

Bab grumbles, "Stealing chances from others is not what I say is luck."

What? First snakes, now stealing. My parents have got to spill actual details when I get a minute alone with them.

But Toros understands Bab's meaning. It's like Bab jabbed

Toros with a stick. He protests, "Hey—" but the rest of his voice is drowned out by an earsplitting mic tap. I say a quick thank-you to whoever intervened before that got out of hand.

I look up to see a man sitting atop a comically tall stool.

He speaks. "Welcome, PakCon Superstars hopefuls. I'm Rob, your tour guide for the evening, here to guide you through the Chicago River."

Rob is what my prejudiced self thought all Chicagoans looked like: a sturdy man with a haircut inspired by Guy Fieri, and a Hawaiian shirt unbuttoned two buttons too low. His voice is jaunty, too jaunty, seeming on the verge of sliding off the rails.

"This is an extra-special tour for all of us. I see we got cameras up all over, so everyone better be on their best behavior, myself included."

There's a light chuckle from the audience, but I'm feeling un-settled; isn't this man supposed to be leading us? At least he's not steering the boat. Between our tour guide's dubious sobriety and my and Vanya's parents' passive-aggressive "death to you" postures, I'm already seasick.

He raises a finger. "Oh, I'm supposed to say this event is sponsored by Big Mike's Hot Sauce, purveyors of the Punch-Your-Gut Ghost Pepper Hottie. Woof, my ulcer says we're gonna skip out on that one. If you're brave enough, the fine folks at Big Mike's have set up a hot sauce chicken wing competition over on the starboard side of the deck. For you non–naval craft folk, that'd be right over yonder." He points to the side of the boat I can't see from here.

I wonder how quickly we can get out of our seats and head over there. Hot sauce isn't my family's specialty, as my mom complains of heartburn, but we need to at least try. Show the judges we're willing to give those wings a shot. I wonder vaguely if my parents have ever had chicken wings.

The boat pushes forward with a light lurch, and there's no stopping it now.

"Well, starting off, this beauty over here is the Tribune Tower, built in 1923 in the style o' the times, art deco."

My dad nods. "Robert"—he pronounces it in a French way, with a silent *t*—"is not quite correct. It is true the lower half has art deco in it, but the style of the tower is described better as 'Gothic revival'. I have read it in that article in the *Smithsonian* on Chicago River architecture prior to this tour."

Toros grunts loudly.

"Is there an issue, Toros?" Bab pushes his head into the aisle and gives the man a stare. I want to get us out, anywhere but here.

"Are you here as fact-checker, officially? If the tour guide not up to the standard, are you gonna report him and get him kicked out? I know you like doing that kind of thing," Toros says, chuckling bitterly to himself.

"*Dad*," Vanya seethes through her teeth.

I don't know what Toros is referring to, but I wouldn't put it past Bab to complain about pedantic matters. I glance over to him and spot a vein in his neck I rarely see, bulging. I shoot out of my seat. This isn't good for Bab's blood pressure, and I'm not going to let him get into an argument with a man who yearns for the days of Ed Hardy.

"Who needs a drink?" I ask, mostly to my parents, but I inch my body toward Vanya somewhat so she knows it's directed at her, too.

"I would love one," Vanya says. I can feel the desperation pulling at her voice. Right now, I know what I promised Mom and I know what she's seeing, but I don't care. We can't all be sitting together waiting until a full-on brawl breaks out or my dad has an anger-induced stroke.

I edge out of the seat, Vanya trailing me, and I'm grateful to have her company but not sure leaving all our parents together is actually a better idea without us as intermediaries. But then Mom heaves out of her seat as well, not losing a chance to chaperone Vanya and me, and Bab follows. Okay, this'll be awkward, but fine. And then Toros stands up and so does Nora, and we're all headed starboard (apparently) to where the drinks are and where the competition is going on.

This should be one of the most visually memorable experiences of my life, sailing past glass and stone while the humidity sinks into my skin. Instead, I'm nauseated by the thought of what horrifying possibilities are to come.

The hot sauce booths pull into view. They've set up six booths to accommodate everyone on the boat who wants to try this out, and there's a bar with a number of bartenders opposite them. The booths each have a judge and someone else who seems in charge, probably a Big Mike's Hot Sauce brand rep, preparing the wings and sauce. All the booths are taken except for one, but I absolutely need a drink first.

The crowds swirl around us, and I feel like there are a couple of familiar people from the styling competition, the too-pretty brunette with the pasta and the *Jackass* bros. The noise of chatter and Rob's commentary—"rebuilt from the ground up, which is how it got its nickname the Second City. Not like you Yankee snobs might think, because it's second to New York"—give Vanya and me some cover. I move toward the bar line but also step closer to her, purposefully brushing my arm against hers, and she glances at me, her eyes delighted by my move.

She says, "When can we break away from all this?"

Every time she reminds me we're in sync, it's both a surprise and weirdly expected, because I'm feeling it before she says anything. I'm struck by a freeing sensation of flying, ascending this boat into a land of only her and me. I tell her, "The second we get off this boat, let's run."

"It's a deal," she replies.

Before I have a chance to internally celebrate this, I sense something's wrong. We're surrounded by people, but I quickly realize the shadow of my parents is missing. I scan the crowd, and moments later spot them, stepping up to the open hot wings booth, with Toros and Nora next to them.

"Oh God, they're doing the hot sauce challenge together," I gasp, not containing my horror to Vanya.

"My dad has some weird throat issue; he should not be doing this," Vanya says, concern coating her words. And though Toros doesn't seem like the nicest man in the world, her worry for him is touching.

We rush up to our parents, and thankfully they haven't started yet. Mom is reaching for possibly the first chicken wing of her life, but the brand rep, whose name tag reads DOUG, is still plating the rest of the wings with a pair of tongs.

As Nora grasps her plate, she asks, "Do these have gluten?"

I catch my mom rolling her eyes.

"They're chicken wings, ma'am," Doug says in an almost mocking manner. I instantly dislike him, with his thin beard and unremarkable eyes.

She smiles. "I know this. Do they have gluten?"

"They do."

Her smile falls. "Oh, I see. Well, for the competition—"

Vanya asks her parents, "What are you guys doing? Dad, your throat. I don't think—"

Toros interrupts her. "Vanya seerelis, you worry too much." But even I can sense the falseness in his voice. He is definitely attempting to hide his own worry.

"Mom, what about your IB—"

"Vanya!" her mom shouts, tiny and shrill as a hummingbird. Then she softens, saying, "Why don't you do with us?"

"Can't wait to say I told you so tonight," Vanya grumbles, stepping beside them.

Realizing I'm in this, too, now, I say to Doug, as shortly as possible, "I'm with them. Hagop's Fine Armenian Foods."

"All right then, everyone keep in mind there's no real winner in this game. It's all about participation. Judges might be coming around to say hi, get to know you."

Right, I remember that from the website. At least one small relief.

Doug continues, "Now grab your first wing. I was telling these folks here that we've got a total of five sauces, and we're starting with a mild barbacoa, great smoky barbecue flavors."

I whisper to my parents, "Are you sure about this?"

My dad chortles. "This nothing; in Lebanon children are raised on Aleppo pepper. Stir it into their preschool porridge."

That's not a story he's ever told me before, and my bullshit meter is going off, but nevertheless, I grab my first wing and take a bite. Doug was right; this one is mild, and the flavor is enticing. One point for Big Mike. And whoever cooked these wings.

Bab licks his clean and laughs. "An excellent piece of chicken. Do you see, Nazeli jan, I tell you it will be fine."

Mom is attempting to pick at hers daintily, dabbing at her mouth with every bite lest anyone spot a bit of sauce on her. I didn't think she'd enjoy a food that required so much mouth-related upkeep. Vanya's parents seem fine with their wings, though Vanya is keeping a watchful eye over them.

The next hot wing passes in much the same way, with a tad more bite, as promised. This one has an unexpected ginger-based sauce that gets Vanya's mom talking about the ginger's health benefits for the stomach and liver. My mom audibly groans.

The third is not what I'd call a nonevent. I'm not sure if it's because our tongues are already pre-spiced from the first two wings, but this third one, Berserkley Dreams, is something of a doozy. About five seconds after my first bite, the spice seeps into the roof of my mouth, pinpricking me mercilessly, spreading to my tongue and throat.

"Goddamn, that's spicy," I say.

"Nazeli," my mom warns. My parents cannot come to terms with me swearing, especially when it involves the Lord's name.

Vanya is nodding, her mouth still closed, unable to speak. Then she comes out with "That was a big step up, bro."

Doug chuckles with a touch of malice. Of course they'd send someone masochistic to oversee this event.

Both sets of parents, though, have fallen silent as they chew.

"Anyone need some milk?" Doug asks, barely hiding tinges of glee.

He offered it early on as an option in case we couldn't handle the heat. With that type of qualifier, it's hard to say yes. I decide I'll hold out for the next wing. "No thanks," I say, wondering if speaking made the flames in my mouth larger or smaller. It's honestly hard to tell.

The fourth wing is about equally as spicy as the third, but my entire body is protesting, and I can't escape the thought *this is my life now, this is how it will always be unless I do something*, so I give in and ask for the milk. No use in pretending this isn't torture and I don't need help. Sweet, sweet relief in the form of 2 percent floods my mouth. It's both heaven and not nearly enough. I can tell the spice is going to be lingering for some time. Plus, there's still one more wing to go.

I'm happy to see that Vanya follows my lead and chugs an entire glass. No one else does, though.

I glance at my mother, her knockoff Fendi sunglasses from the Milpitas Great Mall perched atop her nose, tears streaming down the sides of her face.

"Mom?" I whisper, but she shoots a finger up like "don't you dare talk to me right now," so I back away.

Bab, meanwhile, is pretending to stare at an unusual glass skyscraper that sort of looks like a modern industrial Caesars Palace. He's placed his hand under his chin to complete the "pondering" effect, but with the sweat beading on his forehead and his constipated expression, he's not fooling anyone. Vanya's mom is smashing her lips repeatedly with a napkin, as if that would help anything, but I suspect she understands the futility of her efforts and can't find a better alternative. Toros is shifting his weight from one side to the other, asking rapid-fire questions of Doug, but none of them come out all the way as he shuts his mouth to avoid further pain.

"How long you been working—"

"The hot sauce process isn't at all complicated I—"

Then Doug shouts, "Final wing!"

As I receive my plate, I feel more like I've been given a knife to swallow, and glancing around me, my compatriots seem to feel much the same.

I'm about to say that I wonder if I should sit this one out, when one of the judges—with the gold-plated JUDGE tag around his neck—walks up. Then I recognize him as Big Mike himself, presiding over the event like a mother hen, all his babies being swallowed up by hundreds of new future customers.

Can't chicken out now.

He glances at the bottle. "Oooh, the final: Paula's Revenge. Named after my ex-wife. Part of the settlement terms, she wanted her name on my hottest sauce so I'd always remember her. It's a spicy bitch, so, you know, it fits."

I dislike oversharers, especially those who slander their exes in their first breath. So I kind of hate that I have to impress this guy. Vanya coughs, and I don't think it's all from the spices.

"If you're already at the coughing phase, might want to sit this last one out," Big Mike jokes.

She delivers him a steady smile. "You know, that's a fantastic idea, Big Mike, I think I will. What a gentleman." Vanya steps back from her plate, asks Doug for another tall glass of milk, and chugs that one, too.

"Excellent competition," my dad tells Mike, his voice warbled like an out-of-tune guitar string. My mom nods enthusiastically, crying.

Big Mike chuckles. "Spicy, aren't they?"

"Indeed." My father smiles.

"Not so bad," Toros manages after a cleared throat.

My dad gestures to Toros. "Toros would never admit to such thing, just as he would never admit that our brand has the superior food, that we"—he gestures to me and Mom—"are the best representatives of Armenian Lebanese cuisine."

I want to clap a hand over his mouth. This is not something

the judges need to hear. Good Lord, I wouldn't be surprised if they found some reason to eliminate us now. After his outburst, Bab reaches for some water, takes a sip, and remains completely still, like if he moves a muscle he might internally combust.

But Bab's words light Big Mike up like it's Christmas in June. "Do I sense a rivalry here?"

Oh no.

Nora speaks up, her voice as dry as a desert. "We have known each other very long time."

Big Mike asks, "What'd you say you were, Albanian Libyan?"

Vanya and I answer in unison with varying notes of frustration, "Armenian Lebanese."

He nods. "That makes more sense. Armenia, that's, like, Turkey, right?"

My mom's lips tighten, but that action seems to pain her more, so she lets them go again.

Vanya says, "No, it's not. They're our genocidal neighbors."

Big Mike waves his hand. "My bad, my bad. Anyway, this is great." He glances over to the front of the boat. "Benny! Eh, Benny, c'mere."

While we wait for some unknown reason for Benny, Big Mike asks Doug to hand the rest of us (barring Vanya) our final plate, Paula's Revenge.

Benny swaggers up to us like his arm muscles are so big he can't keep them pinned to his sides while walking. "What's up, Mike?"

Mike motions to the six of us. "These folks here are all . . .

Armenian Lebanese, did I get that right, young missy?" he asks Vanya, who gives him a half smile out of politeness, but the other half is a grimace. "Sounds like they go way back and have a *rivalry*."

What I didn't notice until this second is that the cameras followed Benny, and they're now pointed squarely at us. And after Big Mike's statement, Benny appears like he's been on a long day's truffle hunt and dug up a ripe one. My parents' decades-old feud fits right into the reality TV–style culture the organizers are trying to cultivate.

My mom whips a napkin from the table and begins dabbing her tears. She must be fucking mortified for anyone to see her like this, so I ask, "Are those rolling?"

"Sure are," Benny says.

There isn't much I can do, because I still want to win this thing, so I angle myself slightly in front of my mom so her face is partially hidden from the cameras.

Nora attempts politeness to the judges. "It is not a rivalry, it is very friendly. We are all Armenian, after all."

"Hmph!" my mom exclaims.

I almost whip around, like, "What the hell, Mom, why are you trying to draw attention to yourself?" But that was clearly an involuntary exclamation.

My dad grumbles. "It was not so friendly twenty years ago when—"

Nora interrupts with a pacifying smile. "Let us not drag up ancient history."

Wait what? Are we getting to the heart of this now? I need

to know. I sort of don't care it's happening in front of cameras. I want answers.

Mom seems to have finally regained her ability to speak. "No, Nora, you are only say that because you know you are in the wrong."

"I—"

Bab continues, "Yes, when the Shirinians offered up their industrial kitchen for free, and you"—he is directing this to Toros—"snatched it from our hands using deceptions."

Deceptions? My first thought is I hope my dad is mistaken. Otherwise, what could Vanya's parents have lied about? I don't want it to be true, because if it is, I can't help but wonder if there's a streak of this in Vanya, too. She is . . . pretty smooth. That's not always a good thing.

I dare to glance at Vanya to see what she's feeling. Her face is reddening, and I wonder if she also wants to get as much information as possible from her parents, who have been just as tight-lipped as mine. But she's not liking what she's hearing. In fact, she appears restless, like she's considering walking away from this but feels tied down, like if she stays she could help it from getting worse.

My parents have never told me the story about the Shirinians offering up a space, about another family taking it from them. This family. I think of my parents' humble rented kitchen, how the water is always leaking and the wiring is so old sometimes the lights won't turn on. The early years, especially, were hard. They've made the best of it, though.

Toros grows larger. "Deceptions. You're one to talk. It is not my fault, Baron Hagop, that I am better at selling my company than you are. You think you are a silver tongue, but sometimes simple is better. The Shirinians said let the best man win and chose this best man."

Bab is about to retort, when Nora puts a hand on her husband's shoulder. "Enough, Toros. There are—" She flicks her chin in the direction of the cameras.

Big Mike smiles. "This is gold. But there are also wings still to be eaten. Everyone, please."

While the dads were airing our dirty laundry to the cameras, Benny tapped a young man with a walkie-talkie on the shoulder, asked him something, and the man ran off. Can't be good.

So this is the second time they're in competition with each other? Must be why my parents are so determined to beat the Simonians this time. And Toros's words about *my* parents' deceptions still ring in my ears. There's something more here.

Benny and Big Mike are staring at us intently, and I get it, this is our cue. I raise the wing to my mouth, say a little prayer to the ex-wife gods to have mercy on my soul, and commit only to a small bite. I'm not sure what's worse, to leave a wing partially uneaten or not eat one at all. We're being watched so closely, I want to be a good sport to give us a chance at winning.

The pain is not immediate; that's what I'm learning about hot sauces. They trick you, draw you in with flavor first, an "it's not so bad" mindset, until the assault begins and they unleash an army of flames in your mouth and down your throat. My lips feel bee-stung.

Luckily, it seems, Mom has followed my lead and eaten only

a small bite. My poor dad, one eye on Toros, is chomping at his hungrily as if the more he eats the more likely relief will appear. I make a mental note to look up the best hospitals in Chicago should it come to an ER visit.

The young man Benny sent off returns with a large tray of glass tumblers with milk and ice cubes in them. Well, that was a nice gesture anyway.

I set down my plate and turn to Big Mike and Benny. "That's all I can do. Gave Paula a try, her revenge is not one that's served cold—" I cough. "Can I get some milk?" I motion to the tumblers on the tray and decorum be damned, I grab one before I hear an answer and start drinking.

"Sure, but that's not milk," Benny says.

As he speaks, it hits me—it's sweet in my mouth and the cold and cream feel nice but the sticky coffee flavor and sting of vodka burn my throat in a whole new way.

"White Russians," I say, disappointment palpable. And it's strong. I haven't had one of these since the resident party boy in my college dorm mixed one up for a weekday rager. I'm getting flashbacks of vomiting up a dining hall tuna sandwich while my roommate held my hair back. Never had a desire for the drink since then.

"Well, if it is not milk," Toros says, and reaches for one.

"Indeed," says my father, grasping for a second. "We are vodka drinkers in this household," he says, which is not totally true. I've seen him take vodka shots at Armenian weddings before, but he always regrets it and spends the next day lecturing me on why I shouldn't take shots of vodka at a wedding, even though I wasn't the one who did it.

Vanya says, "Not going to say no to a drink," as she takes a glass.

Nora and my mom grab the last of them.

Benny says, "Why don't we cheers to old friends and refreshed rivalries. May the best team win!"

He lifts his glass to us, and it seems like he literally wants us to clink our glasses with his, so I do, and the group follows suit. Vanya's and my parents take care not to accidentally graze each other's glasses, like doing so would violate some deep-held dignity. Such babies. I cheers my parents and catch Vanya's eyes and tilt my glass to her, too. I drink just enough to soothe my mouth. My parents guzzle theirs down to the great delight of Benny, and he rushes his lackey to get us more.

I'm feeling super weird, and it's not the devastating combination of wings and white Russians. This new information, my and Vanya's fathers' bravado, my mother's quiet indignation, and Nora pretending the whole thing doesn't exist are all making my stomach churn. I want to pull my parents aside and learn more. I want to be with Vanya to hear how she's feeling.

Benny claps my father on the back. "Have a great night, all. Thanks for partaking."

He whispers something to the cameraperson, and I catch, "Keep an eye on . . . rush over."

The last damn thing I want is attention on this mortifying feud between Vanya's and my parents, and I hate that the competition creators are taking advantage of it. But at the same time, I also hate that I recognize it could be a good thing. They're paying attention to us; we're not anonymous in this sea of contenders. As long as the parents behave-ish, we should be okay.

In the distance, I hear Rob the tour guide again, and it's possible he's been talking all along, but my brain has been focused on surviving.

"Goodness, what a beeeeautiful building."

His voice sounds unmoored, and I wonder if he's also being served these ultra-strong drinks.

Just then, the errand boy returns with more drinks, and the parents and Vanya down them far too quickly. I go for a normal glass of milk on the table.

Doug says, "If you don't mind, we need to clear this space for other competitors."

He loves the power, I can see it. It deeply irritates me, but he's right that we should move on. "Needed this glass, and we'll get out of your—" I almost say *hair*, looking at the sparseness on top of his head, feeling mean from all the spice and the secrets. But then I remember Jamie's comments on my physique, and decide that's a hard line I won't cross. No negative remarks about other people's bodies. "Way," I conclude.

ANOTHER GROUP FILTERS toward the table, so my parents and Vanya's naturally saunter away. Everyone feels like they're in a similar dream-nightmare-like state, unable to process the layers of what is happening.

Nora says, "These drinks are too strong."

My mom says, "I am never eating a wing of chicken again. American foolishness."

My heart warms for a moment hoping that they can find some common ground. Armenians love to complain, and I wonder if either will seize the other's objections and . . . agree.

Sure enough, Nora nods. A flare of hope seizes my heart. Maybe this thing between our parents was all a big misunderstanding that they blew out of proportion over the years. Maybe they can be reasonable, which would mean this fledgling crush between Vanya and me could stand a chance.

After Nora's nod, my mom makes no further conversation, but at least there's no more vitriol. It's a start.

I speak to my parents. "You good here? Mouths recovered? I'm going to go wander around the boat."

Mom says, "Stay with us, hokees. We can enjoy the boat together."

So codependent, always. I say, "I'll meet up with you in a bit, going to explore."

Bab waves me off. "Whatever you must do."

His compliance is so unexpected that I worry a bit. He didn't drink *that* much, but he did drink pretty quickly.

I whisper to him so the Simonians can't hear. (They're looking away but are still somewhat nearby.) "We have more competitions tomorrow, so let's cap the drinks, okay?"

"I am grown man," he replies.

I huff and begin to break away from them. But before I do, Mom grabs my arm. "Whatever you do now, do not go with that Vanya girl. Apricot does not fall far from the tree, and I tell you the tree is rotten."

I can only stare at her for a moment. "Mom, seriously?"

But her eyes glaze over, and I take the opportunity to pull away and immediately walk up to Vanya. Seeing her in that sheer pink top, I can't help it, I grab her pinkie and give it a light squeeze, hoping to impart "follow me" with the gesture. Then I head off toward the back of the boat.

It doesn't take long to weave through the crowds of competitors, many of whom are doing the hot sauce competitions, some flailing and clutching their throats, and I feel a warm presence behind, then beside me.

I tell her, "I wanted to give the hot sauce challenge another try, just you and me."

She stares at me in dismay, like maybe she's miscalculated me and is rethinking several of her life choices as a result. Then her face softens into a smirk. "You got me there."

I gently push her arm with my shoulder. "I was shocked you weren't ready to dive back into Big Mike's misogynistic creations."

She shakes her head. "That guy."

We've reached the end of the boat, the river waves frothing and bending out into a cursive V shape as we slice through the water. Chicago's west-facing skyline is reflecting golden orange from the sunset.

"So . . . doesn't seem like our parents are best buds," I say, needing to address the subject, but wanting to enter it lightly.

"They really do hate each other's guts. Especially our dads, my God. I swear my dad isn't the worst, but sometimes, he busts out that Armenian machismo, and I want to disappear. Or, like, douse him in anti–toxic male spray."

"Available at Target?" I ask.

"Exclusively," she confirms.

"I know what you mean, though," I say, not wanting to stray too far from the heart of our conversation. "My dad, too. I've never seen him puff up his chest in that silly way. Might as well have a set of antlers on their heads, butting each other over and over. He's not usually like that."

"I guess some stuff happened with their kitchen? We still use that one, I know the Shirinians own it, and we go to their fancy Christmas party and all that, but I—I'd hate to think they stole it from your parents somehow."

I shake my head, relieved that she doesn't know anything about this, that she also doesn't want it to be true. But there's a feeling deep inside that says the story is likely correct. The way my parents are talking, maybe hers did steal it. "We don't know any of the particulars yet. Now that I've got some details to latch onto, hopefully I can wiggle out the rest from my parents."

She stares out toward the water, where the river meets Lake Michigan, then runs her thumb back and forth across the white metal railing. "The thing is, though, we really need this win, at least to place. For the publicity, but especially the prize money."

I don't say anything. She seems on the precipice of a great exhale, like this has been weighing on her. And it feels strange.

House in Saratoga, river cruises in Europe—not things normally associated with a lack of money. "Lately it hasn't been so great—with the business—we've been in the red for two years and can't get out. Stores that used to stock us aren't stocking anymore. We changed our recipes to cut costs, but it's not helping. We bought VIP tickets to PakCon to try and schmooze every last buyer we could get access to, but it's not looking good.

"Anyway, the stress of the whole situation is getting to my parents, I think. I hope you can forgive them for being assholes. My dad, anyway. I don't know if that's possible, or not cool of me to ask."

So that's why their food doesn't taste so great. I mean, sounds like earlier on it wasn't the best, either, but that was probably why the falafel I got was so flavorless. I appreciated her giving me an explanation for her father's braggadocio.

"Thanks for telling me. I hope it turns out okay for you all. And hey, I'm equally mortified. My dad's been throwing barbs and my mom's said some stuff—" I remember her comments about Vanya's tattoo but obviously keep that to myself. "Whatever happened between them, shouldn't affect, um"—I dare to look at her—"us."

The boat rounds a corner, and her face is painted gold by the sun, her irises blooming as if to take in all its glory. I want to kiss her.

"I hope you're right, 'cause I think you're pretty cool, Naz."

The way she's staring at me, it's like we're back on the rooftop, like she wants me closer. I inch my face toward hers. Her mouth is so beautiful, wide, I want to know what her lips would feel like. A warm breeze ripples against my back as if pushing me toward her. She closes her eyes as I draw in.

Then, over the speakers, there's a tussle of the mic, a couple low *doop*s as if it was grabbed. And then I hear the worst thing possible.

A new voice is over the speakers, saying, "Khallo, ladies and gentlemen, allow me to continue this tour with true architectural knowledge so as to cultivate enlightenment about world around you. As our guide Robert . . ." The name spoken in that French accent, that most familiar male voice in the world, singsongy and definitely sluiced with drunkenness—it's Bab.

"Oh God," I say, whipping toward the front of the boat, though I can't see a thing from here. "I gotta go."

I push through the crowds in a way that's borderline rude, but what does it matter, most of the contestants seem drunk, and I have a feeling I know where all the cameras are.

Sure enough, two giant cameras are pointed at my father, who is sitting atop Rob's high stool. My mom is right by him, listening with stars in her eyes as if he's been crowned king. Toros isn't far away, laughing his ass off, but what surprises me is that it seems only moderately mean-spirited. Part of it is, like, "look at this know-it-all Hagop," but another part is simply amused by the spectacle. Rob, dethroned and drunk, tries once to stumble back to his chair, but Toros holds him and says, "Come on, man, he's doing better than you up there."

Indeed, my father is expounding on the history of the Civic Opera House and the matching yet dueling art deco style of the building across the river from it. I whip around to the other contestants, his audience. They seem to be digging him. I spy smiles of appreciation and the type of knowing nods people do when they're learning a new fact. And Benny has a massive grin on his face, switching between Bab and Toros. Like he was right: he found his new reality stars.

I guess it could be worse.

Chapter Thirteen

As soon as we walk into the Conservatory, I know I've picked the right date-night spot. It's said to be one of the best gastronomic cocktail experiences in the world, and the space is delivering: all blacks, creams, and golds, with a stunning abstract lighting fixture like cursive gone wild. Everything screams exclusive but isn't too in-your-face, either. There's a subdued nature to the whole thing.

I'd like to say I romantically whisked Vanya away after the disastrous boat ride, but the reality was more like making sure my burping and swaying parents made it to their hotel okay (they did) and a series of texts and sneaking around to get Vanya and me to the same Green Line stop. Then our dalliance could take flight, because there is something so sweet about riding a train with someone you're crushing on.

A host seats us in light leather chairs, which are perfectly comfortable, except that they're not close enough together and seem huge and immovable, but otherwise, I know we're about to have a ball. Around us, Vanya and I get a preview of what we're in for, with steampunk-looking contraptions dispensing drinks at people's tables, smoke unfurling from glasses, a roomful of delighted customers.

"I'm so glad you brought me here," Vanya says after placing her slouchy black bag on the floor. "Since I only take my cocktails through Rube Goldberg machines."

"Oh, I was aware when I made the booking," I reply.

We look at the menu, and the prices certainly match the extravagance around us, but this is on me, I tell her. I'm going to land Operation Wolf, get my bonus, and then I can rest. Meaning a long weekend trip, anywhere with a beach. I know it's too soon, but I wonder how Vanya would feel about coming with—

"These names are ridiculous in the best way," Vanya says, scanning the menu. "Definitely have to be a native English speaker or entrenched in pop culture to get them. My dad would be annoyed by it all for sure. Too pretentious."

I gaze at a cocktail name riffing on a Hall & Oates song, think of Toros calling Bab a silver tongue, and have to agree. "And my dad would be outraged by the prices. He'd probably corner someone from the waitstaff and give a sermon on why drinks should not be this expensive. Can't take him anywhere."

Vanya sighs. "Our parents have so much in common; I wish I got more details on what happened. I tried talking to Mom and Dad, but they were pretty useless with information by the end of the boat tour. Mom fell asleep in the car."

"Similar story here," I say, remembering the harrowing journey back to the hotel—Mom on the verge of vomiting, Dad telling us in Armenian how he was holding back gas until he got to the room. The best I got was that they reiterated that the Simonians stole that commercial kitchen from them. Wouldn't say how, just that they did. The memory of that, their finality on the truth of the matter, churns my stomach.

A server comes by and takes our order, Vanya choosing her drink by pointing to the steampunk contraption someone else had in the corner. I decide on something that supposedly comes in a plastic bag, which sounds so lowbrow for a place like this, I need to see what it is. We also order some food, truffle popcorn, a Japanese yam dish, and Russian cabbage stew. I pray that Operation Wolf bonus is as big as I'm hoping.

While we wait, I try very hard *not* to think about my mom's insistence about the poison apricot tree, that Vanya is bad news. Her Mayr Hayastan tattoo catches my eye again. I wonder how anyone with a tattoo like that could be awful. "When did you get that?"

She glances down at it. "This fine lady? Right after our trip to Armenia about five years ago. We went on a pilgrimage—no, seriously, like a religious one with the church. I thought it would be the lamest thing in the world going with a big group and a priest, but it's probably the best trip I've ever taken. You been?"

I shake my head. "Nah, parents are terrified of planes. Bab would never admit it, but I know he is, and Mom has openly said there is no way she'd survive the twenty-four-hour journey to Hayastan. I've had to do my traveling on my own with friends, but haven't found someone to go to Armenia with."

Vanya smiles. "I know a fantastic church group. At the risk of sounding lame, it changed my life."

"Oh? How so?"

There's a couple beside us, and the man, with slick-gelled hair and boat shoes, stands up abruptly, bumping our table and not saying sorry, though his companion glances at us apologetically. Vanya only looks partially annoyed at the disturbance, but continues on with her story.

"We went with my brother and his pregnant wife, which in retrospect was so ballsy of her. She's a badass, though. I like her way more than my brother. The stomach bug I got? My God. I was on the tour bus so fucked up I couldn't go into Geghard Monastery, and I started borderline hallucinating Mayr Hayastan commanding me to bring Armenian culture to the diaspora by way of children's books."

I raise my eyebrows. "You sure that was just a stomach bug?"

"I mean, maybe it was a homemade mulberry vodka hangover from the night before, but I was definitely feverish. I've always loved to write, and to this day my favorite books are my childhood picture books."

As her story is unfurling, I'm finding myself getting sucked into Vanya more and more. I've never gone for a writer type before. There is something utterly different about her; maybe it's that attention to detail. And the fact that she is into kids' books is so unexpected, but in the best way possible.

"So, anyway, I get that tattoo, but I'm home a few months and life takes over and the idea's sort of buried. But now I have two nieces, the cutest little fierce bunnies, and I saw how hard it was to get them great Armenian picture books. In Armenia, the books are all in Eastern Armenian, so there's that language barrier. And I'm seeing that my nieces have the widest selection of picture books in English, on any topic, with the world's best illustrators. The Western Armenian selection is so limited. Like, how is anyone supposed to keep up the literacy side of our culture? I'm probably bitter that my Armenian reading skills suck. But bitterness isn't the worst motivator, right?"

I think about my parents and their newfound interest in entering and succeeding at PakCon Superstars. I nod, allowing her to continue. She says, "I have this idea of bringing our great epics, 'Haig ou Pel', 'Sassountsi Davit', and some of our weird fairy tales into both English- and Armenian-language picture books. This vision to share our culture with the Armenian-American diaspora, with non-Armenian and Armenian kids. I already have three picture books drafted. But"—here her face shifts downward —"it feels like such a hopeless, solo adventure. I have no idea what I'm doing. I mean, do I set up a Kickstarter? I'd rather get traditionally published, but who's going to want our stories?"

She reaches for her water glass, takes a sip. "That's why I feel like a lame ass saying my trip to Armenia changed my life. Like, it gave me a mission but I have no clue how to fulfill it."

She seems downcast, such a change from how she began this story, filled to the brim with energy. It's almost as if she's given up on it already. I tell her, "The solo part, that might be your problem."

At Abilify, you literally can't create anything big without a team, and her dream sounds big. I think of the one-man founder whom we acqui-hired. He had a brilliant product but no marketing skills whatsoever, no way to sell his product. He was connected, though, and ran into terrifying Reid Erikson at a party and got a chance to pitch. Now his data network is what makes Abilify so powerful, and he was handsomely rewarded for it. Point is, you need other people.

I'm about to expand on that, when our server returns with food and our drinks. "Drinks" is kind of an understatement, though. Vanya's is the promised steampunk machine, which our server sets down before her. And mine, it seems, is indeed a glass of liquid inside a clear, sealed plastic bag with smoke furling around it.

The food is also . . . not what I expected. The truffle popcorn portion wouldn't fill up a sparrow—Vanya and I will probably be counting out six popped kernels and splitting them. The cabbage stew appears to be deconstructed and resembles a scene from a medieval horror movie where newcomers are warned not to mess with the ruling nobles or else their body parts will end up on spikes. Each element of the "stew" is stuck upon a metal skewer dripping in what I hope is beet juice. And the Japanese yam must be a mistake, because it looks like a plate of foamy spit with a couple microgreens on top.

Vanya is eyeing the spit dish with a similar blend of revulsion and confusion.

At the risk of sounding like a dilettante, I ask, pointing to it, "And this is the . . . yam?"

"Yes." The server smiles without pretentiousness or malice. "It's a Japanese yam foam."

Vanya says, "Ah, of course."

This gets an amused smirk from the server. Then she tends to Vanya's drink. "We light this Bunsen burner, and that stimulates the smoke in the main chamber, which travels to the antechamber, infusing the wild summer berries with a subtle vapor. Then we pull this lever"—she yanks one near the top—"and your drink will begin to flow downward. Here's the spout where you can pour your drink. We recommend filling only one-quarter of your glass at a time."

"This is exactly what I wanted," Vanya says, plenty of glee in her voice.

"And your drink." The server turns to me and pushes the plastic bag my way. "The bag has been infused with essence of star fruit smoke, coating your drink. When I pop the bag, dip your head in to get the full effect."

"You want me to smell the bag?"

The server nods. "I do."

Vanya chuckles. All right then. I lean close, and the server holds out a large old-fashioned safety pin, flicks the needle, and then snaps her hand, popping the bag at once. I breathe in despite the ridiculousness of it all, and I'm glad I did, because star fruit is now one of my top favorite smells. The ole smell-a-bag gag wasn't as bad as it seemed. Vanya has edged over as well, and there's both amusement and curiosity written on her face. Her nostrils flare to bring in the scent, and she closes her eyes a moment longer than a blink. Next time, I want to be the reason she makes that face.

Our server leaves us and our two contraption drinks, and I didn't realize until now how much I'd been holding in the giggles, but I catch Vanya's mischievous eyes, and suddenly I'm bursting with them.

"I just paid twenty-five dollars to sniff a bag." I laugh.

This ignites Vanya. "My drink thinks it's Versailles, coming in here with its antechambers."

We haven't had a sip yet but I already feel drunk.

Vanya motions to the deconstructed cabbage stew. "I do believe Don Corleone is in the back kitchen trying to send us a message."

"Hey, I'll take it." I giggle. "At least bloody organs make for a substantial meal," I say, nodding toward the popcorn. "And certainly better than eating the sous-chef's spit." I eye the foamed yams.

"Wait, wait, let's try it. You never know," Vanya says, still alive with fiendish elation.

She scoops a spoonful into her mouth, then quickly hands me the spoon, and I do the same, secretly delighted to share a utensil with her. Then I feel the minute bubbles all slimy and popping on my tongue, and perhaps there's a hint of a delicate flavor in there, but the texture, my God. I almost gag as I swallow.

Vanya winces as she gulps. "Honestly," she says, recovering herself, "at this point I'm surprised there isn't a full-on mastication sommelier who baby birds you the food himself."

She mimes someone chewing up food and is partway through pretending to spit it into someone below, but we break into laughter before she can finish. Her face is full of such mirth it makes everything seem even funnier. I'm laughing so hard now it's silent. I cover my eyes with my hands and feel the tears forming.

I open them and Vanya is still in fits of laughter, and we surf each other's waves of elation until they naturally smooth over. I lean my head on the back of the chair, resting from our joy zenith, and she, the minx, curls her arms over the end of her chair, one hand dangling over the edge.

I uncross my legs, then recross them toward her, leaning. I reach out, hold her hand's small smoothness in mine. I carefully watch her face to make sure it's okay, and it only grows with bliss, her eyes blooming into brilliant shades.

But we're too far to kiss. Damn chairs.

"You two seem like you have something really special, good for you," says the kind voice of a woman from the table next to ours. But as well-meaning as the voice is, it knocks me out of the rapturous world of Vanya and me, where everything else had blurred but us.

"Thank you," says Vanya, a high perkiness to her voice, almost postorgasmic. That, I'd love to check to be sure.

The woman is young and pretty, with doe eyes, though without any of the innocence, like she's seen some things. "You make me wish I could hurry up and dump my useless boyfriend. He's in the bathroom doing coke. It's been ages; I bet he cornered some man in there and is having some one-way conversation with him."

"Our condolences," Vanya says. "Why don't you?"

"We're in our last week of our MBA; it'd be so awkward with the friend group. God, I wish I were a lesbian."

"I'm bi," I offer.

"Bi, pan, somewhere in that zone," says Vanya.

Interesting. I had been wondering where Vanya fell.

"I tried it," the girl says wistfully. "Didn't work for me. But anyway, I didn't interrupt your cuteness to talk about my troubles." She leans her elbow on the edge of her chair and it slips off, though she hardly seems to notice, and I realize then that she is pretty tipsy. Makes sense—not every stranger would openly share about their sexuality and rat on their coked-up boyfriends they're hoping to dump.

Vanya seems amused by the conversation, but I feel a longing in her, too, for us to get back to where we were.

"So, last month," the girl says, as if we've been besties for years, "I went to this spot with my B-school cohort, Aaron Lansing set it up, and he is a mood genius. Anyway, I saw you two and thought, 'God they have to go.'"

There was a time I considered business school myself, but realized I'd be putting myself in six-figure debt to essentially party for two years. The degree would be worth a lot, but two years of lost revenue? Eight percent interest rates? Not worth it. I could claw my way up to the top another way. She's confirming that even out here, business school seems to be much the same. But when an MBA candidate says someone is a mood genius, usually they're right, so I listen up and hope she gives us some information.

"It's called Aqueduct, and it's this old warehouse that's been converted into like a Roman bathhouse, and it's the sexiest place on earth. You've gotta go. Tell them Lana sent you."

We thank her just as her eighties banker–wannabe boyfriend shows back up to the table looking strung tight and ready to rock. She gives us a huge wink and turns to her man.

"Did I hallucinate all that?" I whisper to Vanya.

"Blond girl who wants to dump her coked-out boyfriend told us about some Roman baths?"

I nod. "We must be in the same dream at least."

We dip into the food and drinks, which are all way better than we thought, minus the spit yams, while looking up Aqueduct. My instincts were right, the MBA student knows what she's talking about—this place is dripping in sex. I show what I've found to Vanya, who looks like we uncovered buried treasure, and I make a reservation for us online, and we decide that is where we'll go next.

Chapter Fourteen

The building, an old warehouse, as promised, is all brick and dark wood. There's an unassuming worn wooden door with the name Aqueduct carved into it. When it shuts behind us, we're greeted by a hundred candles glimmering in the dim entryway. Sitting on the sides of the room are ten person–long couches with ornate silver teapots, and small stacked cups alongside them. Vanya is staring openly, like she's walked into an elfin hollow.

I check us in and confirm that they provide swimsuits, since we didn't bring ours. Neither of us could have foreseen that our business trip to Chicago would include bikinis.

The receptionist says, "Feel free to choose your style," and flips an iPad our way, with a modest one-piece, an eighties-style one-piece with high-cut thighs, and a bikini. I go the middle road, the eighties style, while Vanya chooses the bikini. My breath hitches.

We're shown to the changing area, and each of us gets a space that resembles a high-end dressing room. At least we don't have to change in front of each other by a cluster of lockers. Not that I would mind, but it's a lot less sexy.

I step out in my borrowed robe—this place has pulled out all the stops, and thank goodness because, once again, it was expensive—and see Vanya has done the same.

"Shall we?" she asks.

I'm feeling giddy and light again—if the lobby and changing room experience already felt this good, I wonder what the actual baths will be like.

We push through a collection of beaded ropes, parting them to enter the bathhouse.

The humidity instantly wraps itself around my body and face. This place wants you dripping. Everything around us feels as if it's melting, too. There must be a thousand candles illuminating the brick and stone. It's larger than it looks from the front, high ceilings and all. Steam rises off the pool in front of us, and condensation trickles off the walls. The entire floor of the bathhouse is wet, warm.

"Ho-lee shit," Vanya murmurs.

"My thoughts exactly."

There are other patrons milling around, everyone in slow motion, but it doesn't feel busy. I spot a rack where others have hung their robes. I guess it's our turn. I take the lead, sloughing mine off and placing it on a hook. I feel much more nude than I am in this mostly modern black one-piece. The eighties style delivered—that ultra-high thigh cut—and as soon as I put it on, I thanked myself for the good wax I got the week prior (when I was still optimistic about Kyle calling me after all).

While I am hanging my robe up, Vanya shrugs hers off and places it over mine. She has a small waist and hips that make me want to consider bringing the word *bodacious* back into my vocabulary. My God.

"So the suit fits, it seems," I say, averting my eyes so I don't stare like a hungry dog.

"Yours too. That's one of the hotter one-pieces I've seen."

It's already so warm in here, but I find myself reddening more. "Leaves less to the imagination than I expected, but here we are."

"Well, you're rocking it."

There are attendants dressed in black linen uniforms, and one approaches us. "If you so wish, you can partake in our Himalayan sea salt scrub before enjoying the pools." She motions a little ways away to a mound of salt atop a table. If she hadn't told me what it was, I would have imagined it was fake snow fashioned into a model ski slope.

I look to Vanya, who gives me a "why not" shrug, so we head over. There are lines drawn in the salt by previous patrons, and while this whole thing is a little ridiculous, part of me wants to sink my fingers in, scoop whole handfuls of it, and rub myself raw.

"When in Rome," Vanya says, grabbing her own handful and running it along the length of her arm. "How many times do you think I can get away with saying that tonight?"

"I'm sorry to inform you that you've reached your quota." I smile.

I dip my hand in, grab a bunch, and savor the weight in my

palm. Bits of salt roll off, but it seems like you're supposed to waste some. I rub it on my arm, and it sends shivers up my spine. A thousand little diamonds rushing against my skin.

"I keep thinking how wild it is that we're here, that you're here," Vanya says. "You don't even want to be part of the family business. You could have just skipped this and gone and done your disruptive software thing at home."

I laugh, grabbing another handful and rubbing it on my other arm, this time visibly shivering. "It's not that I don't want to be part of it. I've always secretly wished I could, but one, I wanted to get experience elsewhere, and two, my parents are immovable."

The truth of my words strikes me as I say them—that I have always secretly wanted it. Being here, taking part in the contest, as silly as parts of it have been, are polishing this hidden idea further and further. I've wanted this; I could be good at this.

But then I remember. "Did you ever have—I mean, I don't know where you went to school or what it was like, but my parents spent every last penny to send me to a fancy private high school where everyone around me was, to put it mildly, super-rich. Their parents fund Abilify and tech companies like it, VCs and all. So, I don't know, did you ever run into a situation where people looked down on your parents' work?"

My own memory of it stings, even though it was over a decade ago.

"Yes." She nods, running her hands up and down her calf. "But I want to hear yours first."

I wonder how much detail to give. I start plainly. "Freshman year there was a swim team get-together at someone's insane mansion with my classmates and all the parents. I was near my parents, checking out the family's Steinway, running my fingers over it, when the sprint star's dad walked up jovially to my dad. I already knew he was a VC—within two months at my school, I inadvertently learned exactly how wealthy everyone was and what they did. Gossip ran fast there. Wild place."

I haven't recounted this story in . . . maybe ever, so I'm feeling a little self-conscious. I scrub my legs harder with the salt.

"So this VC dad asked Bab what he did, and Bab told him about Hagop's Fine Armenian Foods, and the man gave a bunch of hearty laughs. He thought Bab was joking. When he realized it wasn't a joke, the man backtracked and started talking about honest work and salt-of-the-earth types, immigrants who keep our country running. But—"

The damage had been done. I vowed never to do that type of "honest work." I wasn't salt of the earth. I never wanted anyone to laugh at me like that.

Vanya has stopped working the salt onto her body. "You decided to emulate the guy and his career path instead."

I shrug. "I mean, as best I can. I didn't have the connections or pedigree to go work in the VC world, but I've definitely worked my way up a ladder in a short time and am going to keep climbing up there."

There's a shower right by the salt station where you can rinse off. Vanya starts the water and runs her limbs under it.

"I'm sorry that happened to you," she says, water dripping down her arms, chest. "I know how it feels. I had something similar happen—the white families in our neighborhood always feeling superior to my parents. But I'm trying to play their game, sneak our culture into theirs."

She keeps the water out of her eyes. "We bring Armenian-ness to them by masquerading it as health food."

I don't say it out loud, but I'm not sure she's right. She's sanded down the Armenian part of their food so much that it's not even Armenian anymore. What good is it? But I'm not an expert in these matters, and the issue of our parents' dueling brands is so sensitive, I'm not going to bring it up.

Instead, I give a noncommittal "hm, yeah" and step toward the shower. Sprinkles of salt shake off me as I approach. She steps aside, giving me room. And then I remember her books.

"Your kids' books will do that, too, but more overtly, maybe?"

Her pursuit of Armenian fables in English—that sounds like a unique and untapped way of sharing our culture with the world.

She considers, lips jutting out slightly. "That's a good point."

She glances toward one of the pools. "Let's do this."

This first pool, the one we saw coming in, is flanked by thick white marble, but unpolished, raw. The general brick-and-metal mood of the walls makes it inviting instead of pompous.

An attendant is magically by our side again. "Excellent choice. This is the floating pool, as much salt as the Dead Sea."

"Salt and water everywhere," I whisper to Vanya.

"Same as our bodies," she says.

The attendant vanishes out of sight, and I follow Vanya up the couple of stairs. From the top, I spot more pools in the back, glass rooms filled with steam. I can't wait to explore every inch of this space.

I tiptoe into the pool behind Vanya, the water like a second skin around my feet. Less cautious now that I'm assured of the warmth, I wade in, the water stinging the parts of me where I'd shaved recently.

There are two other couples in the water with us, men and women, and one woman is guiding her male partner as he floats, eyes closed, along the length of the pool. I wonder if I can convince Vanya to do that, and I honestly don't know which would be more pleasurable, guiding her or being guided.

At once, Vanya ducks her head under, dunking her entire face and hair into the pool. I've been more cautious, putting my hair up in a ponytail, but I get the point of this place is to be soaked entirely, so it was in vain.

Vanya moves slowly through the water, both arms out like she's greeting a crowd of devotees. There's music, too, louder now than before, feels like it might be from our part of the world. A melancholy wail, drawn out over a distant guitar.

"I think I need to move to Chicago," Vanya says, approaching me. "Right there specifically." She tilts her chin to the ceiling. "Stash myself up in the rafters like the phantom of the bathhouse."

"This place is probably one of the best spots I've been to in my life. Thank you, tipsy MBA woman."

"May she soon dump her boyfriend." Vanya nods.

"Indeed."

Then, feeling the spirit of Aqueduct overtake me, I decide it's time: yank the hair tie off my hair, slip it on my wrist, and dip my head back, letting the water crawl over my scalp. My hair is fairly long, and I feel it circling me like a halo.

Vanya's skin is slick as she rises and recedes from the water. I should stop staring, but she's closed her eyes now and it feels like an invitation. I dip myself back again, letting the water tickle my ears, and push all the way up into a float. It's easy with the salt. The light from the water projects onto the brick walls like an old black-and-white movie.

Vanya's presence is beside me; there's warmth from her head and face as we drift. Damn my false promise to my mom, and her poison tree analogy. I don't believe it. I refuse to. I pull my legs under, back to standing.

"Let me guide you while you float? I'll take you along the pool."

Her eyes flutter slightly open. "That sounds perfect. Take me everywhere."

I lay one palm flat against her back, and the other I dare to move under her thighs. I realize then that we haven't touched since we got here.

Her body tenses somewhat at my touch, but it doesn't feel like a "no," it feels like a "whoa." I keep my eyes on her face, where hers have closed again.

"You can relax completely, I've got you," I whisper.

She does, the slackness of her body upon my hands. The salt does most of the work, but I'm still part of it.

Slowly, I draw myself through the water, walking the length of the pool, with Vanya gently perched atop my hands. She never tightens a muscle to guide me in any way; it's all my direction. With the dolorous music and the darkness, Vanya's closed eyes, it almost feels like a funeral. Or a birth.

Vanya peeks an eye open. Then she says, "Look."

I glance up and see us, clasped together, inverted by the hanging mirror, like something ancient and special, a new zodiac sign. The candlelight dances around our skin while we flow together.

"How long can we stay like this?" Vanya asks.

"As long as you want."

Her eyes close again, and she looks so serene I want to kiss her face, but I won't, not yet. I want her looking at me, to see the wildness flickering there, the fierce yes.

We spend another five, ten, fifteen minutes like this, I'm not sure how long, with my conveying her around every inch. Then there's a small kick of her legs, and she stands. We're at a corner of the pool, and the candlelight splashes against her sleek skin, illuminating half her face.

Wordlessly, she pulls me in toward her, arms around my back, and then our torsos are touching. Our legs begin to tangle under the water, and our heads, once again, draw near.

"Thank you," she whispers.

I skim my fingertips around the side of Vanya's face, against her cheek. "Can I—" is all I get out.

"Yes."

And I do. I kiss her, our lips meeting soft and salty from the water. The softest moan escapes from Vanya, and instinctually I pull her in tighter. I taste a sweetness, too, like warm wet sugarplums sprinkled with sea salt. Vanya's hand twines into my hair, ensuring we're connected, we're not letting go.

My hands, gripping her underwater, feel the mesh on the back of her bikini. I run my thumb under it. I won't pull it off, not here, but I want to feel the hint of it, what it'd be like. She snickers, low and quiet, and we wrest ourselves away from each other at last.

"If we keep going, we're going to get kicked out," I say.

"Fine by me," she says, swooping in for another kiss.

I kiss her back, then suggest we check out a couple more pools, then—"Come see what my hotel room looks like? See if it lives up to the airport Howard Johnson's."

She chuckles. "I'll bring my sharpest critic's eye."

Chapter Fifteen

$\mathcal{H}$er cheek rests on my bare shoulder as we're lying in the hotel room bed, covers pulled up for the first time since she's been over. It's warm and faintly sticky, like my own skin. I place my hand on her head, play with a few of her curls while I allow my breathing to slow. Hers already has, and her eyelids flutter closed. Time to rest now.

That spa-like tub I thought would get no use on this trip? Oh, it got plenty. The desk where my laptop sits, overlooking the Chicago skyline? That got a very NSFW use as well.

Vanya is something else. Like an ocelot that might seem unassuming from its cute appearance but is ready to unleash in times of need. And she needed.

I must have dozed off, somewhere deep, because I wake to her running a finger down the center of my chest, and it feels like hours have passed, but it could also have been minutes.

"Should we . . . keep this from our parents for now?" she asks.

Her voice is less confident than normal; she doesn't want to ask this. But the truth is I was wondering the same, how we would handle it.

"For sure," I agree. "During the competition? It'll be too much for them, too distracting. And for us, too. Let's not involve them until we have to."

A hint about the future, our future.

"I mean, when we get back home, we're only an hour apart. That's really doable. I've been wanting to move out on my own at some point anyway. Dreaming now, but—I've always liked downtown San Mateo."

I didn't think I could flush any further, but I do; there is still fire within me. Once again we're thinking on similar tracks, and she's not afraid to say it. God, I feel myself falling for her so hard. She's so open, so unlike the repressed assholes of my dating past, who could barely tell me they liked me. Her words don't feel like just talk, either; her voice is ringing so genuine and hopeful that we could make this work.

"Only twenty minutes away from my place. Even better."

She climbs on top of me and kisses me, then glances at the nightstand clock, a red glow I've refused to give my attention. I don't want to know.

She sighs. "I can't believe I'm saying this, but I should get back. My mom's an early riser, and we have some Mediterranean diet lecture tomorrow morning that we supposedly can't miss. She'll be knocking on my door, and if we want to keep this between us for now—"

I nod, sad to see her go but fully understanding. "You've got to head back. Of course. Want me to ride there with you?"

"All the way down and then come back up? My white knight, I'd never ask that of thee."

"Seriously, it's fine," I say, both wanting to spend time with her and wondering how I'd ever get out of this bed. I seem to have become fused with it. The exhaustion from several nights of zero-to-poor sleep is catching up with me.

She bounds out of bed, clearly more energetic than me. She leans close to my face. "Don't you worry. Stay here and I'll see you tomorrow."

While she hunts for her discarded clothes throughout the room, I stretch one reluctant arm toward my purse, which I threw at the base of the nightstand earlier tonight. Even this amount of effort is a lot; I'm sort of glad that Vanya's okay with letting me stay here.

I pull out my phone, which I've ignored for hours, a mix of conscious and unconscious. There were definitely times I was *not* thinking about my phone, such as the teasiest Lyft ride over to this room. Vanya and I wanted to be respectful to the driver, so we didn't full-on make out back there, but ran fingers up legs, across arms, and leaned into necks. Goose bumps springing up everywhere. And all with a quietness that could, to an outsider, look like not much was happening. But I'll never forget that ride my entire life.

The warm memory is interrupted by unwelcome unread messages. Jamie.

I swipe to Slack, preparing myself for some chastising.

Her message says, **News: upper management wants to pivot on our position with Operation Wolf and we need to come up with new messaging to match. See forwarded email with details. We need to present something to them by Monday. Let me know ASAP if you are too busy with your family and I'll jump on it instead.**

Jesus H—a major pivot on a Thursday night? Maybe the changes won't be that big. Maybe it won't take hours and hours of effort tomorrow and potentially over the weekend. I switch to my email to skim the forwarded message Jamie sent me, hoping, but somehow knowing I won't be happy with what I'm about to see. I read it and yep, this is a completely different direction. Good God. I let out a groan I did not expect to be audible.

Vanya returns then, dressed but for her sheer top. "I was wondering if you were going again without me." She smirks.

"Not a pleasure groan, unfortunately."

"Well, I'll learn to tell the difference in time."

For a moment the dread of the work to come sloughs off me, and I'm wrapped in Vanya's flirtations. Work armor.

"Looking forward to that. *Not* looking forward to the work I have to do tomorrow and probably this weekend that my boss just dumped on me." Then, not wanting to sound complain-y, I say, "But I mean, this is what I signed up for. This is the path to director and beyond."

Vanya finds the small clump of her top on the floor, stuck under a wheel of the office chair. She yanks it out and begins climbing into it. "So let me get this right. You took PTO days but still worked the whole time—"

"Most of the time," I interrupt.

She barges on, unperturbed. "Now you need to continue to work into the weekend even though you don't want to. And you're telling me this is what you want?"

"I—yeah. I've wanted it for a long time."

Feels true to say. I *have* wanted it. I want the prestige, I want to have a higher salary and more responsibility and more direct reports. I enjoy making decisions, delegating. Even if it is for performance management software.

"I hear the seeds of doubt," she sings as she picks up her bag, thrown sideways on the armchair.

I don't want to hear what she's saying, so I ignore it. Bury it. "Either way," I say, "I pretty much have to deliver this weekend. People are counting on me."

She nods. "Got it. Well, do it tomorrow, not tonight, if you can help it. Cooking challenge is coming, are you ready?"

Right now I can hardly imagine springing into action for PakCon Superstars, but this one should be our forte with my parents' cooking skills at the forefront. I worry that this might be the one where Vanya's family is eliminated, and after what she told me about her family really needing the money, I hope I'm wrong.

Feels strange after being entwined in her in so many ways that tomorrow we go back to competing against each other. There's enough room, at least tomorrow, for us both to succeed. Only one of us will win in the end, but I won't think about that now.

"Nope," I laugh, and fall all the way back into bed. She rushes over, kisses me. Then I feel her body go from sweet to getting pumped full of that heat again, and she's on top of me, purse to the side of my head, squeezing my shoulders, pulling me toward her. I'm responding to her, pushing the covers down so I can wrap my legs around her, though I'm much slower and sloppier than before. I know she needs to go home, but damn.

Then she pulls away. "Ah, I can't believe I'm being responsible, but I can tell you need sleep. I'm not going to keep you awake any longer than I already have. Much as I'd like to."

She untwines herself from me and strides toward the door.

"You're right, you're right," I mumble with a small smile.

"I'm leaving before I convince myself to stay. You are a fucking treat, Naz."

"Best night I've had in a long, long time," I say to her, and also very much to myself.

Chapter Sixteen

$\mathcal{I}$ wake up with a headache, and the sunlight looks weird. Something feels wrong, but I can't put my finger on it. I mean, I woke up before my alarm, so everything should be fine. After those damn drinks at the Conservatory and that unsubstantial goopy food, my body is probably just mad at me.

I should go back to sleep and wait for my alarm, but I think of the mountain of work and events waiting for me today. Last night after Vanya left, I thought I would fall right back asleep, but I kept running over the finer points of Jamie's forwarded email and started inventing new messaging in my head, editing it, making it better, trying to solve problems of efficiency. And then, afraid I would forget everything, I sat up, grabbed my laptop, and started jotting it all down. Jotting turned into full-on writing and it must have been three or so by the time I fell asleep. Even then, it wasn't close to enough, and I'm still stuck with a monumental to-do list. Guess that all probably contributed to the headache.

I roll over, and the nightstand clock weirdly says it's noon, which it can't be. Must have been some power outage. Still a bit confused, I grab my phone and see twenty missed calls from each of my parents and plenty of texts. I bolt up, my body buzzing with fear that something went horribly wrong, and I think about all that hot sauce and the alcohol and oh God I'm a terrible daughter for not checking up on them last night.

I read the texts lightning fast and am immediately relieved to find they're okay, health-wise. But . . . But.

It is indeed past noon and I missed our family meeting with Ned Richardson. I screwed up my family's one chance to get in at True Foods Grocers.

Then I remember I turned off my alarm yesterday because of the time difference, and I guess I never set a new one. So unlike me. I've been so damn distracted this whole trip.

I tilt my head back, and the sense of dread fills me, starting in the pit of my stomach, rising to my throat, feeling like that nasty pink insulation has been stuffed down there.

Then I spring into action, because I need to find a way to fix this. My parents' calls stopped shortly after eleven, which is when they were supposed to be meeting with Ned. So they must have met with him.

I debate whom to call. Mom will yell at me, but Bab will have resigned disappointment and possibly passive aggressiveness. I decide Bab's is worse.

Mom picks up on the second ring. "You are alive, thanks to God. You are okay?"

I brace myself, because after concern comes the anger. "Totally fine. I—I slept past my alarm. I thought I set an alarm."

Then she launches into Armenian, a language more fitting to wash me up and down in chastisements. "How dare you desert your family this way. You told us you would help us, you always ask how you can help, and we give you this opportunity and you squandered it. I can feel my heart, it is pained after these hours of wondering where you were. Aye! Hagop, am I having a heart attack? This is what it feels like—"

I allow her to let the full string of criticisms and guilt-tripping out before responding. There's no point; she wouldn't listen in a real way, and anything I say, she'll easily rebut. Mom could have been a lawyer.

While she's yelling, I realize that it's almost time for the cooking competition, so I rush into the bathroom to wash up. God, my hair is a mess from all of last night's shenanigans. Suddenly, Mom not knowing about Vanya becomes even more important. She might actually have some type of body attack if she found out.

She's switched back to English. "I cannot anymore. Here is your father."

Oh no.

The electric toothbrush is in my mouth already buzzing, but I switch it off and spit out the froth.

"The meeting ended up being fine without you. We did not need your presentation," he says. "We have secured a promise of future meeting with more representative from the company."

Oof. That's cold. "I'm—I'm glad for you guys."

"Indeed," he says. "We shall see you soon for the cooking competition, unless there is more pressing matter for you to attend?"

"I'll be there," I say, more insistently. I'm not going to take this cold shoulder forever. Yes, I screwed up once, massively. Yes, I should have finished my presentation, and it was so messed up for me to forget about the meeting, but . . . they also forgot? Or at least didn't mention it. They didn't talk about it once last night in all the hot wings madness. Whatever. It's not worth arguing the point, because I have to rush to make it to McCormick Place on time.

After we hang up, I am slammed with the rest of the notifications—my parents' texts and calls had covered the screen—and see, painfully, a string of Slack chats from Jamie. I sent her my messaging draft last night at 3:00 a.m., and turns out she has a lot to say about it. That normally would be fine, but if I don't leave right stinking now, I'll be late to the next competition. Okay. I can do this.

The conversation with my parents plus the borderline rudeness from Jamie is making me feel like a little kid who did bad. And I hate that feeling. The only way to crush it is to channel it all into needing to win the next big thing, and lucky for me, there's a high-stakes competition coming my way in less than an hour. I'm ready.

Chapter Seventeen

$\mathcal{T}$his time, I'm the one who's nearly late. My parents made it before I did to the same banquet room (if it could be called that) where the styling competition was held. I coordinated with them, trying to meet up at their hotel beforehand, but end-of-week Chicago traffic is no joke, so they had to go on without me. It gave me enough time to respond to Jamie and pretend like I was totally available and working but not enough to finish what she asked. The second this competition is over, it's back to the laptop for me.

It's 1:00 p.m. on the dot as I'm pushing open the doors to see what awaits.

The room is much the same as last time, our hosts at the front, judges behind a table, giant clock and scoreboard. But there are a lot fewer competitors.

The space is abuzz from everyone speaking to one another, waiting for the hosts to begin. It's easier to spot my parents, who are close to the door, and the Simonians not too far off. Both sets of parents look a little worse for the wear. There's more slouching, and more paleness in their faces than the previous day. A night of drinking and hot sauce taking its toll. Vanya looks like a damn doll, though. Her curls are bouncier than ever, and she's wearing a plum corduroy jumper over a plain white tee.

I try to catch her eye, staring hard at her, and it works. She looks right at me, that recognition budding, her mischievous grin. *We have a secret.* The thrill of it strikes me to the core, cracking away the rest of the scene so it's only us here.

Nora glances my way then, gives me a wan smile, which breaks the illusion. I am grateful for it, though, and return it. At least she doesn't seem to hate my guts, unless she's a master of the art of fake smiles. But given the false way she and my mom greeted each other back in the hotel lobby that first day, I don't think so.

I approach my parents a little slower than I would normally have, trying to make them see me, and gauge their current level of anger. Sometimes, when they get out all their wrath at once, they're weirdly calm and happy afterward like a tornado didn't just sweep through the room.

I sidle up to my mom, who wraps her arm around me with a certain relieved joy, and plants a kiss on my cheek, leaving her sticky strawberry lipstick mark. I discreetly wipe it off while smiling at Bab, who simply looks in my direction and nods. Ugh, that is the problem with keeping in your anger—it lingers.

Then, Benny's voice booms over the speakers, sending a shock through the crowd. "Let's try that again," he whispers. "Can we turn this mic down? All right, all right, testing one, two, ten. It's Benny and Steph and we're back again!"

"Good Lord," I mutter.

"Do not bring God in this," Mom whispers.

Benny gives some bland opening remarks about thanking us for being here and some sponsorship notes. "You're part of the top fifty percent now, and it's going to get hotter than ever up in here, and yes, hotter than those excellent sauces from Big Mike."

He pauses, chuckling, waiting for sycophantic laughter, which arrives in scatters.

"But in the spirit of surprises, for our first competition today, you get to team up with some fellow rivals."

There's murmuring in the crowd. "Oh yes, a semi-collaborative competition—at least for part one. Stephanie's got the details."

She beams. "Thank you, Benny. For the first competition, we've carefully divided you into teams of six members."

My heart plummets to the floor, wondering if there's any chance . . . ? But no, there must still be about two hundred people in this room—there is no way we'd be paired with the Simonians. Because our parents having to work together? We'd be eliminated for infighting before a single vegetable was chopped.

"Doing a classic relay race of food preparation, with a couple of fun Chicago food–themed items thrown into the mix. And we are pleased to announce that the winners of this relay race, no matter how they place thereafter, will be awarded twenty thousand dollars in cash."

A banner in white and gold snaps down from the ceiling reading **$20,000 Cash Prize to Winning Relay Race Team.**

The buzz in the room has elevated to a full-on roar of voices, whooping, and incomprehensible words of excitement.

"Settle down, settle down," says Benny, so full of condescension I wish my mom could give him an earful about respect.

"As you were saying, Stephanie?" He turns toward her.

"Right, glad to see you're all as pumped about the relay race as we are. Like last time, we'll be texting you the number of your station where you'll get to meet your new teammates! Your team will race to finish your tasks the fastest. Quickest team wins. To be clear, no one will be eliminated in this competition. It is simply a chance to win the big cash prize. As for the tasks, let's take a look at what we got."

A black-clad assistant wearing headphones wheels out a silver island counter toward Benny and Stephanie.

Hugo holds up what appears to be an onion and garlic. "Ve start with ze basics. Task one: one onion, diced, two cups. Task two: garlic, one cup, chopped fine. *Fine*," he warns.

Okay, that's easy. I have decent knife skills, though I do prefer using a garlic press. Not as perfectly as my parents, but I can own an onion with a good sharp knife.

The health food judge waves a cucumber at us. "Pickling cucumber, also chopped fine to make relish."

Also no problem. So far it looks like we've got this. Our competitors' skills are the big question mark.

Big Mike holds up a package of . . . hot dogs? "Then we got five packs of Billy's Fine Chicago wieners. We want 'em chopped casserole-style, like this." He has a hot dog and knife at the ready and slices a piece to display to us. "Quarter inch."

Doesn't seem too hard, either. Just weird. Guess they had to "make it Chicago" somehow.

Solemn Nicholas, whom Mom charmed, steps up and picks up a beige ball. "Pizza dough. We want you to toss it into a twelve-inch pizza pie. Everyone will find a ruler at their station to check the diameter."

He begins tossing in a technique that looks effortless and like it took years to master. The back of my neck begins to feel hot. My parents and I do *not* make pizza. What are the chances we'll be paired up with someone who knows how to do that?

And Hugo moves forward again, holding up a raw chicken in what can be described as an indecent manner. "A whole chicken you must quarter, like so."

His knife flies over the chicken, flaying it into recognizable pieces. I swallow. I have definitely not cooked a whole chicken like that before, and I don't recall Mom or Bab doing it, either. But again, who knows whom we'll be paired up with? What if they have shitty knife skills? But maybe they'll have quartered a chicken?

Benny steps back to the middle, lightly shouldering Hugo. "Got it? We've got photo instructions that'll appear on your phones and yes, the judges will be coming by to make sure everyone is cutting to precision. If you cheat by chopping the pieces too thick, you'll have to pause where you are and go back to the person who cut corners, pun intended."

Stephanie pipes up. "Once you've finished, hit the big red button on your table to signal you're done, and a judge will be over to check. All right! Your counter number and instructions are being texted . . . now."

On the mark, my phone buzzes with the official text, and I open it to see counter thirty-one. "Eresoun-meg," I tell my parents. Bab has the cooler with him, and I feel a pang of guilt that I wasn't there to lug it through the endless halls of McCormick Place. His knee. Before he can reach for it, I grab the handle and pull it in the direction I think thirty-one might be. Bab's coolness is palpable; there's an energy about his filial disappointment that is creating a thickness in my throat. I should have been more on top of the Ned Richardson thing. I knew how big it could be for my parents to get in a major grocery chain.

We are in the forties, the second row of several cook's counters, when I spot Vanya and her parents lumbering our way. And then they stop. Right in front of table thirty-one.

Chapter Eighteen

$\mathcal{I}$ whip out my phone to show the Simonian family. "Number . . . thirty-one?"

Toros grunts. Nora immediately begins fanning herself. My father says, "This is an outrage."

Mom whispers to him, "Hagop, please."

Vanya is somewhat unreadable; she seems at once pleased and concerned. A bit like me, perhaps. I see what they're doing. This wouldn't have happened except for our parents' little show last night on the boat. A camera is parked nearby, pointed right at us. A green light near the lens is flicked on.

Before I can say something, Toros shouts generally into the air, "I need to speak to Benny, right now. I refuse. Refuse."

Vanya looks down and hisses, "Dad!"

I stand so that my back is to the camera. "They're filming this right now. We need to be mindful of that."

"There's twenty thousand dollars on the line, and they pair me with him," Toros groans.

"Do not speak back to my daughter this way," Hagop snaps.

"I wasn't speaking to her," Toros retorts.

"Well, you should have been, she address you."

Vanya steps next to me, back similarly to the camera, creating a decent blockade now. Only Toros's face would be visible. "Guys," she says with a smile. "Twenty thousand dollars. Can we try to win this?"

Toros stares longingly toward the judges' table. "Look at how they ignore us. This is *bad management*," he says directly into the camera.

Sweat creeps up along my hairline as I volunteer, "I've never quartered a chicken before, but I'm great with a knife otherwise. I can do the onion or cucumber no problem. Garlic I'm less fast with."

My mom puffs up her chest. "I do the garlic. Nazeli always uses a press," she laments.

Nora and my father shake their heads in commiseration, and I want to tell them to give me a break, but I'm not going to argue with any interfamily agreements, even if they're at my expense.

Vanya steps slightly closer to me then, her hand near mine; I can feel the warmth of it. I lean mine toward her, and the edges of our fingertips brush, then release. But from that one touch, my entire body is lit up, and I need more. No idea how I'm going to concentrate on onions now.

"I do not mean to brag," Nora peeps, doing her part in bringing me out of the moment. "But I use only the farm-raised whole chickens in my household. I quarter once a week."

Mom rolls her eyes hard, but I sense some relief in there, too.

I'm sure they quartered chickens back in Lebanon, but she hasn't since I've been around.

Vanya pipes up. "Dad or I could do the pizza, unless you want to, Hagop."

My father blushes unexpectedly at being addressed politely by Vanya. That's a good sign.

"We got this mad pizza oven at home, top of line," Toros says. "Vanya and me make every Friday night a new variety."

"It sounds like this your special hobby then," Bab says. "You can do pizza." I know deep down his worries about having to throw dough in the air without any prior practice have been alleviated. And I'm pumped that we have someone—two people—on our team who know how. Three cheers for Toros and his mad pizza oven.

Vanya turns to Bab. "That leaves you and me. Cucumber chopping for relish, or the hot dogs?"

She's being so kind, I want to rush over and kiss her right now.

Bab shakes his head, staring ruefully at the hot dog packages. "I cannot in good conscience chop wiener into bits."

Vanya smiles. "I can."

"Perfect," I say, and I can feel my pulse race with anticipation. Maybe we can do this. My family in front and Vanya's bringing up the rear. I address the group. "Me, onion. Mom, garlic. Bab, cucumber. Vanya, hot dogs. Toros, pizza dough. Nora, chicken."

Toros looks around. "Everyone feel satisfied?"

Not surprised he wants to get the last word. We all nod and say some version of yes. I didn't realize it until now, but in the time we've been conferring, a camera has snuck up to the side of us and got a view of our grand symposium. Well, they're not getting the drama they hoped for.

"Twenty grand, man," Toros murmurs. Nora rubs his arm.

"Well, ten thousand. We split," says Bab.

Toros waves him off. "Course, course."

"Unless you want talk about restitution for lost income of the past," Bab suggests.

Even though we haven't made up yet, I can't help snapping, "Bab."

He turns to me. "A friend betrayal was enough, but a daughter's? I am not satisfy with your excuses." Bab shakes his head.

A renewed tide of shame slams against me. I was hoping, with his rivals around, he'd have forgotten about my slipup this morning. I groan and say, much more lightly than I feel, "I said I was sorry. Can we focus on the task at hand?"

Toros sniffs. "Daughter not living up to expectations, Hagop?"

Bab's eyebrows twist in affront, and he leans backward. "How dare! Nazeli is perfection herself." He states it like I'm a God not to be disrespected.

And, I have to say, I almost want to thank Toros.

I laugh uneasily, knowing the cameras are still pointed directly at us. "You heard it here first, folks."

Then Benny's voice calls over the speakers, and I've never been more grateful to hear his pompous tones. "We'll begin our countdown momentarily. You can raise your knives, but not a single chop until the official buzzer."

I scramble to the front of the counter, grabbing an onion and reaching for a chef's knife. A much fancier blade and brand than we got last time. I wonder if they upgraded for this round of competitors. I motion for Mom and Bab to stand next to me.

They do, and the Simonians take their places and prepare their foods in front of them. The naked chicken is plunked down in front of Nora, a funny end to our mismatched relay race.

I look down and concentrate, reminded of swim practice way back in high school when I would stand on the diving board, head lowered, ready to hear that buzzer, not jumping even half a second before. I never won a race (green participation ribbons for life) and had zero talent in swimming, but my parents agreed it was a "safe" sport less prone to injuries, so that was what I did. Now, though? I have to believe we have a shot at winning.

Stephanie's voice, girlish and in charge, counts down. "Five, four, three, two, one."

A bell rings and I'm off. The knife slices through the ends of the onion like melted butter. Damn, they pulled out all the stops for this competition. I'm almost afraid I'm going to accidentally skim myself on it and the wound will be way bigger than it should be because the blade is so sharp. But no time to be afraid now. The onion skin's off, and my eyes aren't watering. Not yet.

"Throw that peel!" Toros calls.

"So fast, this is my daughter," Bab crows.

Then from my peripheral vision I notice Mom is springing into action, grabbing her garlic and sinking a fingernail into the skin. I halt all progress and yell, "Mom, stop! They'll disqualify us!"

"I don't understand," she says. "Is not time for me to chop garlic?"

"Bab, please explain," I plead, picking my knife back up again.

I hear him murmuring the explanation in Armenian to her over the din of the room and pray she'll listen to him. Teams are all cheering each other on, we're not the only ones.

And now, with the onion halved, is where it's really time for me to shine. With my phone set up against a utensil holder, I remind myself of the specified onion dice size. My blade flies across one half, seven or eight slices down the side, then flip and chop-chop-chop-chop into little bits. My eyes begin to water, but I don't take the time to wipe them. I'll be literally sobbing over these onions before I stop.

Vanya lets out a whoop. I don't bother hiding my blush, but don't look over, either. Not done yet.

I scoop the chopped pieces into the measuring cup provided and start on the next half. I pulverize it in record time, and no, my pieces are not all perfectly sized, but they're not bad, and they're all at least the size specified or smaller. I'm using the knife to slough off every last piece of slippery onion stuck to my hand. I check the measuring cup while Toros is yelling, "It's good, it's good!"

He's right. I slam down the knife and say, "Mom, now, go!"

"Do not rush your mayrig," she chides.

I raise my eyebrows in what I hope comes off as pleading, and she must gather how important this is to me, because then she begins.

The head of garlic is huge and looks a little older, so the skin on each clove is dry and ready to be shucked off quick. She uses the knife to slice the pieces off the bulb with one fell swoop, which is pretty clever—if it was up to me, I would have plucked them off one by one. Excellent time savings. Speaking of, I glance around the room and notice most people nearby are still on their onions. I mentally pat myself on the back.

Mom's already chopped two thick garlic cloves by the time I turn back.

"My wife." Bab glances around with pride, and I don't think he's ever heard of Borat, so it's zero percent ironic. "Best cook in land."

"Right, right." Toros bobbles his head in some semblance of annoyance, but I can see that he's also thrilled by Mom's virtuoso-like speed.

"Bravo, Hera," Nora near whispers, and my mom's knife slows for a fraction of a second before resuming its steady slicing.

She fills the container with all the chopped garlic, and instantly Bab picks up his knife and goes for the cucumber. I hug my mom's side and tell her she did incredible work. "Is nothing, what I do every day," she waves me off. But she is smiling.

Unable to help myself, I glare at our competitors again. They are tripped up on that garlic now. The table next to us, three blond heads speaking an indistinct language (Finnish? Dutch?) are near hair-pulling status as they watch one of their fellow teammates, a redheaded middle-aged woman, struggle with her garlic. Their garlic is fresh and the skin is clinging to the garlic meat, refusing to budge.

I whip back to Bab, who has chopped up his first cucumber. "It needs to be thinner, babam," Toros directs him. Annoying, but he's correct.

"Euff," Bab lets out, a very Armenian dismissive outburst. Yet, he does go back to give the pieces another couple vengeful chops that puts them in the correct size.

"All right, Bab!" I cheer. "We're doing so well, keep it up."

The cameras have moved on from us, which I guess means we're getting along better than they expected. In their place, Hugo, who is making his rounds, swings by our table. My stomach tightens, worried that he's going to make us go back to square one, that I didn't chop the onions small enough. But he inspects our goods, nods once, and walks on.

Vanya says excitedly, "So far, so good."

And then, it's her turn.

She's ripping open the hot dog packages and slicing up wieners in a manner that might make a grown man blush. Indeed, my father is looking queasy. His head was down while Hugo came around, so I filled him in on that fact, and that we got the official nod of approval.

"See? I know my relish size was ideal."

Well, he did chop them smaller after Toros asked him to, but whatever.

Toros is half circling Vanya like a helicopter parent slash coach, shouting encouragements and praise her way. While not everything about him is my favorite, I am finding his obvious love of his daughter quite touching.

Vanya's popping the last of the hot dogs into her bin. Nora reminds her husband, "Toros, ready yourself."

He takes to his station, hands placed over the pizza dough with his face intent like he's about to say an incantation to make it levitate. And in a way, I suppose he is.

When the time comes, he pushes down on the dough, morphing it from a round ball to a flatter circle shape with a clearly defined crust. "I need flour," he grumbles as the dough gets stuck to his fingers, but he presses on. He runs his palms inside the dough to spread it evenly, and I am damn relieved we have someone who knows what to do.

Then he holds the thin dough, his palms under the edge, and tosses it into the air, catching it and spinning it once, the fluff immediately expanding. I sneak a glance at my father, who allows his face one bare moment of awe. Then Toros slams the dough down on the table and whips out the ruler, but we can all see that it's definitely at least the specified twelve inches. He did it.

Vanya pats her dad on the back while he brags, "The secret is good dough prep. You only need one toss."

Nora's already working hard on the chicken, a drumstick on one corner of her cutting board.

My eye's on that "finished" button, bright red and garish. We forgot to discuss who would press it, but I'm not going to let some kind of social hierarchy interfere with us getting the win. I'll slam it first if no one else is going to.

But then, there's the sound of a loud buzzer, and I look

around, trying to find out if that means we're out of time. No, it must be that someone else finished before us. Shit.

"I should not stop, no?" Nora asks the group.

Vanya insists, "Don't stop, just in case." So Nora presses on, head down.

A couple of judges stride up to a table near the front, where a team full of young guys are stationed, including the ones I think own that meal-replacement drink. I'm standing on my tiptoes, trying to see. I'm not the only one, either; Toros is poking his head in their direction.

Benny's voice booms over the speakers. "False alarm, their garlic wasn't fine enough. Folks, make sure you follow instructions."

"Knew it," Toros says. "Nora, we are almost there. Chop!"

And right as I am filled with elation that we're about to make it, right as my hand hovers over the red button, another buzz fills the room.

Most likely this second team has made it, but Nora puts down her knife. "I am done," she shrieks.

At once, my hand is covered by Vanya's, then Toros's, which flew to the buzzer right after Nora's proclamation. We are pressing down when Bab joins in, his hand atop Toros's, and we hear it ring out in the halls. We came in second, at least.

Benny himself struts our way, a giant smile plastered over his face, which is weird for a team coming in second, but then, he's a strange dude. He doesn't feel condescending now, more like he . . . knows something?

"Hello, folks," he says. "Excellent work, let's see what you've got."

While Benny picks up my onion-filled measuring cup, I peer over to the other team that buzzed before us, and Stephanie is there, shaking her head as she holds up their lumpy, uneven pizza dough. Which means . . . we might have a chance.

Benny gives his nod of approval and moves on one by one to each of our finished products. He marvels over the pizza. "Fine work," he says, and I swear Toros blushes.

Then Mom asks, "Excuse me, Mr. Benny, are we winning?" This time, I don't stop her, since she previously charmed Nicholas with her innocent intrusions.

"We'll have to see," he replies. He abruptly walks away to confer with the other judges.

A few more buzzers go off, but none of the judges go over to check. Seems like one of us must be the winner.

Vanya says, "We passed muster. Now we have to hope the other team didn't."

Bab replies, "It difficult for me to imagine another team among us had the combination of skill and speed that we are presenting."

And I have to nod along with that. We were damn good, and this is not like one of those chef cooking shows where everyone has been a line cook or whatever for years. I bet many of the people in this room, like the meal-replacement bros, don't cook or work with fresh ingredients for their product. Also, my dad complimenting the Simonians? Calling them skilled? I sneak glances at them, and Toros is shifting his weight from one foot to another like he's unsure what else to do. I wonder if that's him accepting a compliment.

The judges are huddled together; there are some gestures toward us and some in the other team's direction. A few more buzzers sound, but I'm also seeing some teams laying down their knives mid-chicken. They know this is over.

Benny and Stephanie move to the center of the room, and Benny says, "All right, folks, we have a victor."

Stephanie says, "We're pleased to announce that the winner of the collaborative relay race competition is . . ." And here she pauses. I squeeze my mom's hand.

"The Green Falafel and Ha—um, Hag-ope's Fine Armenian Foods!"

Forget the name butchering, we won! We flipping *won* something. Twenty thousand somethings. Amid polite applause, Toros lets out the most relieved, excited screech I've ever heard from an Armenian man, and he clasps Nora in his arms and kisses her on the cheek.

She laughs, "Toros, Toros jan, I am squish." As he pries himself off her, Vanya jumps in.

Meanwhile, Bab has his "I knew we'd win it" smile on his face, and he's looking at me now, like everything from this morning is forgotten. He rests one arm on my shoulder and another around Mom. "Nazeli jan, you told us when we got here to join this competition, and we said no. But you—you were correct."

I must be in some alternate dimension for sure. I'm waiting for the earth to part and for me to be sucked into the molten core, because Bab just admitted *I* was right. For the first time in my twenty-seven years on this earth.

Then Vanya is by my side, and she is coming in for a hug, and screw it, I can hug her, this is fine. When I feel her soft press, there's a strange rush of memories of last night—our heady selves together alone—yet I'm fully aware of the present, with many, many eyes on us. I'm overwhelmed with how to take in both, but I concentrate on one small curl of hers that is tickling my nostril. It grounds me until she pulls away.

It was quick enough, friendly, congratulatory, but beneath it there was a shared layer of intimacy. I try not to be self-conscious when looking at my parents, who definitely saw the hug—I can tell by my mom's mild disappointment, that twitch on the side of her mouth.

Then it doesn't matter because Benny and Stephanie are upon us, mics in hand and cameras in tow.

"We present to you," Benny says, pulling out a regular-sized check from his coat pocket, "the prize of twenty thousand dollars. Congratulations, well earned."

Bab and Toros go for the check at once and each get a grasp on it. They let out low "you must be kidding" chuckles.

Feeling the cameras pressing on us, I say, "Thank you so much, we're shocked and grateful to have won." That was honest enough, and hopefully gave our families a respectable face instead of whatever is going on between Bab and Toros right now. They are staring at each other, wild grins on their faces, thumbs pinching the check. Benny has let go of it, so it's ours now.

Bab says, "Toros, I insist. I have very secure pocket within the lining of my coat. We can visit the bank, cash together."

"No, no no no no no," Toros says with a smile. "I don't want you getting idea about 'lost wages' and deciding to keep some for yourself."

"Come now, I am man of integrity."

"Oh," Toros says, eyes widening in mock incredulity. "You are. Same integrity that lock me out of every respectable board?"

Excuse me, Bab did what? I find myself turning between Bab and Toros, wanting answers.

"Now, now," Bab says, but there's movement around us, restless stirring, whispering.

A middle-aged white man with glasses steps forward, frowning. He yells back, "Fran, it *is* the guy from the boat." Then he faces us. "You people have to have all the attention on you. Isn't enough that you won, now you need to make a big show of it, too?"

A few people around us speak up in agreement, and my spine runs cold. I get that our dads are kind of making a scene, but it hasn't been *that* long, and this guy screams sore loser to me.

Vanya says to him politely, "Now you're contributing to the show, dude."

God, I wish I could scoop her up and kiss her for that. She is so brash, I adore it. I laugh at her statement, the bravest thing I can do here.

"Oh please," he says, giving an eye roll and something that you could call a body roll along with it. I hold my hand to my face and snicker.

"Glad to see contestants so eager to start the next competition," Stephanie chuckles nervously at the middle-aged guy.

And then Toros steps up, leaving Bab holding the check, open-mouthed. Toros is taller than the rude man, but the man has a thicker frame than him. Still, they're about the same age, and I know Toros is hitting the gym. He seems like the type that would enjoy boxing, too. "You talking to my daughter that way?"

Benny does not bother to hide his glee, the gleam of spit shining his freshly bleached chompers. Wait, Benny.

While the man is muttering apologies and backing away, I snatch the check from my unsuspecting father's hand—perhaps a little more forcefully than I would have done before hearing about Toros's accusations—and wave it at Benny. "Why don't you hold on to this until the next contest is over? Might be better that way."

I can see in his eyes, a slight shift back and forth, that he's puzzling over a way to refuse me, but with all the cameras on him, he's unable to come up with any. "Sure, that's, uh, that's a good compromise."

Bab and Toros shift toward Benny, annoyed at this turn of events, because to them it means neither of them won, but they're not ready to fight it. I note again how similar they are, and that they probably don't realize it.

Benny and Stephanie step back to the center of the room. "All right, folks, another congratulations for the winners." More half-hearted applause. "And now, time to say goodbye to your teammates. You're rivals once again."

Chapter Nineteen

We're at new tables now—Mom, Bab, and I—listening to the rules for the competition. The Simonians are a couple of stations to our right. Our counter is clean. An entire crew came up to take the food away and set it up in the kitchen behind us, so thank goodness all those chopped and prepared goods won't go to waste since we're meant to cook with them next. Though . . . who's going to use that many wieners?

And so far, the rules are simple—we make food, judges taste it, and a heart-pounding 50 percent of us will be cut. There are a little more than fifty brands in this room, which means only twenty-five or so will make it to the next round. Pushing the rest of us off a steep cliff.

Now that we've won one major competition, it only fuels me to want more. I don't want to be cut now. Bab admitted I was right about entering; if we keep winning, what more will he admit? That their branding could use an update? I can't help but think about the number of great things we could do for Hagop's

Fine Armenian Foods, if only they'd open their minds a bit. *And if only they'd let me in*, a small part of me thinks.

"But there's a twist," Stephanie says, tilting her head, making sure we heard, that we are worried.

It's working—I am.

"We don't just want you to show off your brand's delicious foods. We want you to get creative."

Oh no, we already established in round one that I am not creative. What if there's no Pinterest fix for this one?

"We want you to use your brand's food in a classically Chicago dish!" she reveals with a blazing smile.

What . . . ? How am I supposed to make Armenian Lebanese food, so light and filled with spices, fit in with Chicago's heavy cuisine? This is going to be a cinch for anyone doing hot dog buns. Also, what *are* classically Chicago foods besides Chicago dogs and deep-dish pizza? Thank God they didn't take our phones away for this; I'm going to have to do some speed googling.

"You'll have forty-five minutes to plan, cook, and plate your meal. Then the judges will come around one by one and try your creations. You will have a chance to explain your dish, and points will be awarded for creativity as well as taste."

I do not get this whole competition. If the point of it all is to land a spot in a Super Bowl ad and share it with the restaurant association, shouldn't they vet the brand for the taste of their actual food? The aesthetics thing makes sense, since you need to make sure they know how to show off the looks of the food. But even then, the owners of a business aren't necessarily the ones with design sense. Most of us in this room paid someone else to make our logo for us (besides Bab, who used some church board connection whose son wanted to become a graphic designer). The true point of all of this seems to be to make us jump through hoops for the judges' own amusement and for some kind of reality TV–style video. I get that they're trying to spice it up this year and they've rebranded, but I think in doing so they've lost sight of some core principles. For instance, does the brand in your commercial make food that tastes good? How can they judge that if we try to Chicago-fy it?

Their mistake, I suppose. I realize I'm feeling bitter about this because I have so much confidence in the actual taste of my parents' food, and now I'm worried they won't get to see that at all when I'm making a monstrosity of a Chicago-style Mediterranean hot dog.

My parents are staring at me, maybe have been for some time.

"What we going to do?" Bab asks.

"Start googling," I whisper.

My parents were both embarrassingly, willfully computer illiterate and leaned on me for everything dealing with a desktop, but as soon as smartphones came out, they took to the technology as if they hadn't missed two decades of tech.

I hear my mom's voice command ring. "Siri," Mom asks with a closeness that suggests she is consulting her brilliant long-lost cousin, "vat are the Chicago foods?"

I shush her while a few of our nearby competitors stare at us in a mixture of shock and annoyance. Luckily, there's enough chatter in the room that my mom's Siri request didn't sound like a glass shattering on a concrete floor, more like one of those unbreakable Ikea glasses—with which my house is fully stocked—clanging around. I spot Vanya peeking at me from behind Toros's mountainous shoulders, with that smirk of hers.

Though it's rude of me, I grab my mom's phone and cancel the request so Siri quiets down mid-explanation. "Where are your manners?" Mom hisses at me in Armenian, and I would love to ask the same of her.

I turn to my own phone, speed type, and start reading an article that promises the "Top 10 Most Chicago Foods." It's some of the usual—deep-dish pizza, Chicago dogs, Italian roast beef, but before I can read further, the mic clangs. I tune back in to Benny speaking in case I've been missing anything. "I hope you all feel honored to be here . . ." A bunch of skippable BS as expected. Yes, thanks, Benny, *we* feel honored.

The list is calling me; there has to be something here. Could we turn lavash into deep-dish pizza somehow? But the bread is so papery thin by design, there is no way it could hold all the casserole-like sauces of a deep dish. What about a hot dog wrapped in lavash? Dear Lord that sounds nasty. No. Or like . . . a dolma wrapped in lavash pretending to be a hot dog? Nah, I'm shuddering even thinking of that. That's not food, that's a kindergarten art project. Maybe an insult to kindergarten art projects.

I keep scrolling, when I see number ten on the list. "Tavern-style thin crust pizza . . . square-cut pies." I am reading with fury. Apparently some pizza joints in Chicago dispute that deep dish is the original Chicago-style pizza, and say that the thin crust is more authentic to the area.

This could be it. Lavash's size and shape look exactly like a rectangular pizza pie with those square-cut slices. (And truth be told, I love a square slice; in California it feels like a delicacy.)

The buzzer rings through the hall and I slide up to my parents, who are deep in their phones, as I was.

"Mom, Bab. I have an idea."

I tell them about what I've found with the flatbread. Mom twists her mouth. "Are you sure this work? Lavash is so delicate, it break right apart after cooking with cheeses."

She has a point, so I think it through.

"It should hold if we don't overload it with toppings."

"Perhaps it work," she muses.

Bab shrugs. "I have found no better solution in my readings, hokeesner."

I mean, I feel the same way. It's not perfect, but it should do.

"Ah!" Mom exclaims. "How cute it be, what if we put little falafel on top like sausage?"

I want to hug her; that is a perfect idea. "I love it. This way we get to show off the falafel and the lavash."

"And the manti," Mom adds.

I ask what she means.

"Well, the handsome judge he say he want to try my manti, so this morning I use the microwave and coffee maker hot burner to make some for him. It turn out perfect."

She whips out a Tupperware from the cooler, and sure enough, a dozen manti pieces float in their red tomato butter sauce, a dollop of minty yogurt on top.

"Mom that's—" I want to say *presumptuous*, like what if he doesn't even make it over here, or he was simply being polite last time. But you know what? Mom's instincts have gotten us to this point, so I'm not questioning her. I finish with a lame "Great."

"I never leave behind person who ask for my food. Never."

I nod, and we start to plan. The only thing we need to make is the pizza sauce. I look up a recipe and wonder if Vanya's family is also taking advantage with the pizza-making skills. I bet they make a kick-ass sauce. Meanwhile, we've never done this before.

We've got our ingredient list, and I tell them like last time that I'll go shop. Mom says she'll plate the manti and Bab will chop the falafel into sausage-like pieces. Another advantage of flatbread pizza is that it'll take a lot less time to cook, so the hour we have feels almost luxurious.

Still, I run toward the kitchen, hoping I won't need to elbow anyone in the guts for grated mozzarella. I'm by the spices when I spot Vanya, by the condiments refrigerator. She grabs two types of mustard and is about to run off when she locks eyes with me.

"This one is ridiculous." She shakes her head.

I'm about to agree, when a skinny bro nearby pipes up. "Right? How the hell am I supposed to turn an elite macro protein bar into a fucking hot dog?"

Guess we're not the only ones. The energy in the room does feel more frantic and, dare I say, negative than during the food-styling competition. More furrowed brows and muttering.

Not everyone, though—there's a woman about my age with a smile plastered on her face, humming happily while selecting a package of pepperoni, and I can't help it, but the inquisitive part of me needs to see what counter she ends up at, what her brand is.

"It's going to be a long shot," I agree with them both. The bro grumbles, then runs off.

Vanya raises her hand to her temple, "Morituri te salutant." Then she salutes me, totally seriously.

I stare at her wide-eyed. She explains, "'We who are about to die salute you.' What? You didn't take Latin in high school?"

Okay, not another word from my mom about how Vanya isn't accomplished enough. Dear Lord.

"Forced to take French since my parents knew some from Lebanon. Language of the elites."

Vanya says with satisfaction, "They pulled that on my brother, but I, the baby, got to do what I wanted."

That was true in our household, too—my brother took Japanese, which didn't even have an AP course (gasp). I always thought it was because he was a boy and athletically talented, but maybe it's just a younger sibling thing.

"Spoiled brat." I wink at her.

"You love it," she says as she darts away.

Right. We're in the middle of a food competition here, and not a flirting one.

After gathering all the ingredients, I meet my parents back at the table, where Mom has prepared the manti on a plate, ready for Nicholas, should he happen to come by. The need to focus on aesthetics yesterday must have sunk in somehow, because I have to say she arranged them well. Much better than our usual haphazard presentations.

The three of us get to cooking together, and we feel incredibly in sync, making the slightly Lebanese take on pizza sauce (with mint instead of oregano), which takes a good twenty minutes, but then it's done. We spread the sauce, Mom sprinkles the cheese over the bread, and then Bab takes it to the oven. He and Mom squat down, checking to see the exact moment they should remove it.

I catch someone running their hands through perfectly blown-out hair and realize it's that beautiful smug woman from before who seemed so confident about this round. She's a few tables ahead of us, with several jars on the countertop. I squint and make out MARINARA SAUCE written on the label, and then I remember her spaghetti from the food-styling competition. Well, no wonder she's swishing that tail like a well-satisfied cat. Her brand's food easily gets to shine. The meat brands, too—any sausages, pepperonis. Hot dog bun makers, sandwich bread makers. It's pretty obvious who's going to make the cut.

I dare myself to glance at Vanya's table, but can't see what's happening on their counter. I catch Vanya with her eyes hooded, appearing defeated. Toros is jumping around with staccato-like rhythms, and Nora, while her back is turned to me, has her shoulders slumped. Even though we're in competition, and I knew the food-tasting portion would be a long shot for the Simonians (I internally wince just thinking it), I still want them to advance. The $10,000 is an awesome start for them, but it sounded like from what Vanya said that they're going to need a lot more than that.

"Hima, hima!" Mom shouts at Bab, and he dutifully opens the pizza oven and rescues it at seemingly the perfect time.

It turned out beautifully, and I tell them as much. And we've got over ten minutes to spare. Coasting. "Time for the falafel topper?" I ask.

Mom nods, and pushes the bowl with the chopped falafel toward the lavash pizza. But she pushed a little too hard, and the steel surface of the counter was more slippery than our rough tiled one at home, and the bowl crashes into the pizza, cracking it.

"Vai Astvadz," Mom exclaims, and I know she's taking this seriously when the Lord's name escapes her lips.

I glance at the clock. Ten minutes left. "We can make another one," I say, trying to keep my voice as calm as possible. Endless fire drills at Abilify have prepared me for this.

"Yes," Bab says. "But vait."

He takes a knife from the rack and cuts another corner of the lavash pizza, and it cracks unevenly, not respecting the blade of the knife in the least.

"I see what your point. Even if we make another one, we can't slice it like pizza."

"It break every time," he says, painfully demonstrating again.

"Hagop, no more," my mom cries.

Lavash is not meant to be toasted. This was all my fault. Unless we precut the slices completely, but that would look more like slices of lavash toast, not a pizza. Except . . .

"Why don't we pre-trace some slices on the bread so that when we cut into it, it's more likely to slice and not crack apart willy-nilly?"

"Again, a charade?" my father asks.

"Exactly."

Mom nods. "I do this now." And true to her word, she whips out a fresh slice of lavash and precuts soft lines where we can slice into it later with hopefully more success than our first attempt. We do the whole song and dance again of pizza sauce and mozzarella and pop it in the oven.

While Mom and Bab watch the oven, I watch the clock nervously as it ticks down to two minutes, then one.

"Are we close?" I ask them.

"'Be joyful in hope, patient in affliction,'" my father quotes at me, hoping I will revere the Bible verse as he does.

"The clock isn't going to be patient for our afflictions. Yallah."

Then my mom springs to action, whipping open the oven door and ordering Bab to take out the lavash. He treats it with such tenderness I haven't seen since my little brother was in a swaddle.

Mom grabs a palmful of falafel bits and scatters them over the pizza as the clock ticks three, two, one.

The buzzer grates on me, lasts a few seconds too long. But we did it. At least, we'll see what happens when the judges try it.

"Tools and hands down, everyone," Benny announces.

"Now we get to the fun portion of the day," Stephanie says, and I wonder what she thought the rest of this was. "We're going to approach one by one and try your food, and our cameras will show what's going on to the room so everyone can enjoy your creations."

For some, it will be humiliation for the world to see—it sounds like the judges will have a grand time with that. God, I hope our lavash holds.

"This time, we'll make notes but won't announce our final decision until we've tried all fifty-two teams' creations."

They start from the right, which means we're about twenty people down the line, and Vanya and her parents will go ahead of us.

One by one, we witness people's relative successes and failures. A pickle company showed off their gourmet hot pickles in a Chicago-style dog, which all the judges seemed to like. Polite nods and a few *yum*s.

A chips company tried a devastating deep-dish pizza with a crumbled-chip crust, which got soaked through by the filling. The bottom fell out, nearly splattering the health food judge's white blouse.

I hadn't been considering what the sweets manufacturers were going to do, but during this process I learn that there's a big popcorn company in Chicago that is considered a Chicago staple, so any brand making sweet stuff seems to have seized on it. An applesauce company cooked their applesauce with some sugar and attempted to make kettle corn but does not seem to have succeeded, judging by Stephanie's face. A chocolate bar company seems to have done it by drizzling their chocolate over sweet and salty popcorn.

It goes on like this until the Simonians' table is next. My stomach clenches for them when I see Vanya up on the screen. Then tighter, when I see what they've created.

"For you, a Mediterranean vegan Chicago dog," Toros exclaims.

Oh no, my initial idea, which I thought was ridiculous. They've executed it.

A piece of dolma wrapped in lavash with falafel sprinkles, pickled red onion, and according to Toros, sumac. I'm impressed they found sumac among the spices. There's also a small topping of yellow mustard, which has to taste horrible with that combo, but without it, there's nothing Chicago about this dog. I mentally wave goodbye to them as competitors.

But again it's the health food judge who takes the lead with them, and she claps her hands in delight as Toros and Vanya explain their creation. Nora interjects about how all their foods are locally sourced in California and organic, and the judge beams. On the big screen, the judge raises the lavash-dolma dog to her mouth, takes a bite, and her face is left a puzzle, assessing.

"Fascinating flavor. The texture, too. Never had anything like it. The pickled onions are a great touch, and so is that sumac. The mustard I could do without, but overall, I am loving the fresh concept of this vegan hot dog. Great work!"

The Simonians' faces lift with relief, and mine washes with confusion. I guess they pulled it off? We'll see what the other judges say, though.

"Anyone else want to sample?" the health food judge asks the rest of the panel. So far, anywhere from three to all six judges partake in tasting the creations. This time, only Stephanie pipes up. "Sure," she says.

She takes a mouselike bite off the other end, chews a couple times with her hand over her mouth, and says, "Agree with everything you said."

Huh. Maybe it wasn't so bad. Strange that none of the other judges jumped in, especially at the chance to excoriate someone's choices. Hugo went to town on the applesauce team. I'd think Big Mike with his love of wings would have something to say about a dolma plopped into lavash bread and called a hot dog, but he's already looking toward the next table.

Still, despite my gut telling me something's off, I'm happy for Vanya and her parents. They're giving each other high fives when the camera moves off them.

A few more competitors go by, including the attractive pizza sauce woman and her partner (a similarly handsome young man with thick hair), who own Tossed Sauce. What a terrible name. She gushes over the secret recipe "from my nonna and nonno in Italy." She makes sure to beam her eye contact directly into judge Nicholas's gaze. Everyone tries her and her business partner's deep dish, and the judges each deliver a unique compliment.

Then we're up.

The judges seem larger than usual up close, all of them together. I tell myself to stop being intimidated. I am the senior product marketing manager at Abilify; I am a polished professional. Far more so than someone like Benny or Big Mike.

"What do we have here?" Big Mike asks.

I'm prepared. "As we all know, when we think of Chicago pizza, we think of deep dish. However, Yodel's Place on the west side maintains that, actually, tavern-style thin-crust pizza cut in squares is more authentic to Chicago."

Big Mike interrupts, "I do love that joint."

I inwardly curse myself for bringing up the square-cut pizza. Our little trick dotting the lavash isn't necessarily going to work, and now I've set up squares in their minds.

"So," I continue, pretending everything's great, "we decided to create a thin-crust pizza on our own using Hagop's Fine Armenian Foods' lavash, with a Mediterranean-inspired pizza sauce we cooked up right here, and topped with mozzarella from your fridges and some of Hagop's own falafel as a sausage substitute."

Bab pats me on the back. I can feel the energy from Mom's smile without even looking at her. This kind of thing? That's my jam, and it feels good to have them acknowledge it.

Benny speaks up, "Let's give it a try. Cut us a slice?"

I glance at Mom and Bab. We didn't discuss who should do it, and I don't think any of us want to potentially rain down ruin upon us.

Then Mom picks up a knife. "I shall cut," she says.

She raises the knife above the pizza, and I swear it feels like the room quiets. I bite the cuticle on my thumb, then immediately stop when I remember we're on camera. I suck in my breath and try to look natural.

She slices down, and the first cut is a perfect line along our pattern. She tries the other side, and it works, too. Now one more and we're home free. I hear the crunch of the lavash and expect to see lopsided cracks, but it cuts through very closely onto our pattern, what anyone who wasn't a perfectionist would call a square. It's done, oh, thank goodness. Bab lets out a heavy breath, ending in a smile. Mom looks borderline haughty with pride. Now, to taste.

But I shouldn't have worried about that. Benny is smitten with the flavor, as are all five of the other judges, who want to try a piece. Mom is cutting faster and the lavash does crack off slightly, but by now, no one notices.

"It's kind of like toast, but different" is the deep insight Benny comes up with.

"Totally refreshing," says the health food judge.

Mom leans over and taps Nicholas on the shoulder. "I promise you to make manti, here it is." She offers him the plateful with a fork and napkin, and he registers surprise even while he takes it into his hands. "Oh, right. Thank you," he says.

Mom winks. "Not part of competition, just for fun."

My God, Mom, so good.

He smears the manti full of the tomato sauce, then dips it into the minty yogurt and takes a bite. His eyes light up, and I notice that the camera is capturing and displaying this for the whole room to see.

Bab notices, too, and whispers to me, "This broadcast is make Toros red in the face, I know it."

"Dad," I whisper, not wanting to betray Vanya, but I still smile. Mom's cooking *is* the best, whether done in her industrial kitchen or on a coffeepot burner.

Big Mike asks, "What's that?" to the plate of manti, but Nicholas turns his back. "Not for you," he says, shoveling in another mouthful.

Mom looks prouder than the day I told her about my UC Berkeley acceptance. I'm not too hurt; she deserves to feel impressed by her own work.

The judges move on, while Nicholas finishes up. He leans toward my mom. "I would lick the plate, but my own mom taught me better than that."

"She teach well." Mom nods.

Mom always chastised me for doing that, but she didn't beat it out of me—one of my great grown-up pleasures in life has been to lift up a bowl of something particularly delicious and saucy and lick the whole damn thing clean.

The last teams' creations get their notes and remarks (and some receive mortifying censure), and then the judges move back to their table to confer.

At this point, I'm starving, so I dig into the rest of the pizza. The judges were right, this is unique. The crispness of the lavash with the melted cheese and the tangy bite of the minty pizza sauce is excellent. The falafel's a nice complement, too. We should open up a place and sell this.

"All right, everyone." Benny's familiar voice echoes through the hall. "We've made our choices, and as always, we'll share them for you on the scoreboard."

Our brands' names, only fifty-two of us now, appear on the board, with an empty checkbox next to each. Just like the aesthetics competition.

Stephanie says, "And the results will appear . . . now."

I take a sharp breath. Nothing happens. She clears her throat, turns toward the rest of the judges. Big Mike throws his hands up quizzically. A PA rushes toward them, taps on Benny's iPad.

Then the screen lights up, green checks and red x's all at once, fifty-two dings and buzzes. I search for our name. Green.

I give Mom a huge hug, then Bab, and mid-hug, I eye the board again.

The Green Falafel? Green check mark. Looks like we'll be seeing the Simonians at Navy Pier tonight. I hope, though, I'll get to see Vanya even sooner.

Chapter Twenty

$\mathcal{I}$'m reworking some Operation Wolf website copy in my head when Vanya strides up to me right outside my hotel. Behind her, there's a large bush of blue hydrangea, and the way they're spread makes it look like they're her wings.

It's an hour or so before the Navy Pier event starts, and even though I still have a mountain of work to do, I couldn't pass up time with Vanya. We texted after the competition and agreed to meet up. I squeezed in some concentrated work right before this, rewording page after page, per Jamie's directives. I'm confident it can be finished by Monday and that I can take this time away from my laptop, even though part of me is still a little worried that Jamie might be pinging me nonstop during Vanya's and my mini-date. I silence my phone.

Work is still thick in my mind, but I try to shove it away, which is easier to do when Vanya speaks.

"Another sneaky meetup before being around our parents all evening, how did I get so lucky?" she asks.

"I was asking myself the same thing."

We hold each other, then kiss. Then kiss deeper. I didn't realize until now how much I needed it. Both what a relief it is to be with her after work stress, and how I had been holding in desire for hours and hours while we were at the competition.

"I'd been waiting to do that all day," she says.

"Same here," I say, practically sighing from satisfaction.

Then, I muse aloud, "That was our first daytime kiss."

Immediately I'm embarrassed, but she says with an easy smile, "I'll mark it down in the Vanya and Naz milestone book."

"Oh gosh," I say, covering my eyes for a moment.

"Don't," she says, taking my arm. "It's sweet. And I find I enjoy daytime kissing as much as nighttime kissing."

I lean into the warmth of her skin and revel in the fact that we get to spend quality time together. Discovering, chatting, getting to know everything Vanya.

"You said there's a beach?" I ask.

She begins walking, and I follow. "I mean, not a Pacific Ocean type of beach, but apparently, yes, on Lake Michigan there's an actual beachy type of beach. Thought we Californians should see it with our own eyes."

"Then let's do it. So happy to leave work behind for this."

"You were still working?" she asks as we begin our walk.

"Ugh, there's such a tight deadline, every spare second is going to have to be spent on it."

She pauses. "Are you sure you don't need to go back and finish?"

I shake my head and continue on, showing my resolve. "No, no, definitely not. The work is the type that can't be finished in an hour anyway. I'm waiting to hear back from people. And I'd much rather be with you. It's still on my mind a bit, but I know it'll fade away." I try to keep the strain out of my voice, but I'm not so sure I succeeded.

Vanya rubs my back. "Allow me to help. Let's look around; I have a feeling this is going to be a pretty little hike."

She's right. We saunter down the summer streets of Chicago. Every restaurant seems to have an outdoor space, and most are full, with patrons pouring drinks from pitchers and laughing at one another's jokes.

"Everyone seems so happy here."

"I bet it's because winter is so cold, this must feel like paradise."

"Not just for them. Coming from SF, it definitely does to me, too."

We walk like this, two tourists through the warm, tree-lined streets, saying aloud any signs and storefronts and new sights we spy. It's comfortable and thrilling at the same time.

Then, as we're strolling in front of a brightly colored teal-and-white shop, a woman about our age with short-cropped hair and a friendly but frantic smile dashes out of the open door and stops us.

"Hey there, do you two like cupcakes?"

"Uhh," I stammer, and Vanya gives a similar noncommittal response. I assume she's thinking the same thing I am—we are not about to get conned into something.

The lady shakes her head. "Sorry, I meant, like, for free. We accidentally misread an order for a wedding and made too many rainbow cupcakes. We unloaded a bunch of extras on them, but they said we could keep a few dozen and give them out. Spread the love. We're closing soon and I only have a couple left, and when I saw you two walking hand in hand, I thought, 'Yes! These two fine people require some rainbow cupcakes.'"

"Well, in that case," Vanya says, grinning, "I absolutely love cupcakes. Especially extras from a—queer? Wedding? That, or unicorn enthusiasts."

"The cutest queer couple," the cupcake woman assures. "Well, maybe not the cutest ever. You two are certainly in the running." I find myself blushing hard, but happily notice that Vanya is, too.

The woman offers the tray with two remaining cupcakes. Admiring the rainbow frosting, I say, "These are lovely, thank you."

"Wait till you taste them." She winks.

We thank her, and when she goes back inside, we giggle at our good fortune. Luck seems to be following us everywhere in this city.

Cupcakes and napkins in hand, we dive in. I take a sideways bite, trying hard not to get the frosting all over my face, and failing. Vanya hasn't fared much better, and it is adorable. The flavor, though? Our cupcake fairy godmother was right: absolutely delectable. Vanilla with hints of citrus, sweet but not overly.

As I think about the wedding from which these cupcakes originated, a thought floats into my mind, and I realize Vanya and I haven't discussed this aspect of ourselves yet. I say, "Do you mind if I ask—and feel free to tell me it's none of my business—are you out to your parents?"

She swallows, then dabs at her mouth in a gesture that reminds me a bit of Nora, and then speaks. "I am, and it's surprisingly okay. My mom at first was all worried during the conversation, like I was some fragile piece of glass that could break if she said the wrong thing, which was touching, actually. And Dad said stuff like, 'Whatever, whatever, just don't share details.' He was weirdly distant from me for a few days and Mom was in that worried state, but then we were back to normal. Not exactly heartwarming, but way better than other Armenian dads I've heard about who disown their kids for being gay."

I nod, thinking about an Armenian friend of a family friend who stopped speaking to their college-aged son when he came out, and still to this day hasn't changed their stance. "Definitely could be worse. Same with my situation. For as religious as my parents are, they . . . well, they seemed to care more about keeping me around, keeping our relationship the same, than what Orthodox Christianity teaches, I guess."

I hadn't considered that until now, that I am more important to them than the good word. True, they're not like my ex's parents, who welcomed her queerness with open arms and a celebration, but Mom and Bab's ultimate acceptance means a lot. This is a type of luck, too.

The trees are dense on these city streets, and the buzzing sound of cicadas increases in intensity.

Vanya licks some pink off the top of her finger. "Pretty big hurdle for us both to have jumped."

I nod. "The pathway has been cleared."

"It's just blue ocean from here." She smirks, and I see what she's doing.

"Uh," I stammer, trying to think of another metaphor. "Three, two, one, ready for liftoff?" I say with both uncertainty and levity in my tone.

She laughs. "Not bad, Naz. I was wondering how long we could keep it going. But if I may speak plainly." She drapes her arm over me, pulls me in, nuzzles my hair, and then kisses by my ear. "I am very happy we met."

I flush a deep red and savor her touch, the trails of sweetness left on the edge of my cheek. I lean into her.

"So am I. I'd say we make a good team."

"A great one. You were amazing during that cooking challenge. Taking charge but also diplomatically handling two sets of Armenian parents. Not easy."

The city streets give way to openness, and it feels like we're getting close to the lake.

"I could say the same for you—you were so cool under pressure."

She pretends to adjust a bow tie, breaking our embrace. "Why thank you, ma'am."

"Seriously, though," I say. "And that was amazing how your dad out of nowhere tossed the perfect pizza crust. I guess not out of nowhere for you—he said you two have pizza night every Friday?"

She wipes a few green crumbs from her top lip and smiles. "It's the most fun we have together, which is saying something, because when he's not competing with his greatest rival, my dad's a super fun guy. I sometimes wonder if we should take the pizza thing out of hobby zone and into the business, but it clashes too much with the current brand."

I nod. "That would be a huge undertaking." But thinking of how it could actually be better for them, considering their less than ideal product, I add, "Though it's sometimes a great idea to follow a passion and turn it into something bigger. Anyway, you should bring it up with them, if you wanted. See what you all come up with."

She considers. "I should. They're usually receptive to my ideas, even when they're daydreamy, like this one."

The cupcakes are done, and we toss the wrappers into a conveniently placed trash can; first hers, then mine.

"You're lucky there," I say. "I know I mentioned it before, but my parents' MO has been to shut down my suggestions, even though any advice I give comes from specific experience. A proven track record, like we say at work. But this competition? I feel like it's changed things a bit. They're seeing how I can help them, and to be honest, I'm seeing more of their strengths, too."

I wonder if I've been as dismissive of them as they have of me, if that's been the real problem. But now, our hard outer shells have cracked a bit, and we're peeping out and starting to see each other as we really are.

"Well, shoot," Vanya says. "Maybe you're destined to work in the family business after all."

"Maybe," I say, spying a hummingbird busying itself in a long red flower.

Just then, our street ends in a pedestrian tunnel, and Vanya says that's our next destination. We walk through it, along with some teenagers, and a mom with a whole troupe of giddily shrieking children, and then climb up some stairs. Then, there it is: water.

I can't see the other side, and given how flat and wide and open everything is, Lake Michigan feels more like an ocean. I knew in theory there were lakes this big but hadn't ever encountered one. It's wonderfully surprising and makes me feel like a kid again, knowing there are still new things to discover about the world.

Vanya and I amble along the walkway while the deep blue water splashes up against the break wall. After a few minutes, we arrive at an actual bona fide beach, with sand and lake water lapping up against it. Some of our tunnel companions are nearby, all the kids yipping with joy, and it only adds to my happiness.

"Whoa, turn around," Vanya says.

I do, and I see why her tone was so reverent. There's Chicago's skyline, the Hancock Tower looming large among the other skyscrapers, old and new mixed together.

"I've never seen so much metropolis practically right on top of a beach. So into it, though."

"Me too," she says, and takes my hand while we stare, our chests rising and falling in unison.

Then I pull her hand and draw her in for a kiss. When I close my eyes, I can still see the towers, and I'm feeling Vanya's softness, and it's all so perfect.

Then something wet lands on my shoulder and hair. Did the waves flare up somehow? Or maybe a kid's water gun?

I pull away from Vanya, and she questions the concerned look on my face. "What's up?"

"Nothing," I say. "Just some water startled—"

But I've touched the wet spot and looked at my fingers, and it is white and gray and sticky slimy and—

"Oh God. A bird pooped on me!"

Vanya is both chuckling and attentive at once. "Oh my God, Naz. I'm sorry. Let's see what I have in here—" she says, rifling through her shoulder bag. "Now I wish I hadn't tossed that napkin. I have a receipt here from the ATM. Don't look, you won't be impressed anyway."

I laugh while she's wiping at my shoulder with the thin strip of paper. "I'm not trying to be a diva, but ew, ew, ew, I feel so gross. Even if my mother insists this is good luck."

"My mom says the same. Maybe PakCon Superstars is going to go your way." Then she knits her brows. "This isn't really working. I think I made it worse, actually. And you're definitely not a diva. I don't think anyone is delighted at being a bird's bathroom."

"Pardon me, did I hear you say 'a bird pooped'?" a woman's voice calls out with a slight Midwestern accent. It's the mom from the tunnel, the one with something like five kids with her.

"You did," I say stiffly, feeling like if I move, I'm at risk of getting more of it everywhere.

She whips out a bottle of antibacterial wipes.

"Let me see, dear," she says. Feeling safe in her presence, I proffer my affected shoulder, and she pulls out a wipe. "Oop, if I may." I nod. "Believe me," she says, "this isn't even the grossest thing I've cleaned up in the last hour."

"Oh gosh, you are too, too kind," I say, really meaning it as she wipes up my shoulder, then gets another wipe out and works on my hair.

"You are good at this," Vanya says.

She gestures toward her kids, the youngest-seeming of which is now throwing sand at the older ones. "Years of experience. Hey, Dax! You stop that now, okay? Sand is for making castles, not for throwing."

Dax magically obeys.

"And good at that, too," Vanya adds.

"Oh no, surely not," she says. She hands me a wipe for my finger, and suddenly, I'm feeling optimistic again.

"How can I thank you? Can I buy you a coffee or something?"

"No, no, I'm all set," she says, pointing to a massive iced Starbucks drink. "Just enjoy your day, that's thanks enough."

We thank her again profusely, her waving it all off.

When we're a short distance away, I say, "People out here are so nice. Giving suggestions, giving free food, giving help . . . just because."

"It feels like a magical city," Vanya says, looking right into my eyes. "I wonder if it's you, or us, maybe. Good vibes begetting good vibes."

"I like that." We sit on the sand, bodies pressed against each other, leaning on each other's weight.

We breathe it all in for a moment, and then Vanya turns to

me. "Can we promise each other something? No matter what happens with the competition—I mean, we still have tonight and then tomorrow's final round, and there's only one winner. So whatever goes down, we won't let it interfere with us. This feels too—I don't want to come off too strong, but I like where this is going."

The lake breeze tickles my face as I lose myself in Vanya's eyes, her startling conviction. "Yes," I say. "Absolutely yes. We won't let it get in the way. And I am sincerely wishing you all luck."

"Me too," she says, and I know she means it.

Chapter Twenty-One

An hour later, I'm at Navy Pier. The PakCon Superstars organizers have roped off a prime area close to the Ferris wheel and carousel for the finalists to congregate. They've fenced it in with potted trees full of colorful lights that are sure to only get prettier as the night falls. There's a gigantic bar, and even still there seems to be a steady line. Like in the great hall today, there's a large projector screen set up that's showing clips of all the event goers. People chatting, drinking, slapping one another on the back. Chicago continues to be a summer paradise with its perfect seventy-five-degree weather this evening, no jackets needed.

I hope to see Vanya in the crowd, but I don't from my vantage point. We arrived five or so minutes apart, and I let her go first, so I know she's around.

As soon as Vanya and I parted, I checked my phone, and there were no fires or nonstop texts from Jamie. That date was totally, completely worth it. It's late Friday afternoon in San

Francisco, and everyone is clocking out, so I'll finish the rest of the work this weekend.

My phone buzzes, and I feel my heart sink when I see it's a Slack message from Jamie. **Time for a quick sync on messaging progress?**

Ugh, it'll never end. I thought we were in a good place for me to take over and finish this weekend, but I guess not. I type **yes**, and then she calls me.

She begins speaking as if in midthought. "It's Friday afternoon and I'm getting nervous about the work being done on time. We *cannot* drop the ball on this."

As if I would simply not do the work and show up to the meeting on Monday without anything. What in my performance record has ever suggested I'd do this? I'm no athlete, but I know I'm not a ball dropper.

"I'm on it, Jamie," I say, only thinly hiding my annoyance. "The work is nearly there, I've checked out best practices from Delphi's messaging—"

Jamie interrupts me. "You already did?"

Delphi is, I guess you could call them, a competitor, but they're a gigantic public corporation with billions of dollars in profit a year. Their performance management software is like the pinkie toenail of their business. Still, if they're doing something, we better be doing it, too, even though their overall look is outdated and clunky.

"Yes," I say, and give her a rundown of my analysis of their messaging versus ours. ". . . which is how we compare." I end my soliloquy.

She snorts. "Except our product is *actually* good."

"Right, well—"

Sort of true, but I'm itching to get off the phone, not talk smack about Abilify's competitor. I stare longingly at the competition participants, imagining Vanya among them, hoping Jamie is done.

"Just promise me you've got this. You haven't been as available lately, and it's making me nervous."

I stifle my exasperation properly this time and put on a fake smile. "I've got it. I promise. I would never do anything to compromise Operation Wolf."

She gives a half-hearted reply, and we hang up.

My nerves are frayed; I am so ready to wash away Abilify for the evening and relax. I wish I could jump up and down and slough off this jittery, maddening feeling.

A waiter steps up to me with a tray of drinks. "Chicago Fizz?" he asks. Well, sounds like the universe was listening to me after all.

The rather hefty glasses are full of ruby-colored foam. At least I know the foam is from egg whites and not some weird yam processing that turns it into spit. I trust in egg whites. The drink looks refreshing, and it is *exactly* what I need. Anything to drown out KPIs and target-oriented incentives and Jamie's nasally voice in my head.

"Absolutely," I say, snatching a glass, its smooth iciness pressed against my fingertips. "And one for a friend," I add, grabbing another. I make a promise to myself that if I see my parents or Vanya before I finish drink one, drink two is theirs. If I don't, drink two is mine.

Perhaps pushing my destiny along in the direction I desire, I gulp down drink one. It's rummy and sweet with grapefruit and sugar, cold to counterbalance the humidity. I'm halfway through drink two when I spot my parents. I approach them, and we hug and give our two cheek kisses as usual.

"Have you hear what the challenge of the evening will be?" Bab asks me.

"I haven't, just got here," I say, hiding the empty glass behind my back. They need some tables around here to set down used items.

Bab grins. "It is hot dog eating competition. I have it from Benny himself."

Oh no. More opportunities for bad behavior. Something in me is sure that Toros will want to partake in this event, and Bab won't be able to resist. "Bab, I'm not sure you should do that."

Mom barges in, "I agree with you, Nazeli jan. Hagop, we are going to have to go to doctor after this trip, and they know nothing, then we will have to wait one more week to see gastro specialist and you will be in pains this whole time. And who will be waiting on you? Me."

"She has a point," I say, finishing up my drink.

I sense a typical argument brewing between my parents, and I don't want to get caught in the cross fire, plus I now have two empty glasses I need to set down. So, silently, I back away and let the two of them go at it while I look for some type of table or busing station.

The skies are beginning to pastel, splashing colors onto one another. It feels so inviting here, like if I leaned back, Chicago would find a way to catch me. Or maybe the fizzes are sneaking up on me.

Finally, way back by the entrance, I find a table filled with what looks like leftover supplies—tape, wiring, speakers. I place the glasses there, though it's not ideal. Then Benny materializes out of nowhere, behind me.

"Hey there! How's it going?" he says.

I glance around to make sure he's talking to me.

"Me? Oh yeah, I'm good, great. What a night," I say, hoping I salvaged my small talk with that last sentence.

"You guys, sorry, forgot your brand name—oh wait, right, Hay-gope's—really shone through in that round. First the relay, then your thin crust pizza."

I'm not sure why, but I'm uncomfortable being buttered up by Benny. I'm not getting the sense he's hitting on me, but I'm not sure what my weird feeling is. Then I think, well yeah, he has a good point, we did shine, we absolutely radiated in that round. We won ten grand and found a way to somehow make our Armenian Lebanese food fit into the Chicago pizza mold. Maybe Benny's been secretly rooting for us this whole time. He might give me a hint about tomorrow. Maybe he's about to drop what question our team is going to be asked.

Benny smiles. "You can stop looking so worried; I'm just some dumb guy."

It's so unexpected that I find myself laughing. Did not think Benny would be the self-deprecating type, and certainly not enough to make me laugh, but maybe it's the booze. He goes up a small notch in my book, regardless.

"Are you prepared for tomorrow?" he asks me.

Here it is. I will myself to concentrate and stop being tipsy. I better remember every sentence of this conversation. Somehow it feels like being grilled by Jamie, though he's not nearly as intimidating. Still, I steel myself as if I were talking to Abilify's board itself.

I puff up my chest a bit and say, "As much as I can be. I know all the ins and outs of our brand and can speak to it in any way."

Benny gives an airy smile. "Like how you're better than the other Middle Eastern competition?" He punctuates his words with meaning so that he must be talking about the Green Falafel.

I snap back, "You mean how our food is actually good?"

It came out so fast; I didn't mean it to. Jamie's words, parroted through me about . . . about Vanya's family business.

He laughs heartily. "Oof, I know what you mean. They skated by one hundred percent on creativity this round. That and Melody insisted on including a vegan option. You know, for diversity."

What he's saying, while painful to hear about Vanya's family brand, is true. But I don't want him to think I'm callous. That wasn't me. That was a Jamie parasite that crawled into my brain. "I mean, it's not—their stuff isn't that bad. I had it once, and the dolma was dry, not enough spices, you know, standard stuff you find in a grocery store."

Oh God I'm making it worse, I have to stop.

I wave my hands in front of my face. "Forget I said anything. They're great, the Simonians. Doing the relay together? That was definitely a highlight. Good people, great kitchen skills."

I sound so lame. Great *kitchen* skills?

Benny rounds on me, and I see his large, sweaty face. "Now, no need to be diplomatic. You know I love to see the real side of people. Thanks for showing it."

I laugh uneasily. "No, no, that wasn't real. I was being—too much gin, I mean Chicago Fizzes. They're really good by the way. I'm gonna go and try to find another. Feeling parched all of a sudden."

And I slink off, praying that that conversation stays between me and Benny. With his penchant for drama, I'm not too hopeful.

Chapter Twenty-Two

*W*hen I finally spot Vanya, I'm feeling epically guilty, and I hope the heat rising in my face reads as an alcoholic flush instead of "I talked shit about your family's food to the event host behind your back."

She's with her parents by the hot dog competition sign-ups, chatting with Big Mike, and I sidle around so that she can see me without me calling out her name and having to say hello to her parents. I don't think I can face all the Simonians right now.

It works. Vanya darts her head to the side and sees me, and her face glows. Ugh, I don't deserve her.

She steps away from the table where her parents are arguing—Nora seems to be politely disagreeing with Toros, who looks like an overgrown toddler.

Vanya nods toward them. "Big Mike is trying to coax my dad into entering. Said we need strong men like him. Might as well have fed him catnip. And Mom's worried about all the nitrates. I'm personally thinking about his throat issue again, but I seem to be the only one."

"If your dad's doing it, mine is probably not far behind."

Vanya is shaking her head in annoyance at both our fathers. Somehow, though, instead of getting annoyed at the dads, or letting myself roost in guilt, I feel the animal in me rising up and crushing my elevated superego under its mighty weight, wanting to back her into a dark corner somewhere. I reach for her waist, and my thumb slides under her shirt against the smooth skin of her torso.

"Not here," she chastises with a smile, pushing my hand away gently.

"You're right, you're right," I say, eyes downcast, embarrassment plucking at my cheeks.

"But," she says quietly, flicking her chin toward the carousel, "what about over there?"

"Yes, absolutely."

She leads and I follow a couple of paces behind her, making sure neither of our parents see us. The Simonians are still in talks with Big Mike, and my parents are approaching the sign-ups just as we round a corner out of sight.

The carousel must operate during the day only, because there's no line, no rope, no kids, no one stopping us from hopping on. I must be in a dream; this is exactly the type of place I imagined kissing her. Too public for anything *really* risqué, but hidden enough that perhaps a hand could slip here or there.

I climb aboard, searching for the best place to steal away among the unicorns, ponies, seals, and sleighs. Then she pushes me against a horse's purple saddle and kisses me.

"How is it," she breathes against me, "I kissed you fifteen minutes ago and I feel like it's been days."

"I know exactly what you mean." I kiss her again, trace her neck with my nose, nip her collarbone. She is moaning now, not hiding anything, and I feel desire rising in me, ready to throw the publicness of our make out to the wind. Then my phone buzzes in my pocket. I ignore it and bring my mouth back to hers, concentrating on her long breaths, her heavy sighs.

My phone buzzes again, and I want nothing to do with the damn thing, so I pull it out of my pocket, trust that the case and screen protector are working as advertised, and toss it to the floor with a thump.

"You're nuts," she says to me, smiling, kissing me again.

"No interruptions," I murmur.

My fingers are tangled in her hair, lightly pulling while she kisses my neck, when we both hear it, over the loudspeakers.

"Our first challengers are the winners of today's collaborative competition. Tur-ohs and Hag-ope! Everyone give them a big round of applause."

We both pull away from each other the second we hear our fathers' names. Goddamn it—Mom, forgive me—can we not get just a moment's peace?

Vanya looks similarly irked. Her face is deliciously flushed, but her expression is fallen. "We've got to stop this. Or at least, I don't know, coach them from the sidelines not to make themselves sick. My dad—so damn stubborn."

I'm shaking my head. "Mine too, these absolute babies needing to one-up each other. When they could be getting along instead, like us."

"Well"—Vanya smirks—"maybe not *just* like us."

I laugh and hop off the carousel.

"Wait," Vanya calls. "Your phone." Oh, right. She bends down to pick it up, but then freezes.

Her voice is low, in a register I haven't heard yet from her. Guarded. "Who is Kyle?"

Oh no. Of all days, of all times, he decides to text me *today*? He hasn't said a word since his dismissive "have fun" and he decides now is a great time.

"He's—he's no one, honestly."

She hands the phone to me. "Honestly?"

There are two messages previewed on my phone's home screen.

The first reads, Missing you tonight.

The second reads, Wish you were here.

What. The. Hell. He dumps me in a meeting right before my massive presentation, and now he misses me? Not a word about how, you know, he told me it was over. So, we're done, but he wishes we were together? Oh God, right—it's Friday night, our usual get-together time, so he's feeling lonely and probably horny. I shake my head.

Forgetting Kyle, there's the immediate problem that Vanya read both of these messages, which make it very much seem like Kyle and I are still together.

"He *was* a someone, but now he's a no one. Ex-boyfriend, if you can even call him that."

I'm watching her face shift into various levels of suspicion. She isn't angry, but there's a furrow to her brow that suggests she's not pleased with all that, and I don't blame her.

"He dumped me. I can't believe he's actually texting that he misses me after that."

And, to show that I have nothing to hide (and throw my dignity to the wind), I hand her my phone so she can see my text exchanges with Kyle. How he didn't know where I was, how I told him I was here, and his curt well, have fun text. If she scrolls up, she can see a humiliating string of texts from me inviting him to brunch and him turning me down, then sucking up to him about his "insights." Ugh, I can't believe I ever let myself be like that.

She doesn't scroll up much, seemingly satisfied. She hands me back the phone.

"I don't think anyone's let me read their ex's texts before. Did you—was it serious with him?"

That one is easy. My face contorts. "Not at all. I liked him a lot, I did. But he always kept me at arm's length, as you can see from those texts. I'm ashamed at how I let myself be strung along like that. I didn't realize how bad it was until I met you. You drew me in; you weren't afraid of diving in with me."

It's a shame that I couldn't have figured this out on my own, and deep down I worry that if I had never met Vanya, I might be back home, running to him after those texts. How did I completely lose my self-respect around him? Either way, I'm glad it's back now.

Vanya's face softens somewhat. "I get—I mean, of course we

have pasts. I just didn't expect the past—the pretty recent past—to start texting."

I shake my head. "Neither did I. Usually when someone callously says, 'It's over,' right before your most important meeting of the year and doesn't hear any counterarguments, that means it's damn well over."

Vanya nods at the phone. "Thinking with his dick, probably."

I can't help but smirk. Thank goodness her mood is lightening, and I seem to have regained some of Vanya's trust. I add, to keep up the levity, "And with whiskey brain."

"Classically lethal combo." She smirks, and I have never been so happy to see it.

Then we hear over the speakers that the hot dog eating contest has begun. Benny says, "And three . . . two . . . one!"

"Damn it, our dads," Vanya groans.

With that, we bolt toward the competition, hoping to quell this next disaster.

Chapter Twenty-Three

$\mathcal{W}$e are not nearly on time when we reach the stage, upon which two tables full of hot dogs stand. Bab on one side, shoving a hot dog sideways into his mouth, and Toros on the other, red-faced and chomping maniacally at a hot dog. There's a timer above them counting down. It's currently at just above four minutes, and I say a little prayer that this isn't a fifteen-minute competition. I'm hoping Bab will only reach maybe three hot dogs max. Nothing to send him to the emergency room.

Most of the PakCon Superstars finalists are beneath them in the pit, cheering them on. Benny is doing his best pump-up-guy impression, telling everyone to yell louder, asking them to cheer for who they think is going to win.

The screens behind and in front of the stage are showing truly unfortunate close-ups of our dads' hot dog mauling escapades, interspersed with scenes from the event. A couple cheersing their glasses, someone bursting out laughing at a joke, someone waving hello to the cameras.

I spot Mom, cross, with her arms on her hips, standing off the stage, near Bab.

"Catch you soon?" I ask Vanya.

"It's a post-father-mortification date," she says.

"My favorite kind," I reply, starting in the direction of my mom, but lingering just long enough to catch her amusement.

When I reach my mom, her position is unchanged, eyeing my father with disdain, stone-faced amid the raucous crowd around her. "I am only glad your grandfather was not alive to see this," she says. "Khent." She caps off her burn with a nice one-word insult.

"I'll try and stop him."

Mom keeps her icy stare at Bab. "Is too late," she says, then adds in Armenian, "this is our shame to bear now."

I'm undeterred, and notice Vanya is walking up the steps on Toros's side to speak with him. Maybe I can do the same. Bab's side of the stage also has steps, and Benny is nearby asking, "That's all you can do? Come on now, be men!" and a couple of people in the crowd increase the volume of their whoops.

I sidle up to my father, right when Vanya approaches hers. "Hey, Bab, maybe you don't have to win this one. Mom's pretty mad."

He shakes his head and speaks with his mouth so full I can hardly understand him. "This major competition. We'll see who the most fun."

He grabs a large glass of water and takes a gulp, then stares straight ahead and starts coughing. He's turning red. "Bab, are you okay?" I ask, alarm rising.

His eyes are fixed ahead. I turn to where he's staring, and then I see it.

On the screen in front of us is footage of Vanya and me, pressed up against the carousel unicorn, wildly making out. Everyone below us is staring behind me, and I realize the screen behind Bab and Toros is casting it, too. Then their eyes quickly shift to me, onstage. Vanya and me.

She's seen it, too, and rushes to Benny. "Hey, that is a private moment. Take that down." She yells fruitlessly into the audience toward anyone in charge, "Take it down, now!"

Benny waves his arms in surrender. "All right, all right. I didn't pick what goes up there."

He even says it like a lie, like he wants us to not believe him. Vanya is still on him, telling him she knows he has the power to do something, so to hurry up and do something.

There's a bucket next to Bab, and he turns toward it and spits out the contents of his mouth.

Toros has his hands up in front of his face. "C'mon, man, that's my daughter, I don't need see this."

Then I look down at Mom, who is viewing the footage. She crosses herself once, twice, then stares at me. Her hands are balled tight, like they're gripping daggers, ready to be flung. The one thing she asked me, I lied about, and now it's splashed all over two giant screens for the world to see. This could not be worse.

Vanya's tirade must have worked, since Benny motions with a spin of his fingers to someone we can't see, and the footage changes to someone eating ice cream—back to their pleasant, G-rated programming.

"I'm so sorry, ladies, really, my bad," Benny says, practically half smiling.

I'm ready to axe this man, and I know Vanya will be right by my side for it—she is fuming, her eyes narrowed into slits—but there's still the competition to think of. Still one more day.

"Benny," I begin, trying the same voice I used on the Abilify director who undermined his direct reports and ended up causing chaos for us right before a client project closed. "I'm not pleased with—"

Then I hear Benny's voice, loud, on the screen. I turn to look, a deep rumble of fear inside me, because the words, the timbre of his voice, I have heard them before, and I know before I even look this is going to be—

It is. I see myself, in profile—the camera must have been just out of sight when I was talking to Benny. And whoever set this video up found the time to add *captions*.

I see myself on-screen saying, "How our food is actually good?" Then someone has edited out Benny talking shit about the Simonians, and it cuts to me layering on more insults, calling their food dry, lacking spices. Then it cuts again to me laughing, but that was me laughing at Benny's self-deprecating joke! Not an evil laugh about how much the Green Falafel sucks. Oh my God, I'm going to murder him.

But before I can do that, there's Vanya. Her face has entirely fallen, whitened, and without looking at me or saying a word, she storms off the stage.

I give Benny my most vicious stare and say, "That was totally crossing a line, and you know it."

I don't wait for him to respond, and then rush down the stairs, trying to find Vanya. She disappeared quickly, but I spy the ends of her curls snapping in the wind, behind one of the decorative trees. I follow, slowing my pace. I reach her, and she's examining the potted tree, the gray gravel stones at the base. She turns one over.

"I'm not sure why," she says, face slowly turning toward me, "what you said somehow feels like a bigger betrayal than if you actually had that boyfriend."

Shit, I knew she was hurt, but the word *betrayal* still cuts. It's what I did, I know, but hearing it from her mouth makes it burn again. I start, "I, I mean—" But she cuts me off.

Her eyes are fixed upon the gravel again. "Maybe I'm not even sure you were telling the truth about that guy. I remember you saying you've never tried our food."

"That clip was misleading," I say gently, trying not to sound defensive.

She picks up a stone, turns it over in her pinched fingers, and then throws it back into the planter box. "Like, I get it, we could be doing a better job, but damn, you had some opinions, and you weren't afraid to share them with *Benny*, of all people."

I feel myself swaying, reddening. I want to gather an army at my defense, a troupe of lawyers, anyone who can help me talk my way out of this. I'm usually able to be persuasive in a hot spot, but there isn't much to defend here. I have to tell her the truth as best I can. "I was tipsy and it came out all wrong, just like this is. Okay, yes. Yes, I had tried the Green Falafel before and I wasn't the biggest fan of it, but you're right, I should not have been spouting that to god-awful Benny."

"Unless . . ." Now she looks at me. "You were trying to get close to him, being all buddy-buddy before the final round?" She throws her hands up. "I don't even know what to think anymore."

I shake my head vigorously. "Nothing like that. It was what I said, a drunken mistake."

"Your laugh—it was so, so fucking hearty. It really hurt, hearing that."

"That I can defend!" I practically shout. "The laugh was cut from earlier and tacked on at the end. I was laughing at something else."

Vanya steps close to me. "I have no reason to believe you at this point. I'm just pissed at myself for thinking, for hoping— God, I'm an idiot."

"You're not an idiot."

She seems larger, worked up, a tornado taking shape before it lands. "It all makes sense now: get close to your competitors, then tear them down. Should have known, with all that talk about clawing your way up the corporate ladder, all the sacrifices you make to get there no matter what. You'd do the same thing to me. We made that promise, at the lake, and it meant nothing to you."

I know that Jamie's words infiltrated my brain, but it wasn't intentional. "It did, I swear. What I said, it wasn't—I wasn't trying—I like you so much, I'm wrecked that this happened. I had hope, too."

She shakes her head. "You don't get to do that. I'm sorry. We're done."

She rushes away, her hands rising to cover her face. I jog after her, but she calls back, her voice breaking, "Do not follow me."

I'm not sure what else to do but listen to her.

I TAKE MY time heading back to the crowd, letting Vanya take a wide lead. I'm not sure if she's going to grab her parents and leave, or what, but I don't want to see it. Part of me wants to see her, be around her, no matter how she's feeling, but knowing that all her pain is caused by me, that's what I can't handle.

I amble up to the back of the crowd. My father and Toros are no longer onstage; there's a new pair sitting in their stead, waiting to begin. Benny is still there, announcing their names, entirely unperturbed. I find my dad first, the back of his salt-and-pepper hair as familiar to me as anything—it's been that color and in the same cut for over a decade. He and Mom are speaking to each other low in Armenian at the edge of the crowd.

What do I say to them? "Sorry you had to watch me make out with your enemy's daughter and that it was broadcast to like fifty people who are also our competitors"?

I go with an oldie but goodie. "Hey," I say.

Bab turns, lets out an exasperated huff.

Mom looks at me, and her eyes are red and wet. Oh no, I cannot stand to see her cry.

"I'm really sorry. I didn't know it would be . . . televised."

And that is what I'm sorry for—not that I kissed Vanya, that I've been kissing Vanya, but that they had to see it all in such a public way. Pretty sure even parents who are rooting for their kid's new crush wouldn't want to see the details.

"I'm going to try to figure out if there's any recourse or, I don't know, who Benny's boss is, and get this straightened out."

Mom glares at me. "I asked you one thing, not to go with that girl, and you said yes."

"Well, Mom, it was a completely unfair thing to ask."

"So you lie?"

"So I lied. Yes."

"This our daughter?" Mom asks Bab, then turns back to me. "This how we raise you?"

"I mean, sort of. You kept the Simonians' existence and your grudge against them a secret for years."

My mom's eyes roll back like she is putting on a fainting spell. "And how you insult their food for the world to hear!"

I'm about to say that I agree, what I said was terrible, when my brain catches up to the situation. "Wait, you're embarrassed by that?"

"Of course we embarrassed! Now everyone think you're . . . anshnorkov agchig."

She and my father flinch at the mere thought of me being a rude, improperly raised girl. There is no worse insult, other than going all the way to poz (slutty), and considering the footage of Vanya and me, I'm sure that word is on the tips of their tongues.

"But you said their food was like cardboard."

My father wags his finger. "Behind the locked door of hotel room. That is different."

I let out the most frustrated sigh.

Mom leans against a white post, her gaze overlooking the lake. "How we going to show our faces to them again? First the sex tape, then the insults."

"Oh my God, Mom, it was just kissing."

But then I do think she has kind of a point—about the insult, I mean.

"But okay, you're right. I should apologize to them tomorrow, especially considering how their business isn't even doing well."

Bab turns to me. "Their business not doing well?"

It's something I'd never dream of telling them before, but at this point, I want to put all the cards on the table. "Vanya mentioned it. They're on the verge of shutting down; their products aren't selling."

Bab shakes his head to himself. "After all that head start."

"You mean with the kitchen?" I ask.

"Hagop," Mom snaps, and her eyes are full of fire. "This not the point."

"You're right," I say, challenging her. "It's my anshnor-koutyoun and pozoutyoun."

I throw their words about me back at them, and it visibly stings my mother, who winces. "I am tired of talking. Let's go back to hotel, Hagop."

Her tone is exasperated, quick snaps of speech. That's it, this conversation is over, and without saying goodbye to me, for perhaps the first time in my life, my parents turn their backs and go.

The loneliness yawns deep in the pit of my stomach. First Vanya, then my parents. Vanya's demand for me not to follow rattles around in my rib cage. I'm going to see her tomorrow—the final competition—but I'm not hopeful that a good night's sleep is all that it's going to take to make her want to talk to me again. Still, there has to be a way. I cannot lose them all; I need to figure this out.

Chapter Twenty-Four

It's Saturday morning, and I should feel well rested after finally getting a free evening, but I don't. My head feels light and detached with a dull pain behind my eyes. My body is buzzing with tired energy. I must have woken up twenty times in the night. I had terrible dreams where I was forced to eat a bunch of hot dogs while Vanya laughed at me.

Vanya.

I texted her last night when I got back to my hotel room—I couldn't help myself. I assessed that I was sober enough, then reiterated most of my apology, and included more about being incredibly sorry about how hurtful my words were.

She didn't respond for a few hours, so I asked, Still seeing you tomorrow at the final round?

When I got her response I wished I hadn't sent that question. She said only, Unfortunately.

So that's that. I tried to use work to take my mind off everything, but my brain wouldn't focus on my tasks. The weight of my unfinished work keeps threatening to suffocate me, but I'm pushing it away for now. I can't bring myself to do it. Plus, I wasn't getting constantly pinged by Jamie because yes, she's a workaholic but prefers to use Friday evenings to network. I don't know how she finds them, but if she's not at the office happy hour, she's always at some mixer for professionals.

Instead of finding the right words for my Operation Wolf messaging project, I found myself trying to gather the right words for today's event. If Benny asked me the exact same question he asked me yesterday, how would I answer in front of an audience? That, I'm starting to perfect, since the competition could still be life-changing for my parents—plus, I wonder if I can sneak in a subtle apology to Vanya via the speech.

And speaking of words, my parents haven't said a word to me, and I haven't reached out, either. I'm in the right here, at least as it concerns Vanya, and they need to be the ones to apologize.

I did not reply to Kyle.

There was a moment, in the dark and lonely night, when I did miss the way he'd rush at me to kiss me, and I felt it again, his arms and his lust for me. I thought about replying, but didn't. I held the phone, reread his message, and wondered how nice it would feel to be swept up in Kyle again. But then I didn't. I'm holding out hope that I can change Vanya's mind today. We are going to see each other at the event; I will find a way to show her how sorry I am.

It also might not hurt to spend a little extra time on my hair and makeup and choose my outfit carefully.

*   *   *

I CREEP TOWARD my parents' booth in the great hall, relieved to find them there. Their coldness yesterday put this idea into my head that maybe they left the convention and Chicago completely. Seeing them now, Mom smiling at strangers and Bab rearranging the pamphlets on the table, warms this sense of normalcy in me. Things might not be perfect, but they haven't left everything behind. Or me behind.

"Hi, Mom, Bab," I say.

Mom jumps at my voice. "Amah, Nazeli, you scare me."

"Sorry," I say. Hoping at some point she will say the same word to me.

"Parev, Nazeli," Bab says, nodding at me with an awkward smile.

There's an air of politeness in our interactions that isn't our usual mode. Our family is a lot of things to one another—loud, messy, loving—but *polite* is not one of them. I wish I could pull out my laptop and work under the table so that simply being around one another would slowly dissolve the tension. But I guess we need to talk instead.

"I'm feeling like you're both being unfair about the whole Vanya thing."

Mom waves a hand in front of her face. "Euff, not now, please."

"No, now." I look to my dad. "Bab?"

"I don't like to talk about them," Bab says, only a thin veil over the falseness of his words.

"Yes, you do. Yesterday when I told you their business wasn't doing well, you were on the verge of saying something. You both always are. You call them snakes, say they stole from you, but won't tell me any details? Then expect me to listen to you about their daughter? Who is . . ." My voice catches. "Wonderful, by the way."

Bab sighs, "Nazeli jan, you do not understand."

"So help me understand. What happened with that kitchen? You said some guy, Shirinian? Offered it for free?"

Mom puts her hand on Bab's arm. "We do not need get into this now," she says, nodding toward the convention hall. "Potential customers everywhere."

Bab shakes his head. "We do, Hera jan."

For once, I silently implore my dad's stubbornness to push forward, not listen to my mom. I ask, "Who is Shirinian, first of all?"

"An airheaded man who got lucky."

None of us are sitting in the single chair they have behind the booth. I lean on it. "Going to need a few more specifics, Bab."

He sighs. "He came to America a few years before my arrival, got involved in a real estate scheme, and had become rich from it then—1997, it was. The commercial kitchen was part of his earning, but he did not need."

This is a promising start. Bab is looking beyond Mom and me, and I know he has more to say. "When Shirinian said he had that extra space, he told me and Toros both. That was first problem. He was wealthy suddenly, like I say, but not popular."

Mom puts a hand on her hip. Her other wipes away a tear. "Hagop, we do not need to live the past again."

But he doesn't listen.

"What he did need," Bab continues, "was companionship. And status."

Mom scowls, the sadness morphed into anger. "He tell both us and Toros and Nora he have the kitchen. That's when Toros start acting strange with us. Nora, too, she avoid me at the Easter luncheon. Very rude."

My mom holding a more than twenty-year grudge after being snubbed at an Easter luncheon in 1997 is so her.

Bab is practically pounding on his chest. "By that time, I been a member of the Armenian church board for many years, I have many connections."

He's dancing around what he's really trying to say, but I'm feeling for him anyway. Like he has to defend himself against something.

Mom intercedes. "Then Toros take out Shirinian to his cigar club and khorovatz night, that was when Shirinian made his choice."

Bab scoffs. "These thing do not interest me. Men with their cigars and their meats."

Oh my God, my dad is hurt over being less popular than Toros, over being given the message that Toros was a lot more of a fun guy than him. Is that it? My dad's insecurities? But then I remember, Bab came from a village in Lebanon, his family wasn't academic at all, they were cobblers, and he worked so hard to give himself an education, something he truly prizes. And then Toros sweeps in with his cigars and bro-time, and says none of that means anything in matters of real life. I suppose I kind of get it.

Bab continues before I can ask. I don't want to interrupt him since he's finally in a sharing mood. He says, "And this was that. Shirinian told us Toros had more compelling business plan so he give the kitchen to him for free for first two years and then discount after that. And Shirinian get to be part of Toros's friends."

I'm dying now; I can't keep it in. "Wait, so how does this make you absolutely hate Toros and Nora? Vanya?"

A convention-goer strides up to our booth, but upon beholding the grumpy faces, steers toward the next table.

Mom puts on her defensive voice, slightly louder, words coming out faster. "Toros gloat to your father at the first Mount Davidson ceremony on Abril ksan-chors."

Oof, if that's true, that is bad. April 24 is Armenian Genocide Remembrance Day, an extremely solemn occasion. There's usually a ceremony at Mount Davidson, where there's a gigantic cross, and the priest and the whole community are there to say prayers and make speeches and remember our ancestors who were killed by the Ottoman Turks in 1915.

I remember this event. It was the very first one at Mount Davidson, and I was seven, so there was no way I was concerning myself with my parents' sometime friends. I do wonder, though, was Vanya there, too? *Vanya.* The thought of her grips my heart.

"Unacceptable," says Bab. "From then on we make decision never to speak of them."

"Did he really gloat?" I ask. Considering the seriousness of the day, I feel like even Toros would tone it down.

Mom answers this one. "You should have heard Nora." Now she does a pinched voice, imitating Nora. "We are so please to have been given this kitchen, what opportunity, we are so grateful."

"Mom, that doesn't sound like gloating."

She shakes her head. "It was, trust me. You know I hate two-face people, especially who try and be so nice and innocent."

They seem to be stuck in time with this feud. Mom has fixated on Nora not saying hi to her at the Easter luncheon and being reasonably grateful for an opportunity, and has taken it as this woman being sneaky and awful, so her daughter must be, too. Mom often has more criticisms of meek women, and Nora does come off as less of a strong personality. But Vanya's the exact opposite! And Bab—Toros stuck his finger right into my dad's greatest insecurity nerve.

I say, "Don't you think you should have been hating that Shirinian guy instead of the Simonians?"

Bab shakes his head. "I still do not associate with the man, he imbecile anyway."

I can't help but laugh, though it's not mirthful. "If you don't mind me saying, I think part of this rivalry is a little overblown. It wasn't fair that they got the kitchen, because the manner of the competition was messed up. But you've created so much on your own. I mean, your business is doing well. Theirs isn't."

Bab drags his toe across the industrial carpet. "Hm. Yes, with all that head start they still could not make it."

Seeing Bab's mood leaven empowers me to dig into the other thing that's been nagging at me. "But, uh, I have to ask. What was Toros saying about you locking him out of all the respect-able clubs? Boards?"

Despite trying to seem nonchalant, I'm standing stick straight, because I do suspect Bab has done some wrong here, otherwise why would Toros dislike him so much?

"Oh." He waves his hand dismissively. "Toros tried to get on the church board one time, we had vote, we vote no."

"And you had . . . nothing to do with that?"

Bab's expression hasn't changed to one of defensiveness, so that's good. "I not saying that. All I do, I lay out his character with the group, and they make their own decision."

I press him. "What about the other boards? Is Toros just ex-aggerating?"

"Well, on church board is Sako Berjian, who is also on ARF board, and then we have Garo Terkhanian, who also on the school board, and so on and so forth. Very close group."

Ah yes, the older male gatekeepers of the Armenian Bay Area organizations.

I tread slowly. "Do you possibly see why Toros might be mad at you about that?"

"Of course. But nothing more than he deserved."

"Bab . . ."

He sighs. "I still say it's fair."

I shake my head. Fine. Fine for now. At least I got some answers from him.

Then I turn to Mom, who has been refilling samples and pretending not to listen to this part of the conversation between Bab and me. I keep my voice as even as possible since Mom does not ever, *ever*, like to admit she's wrong. "Mom, I truly don't think Nora was being rude to you at that Easter luncheon and at Abril ksan-chors. Maybe a little shortsighted in not understanding how their taking the kitchen would affect you, but—"

Mom chokes out a sob, shocking me into quiet. I hadn't noticed, but she must have been holding so much in this entire time. Her face is so heavy, it breaks my heart. "They took the kitchen from us, I did not want them to take . . . our daughter, too."

That's what . . . ? That's what this has all been.

I step toward her. "I'm not a kitchen, though, Mom. I'm not one person's or the other's. No matter who I'm with, I'm always your daughter."

She nods, wiping her eyes. I hug her, feeling myself consoling her, wishing I could do the same to myself. I'm talking as if Vanya and I have a shot, which, as of our latest interaction, I'm not so sure we do.

"Doesn't matter," I say. "Vanya doesn't want to have anything to do with me."

Mom releases me, pats me on the arm. "I am sorry for that, hokees, I am. I can see your hurt on your face."

An actual apology from my mother. I'm so surprised I don't even know how to respond, but automatically wipe away a tear that sprung up on me. Shoot. I'm on the verge of being a mess.

"It's the last day anyway," I say. "We're all going home tomorrow." I try to adjust my voice not to sound like I'm giving a eulogy, but it doesn't quite work.

"How many samples do we still have?" I ask, feeling this conversation has reached its peak and is coming down.

"Vai," Mom gasps out of nowhere, and I fear for the state of our samples until I see what's caught her eye. It's Nora and Toros, several feet away, chatting with another vendor, their backs to us. And Vanya? She must be nearby. My pulse quickens at the thought, my vision sharpening as I scan for her. She is nowhere, but my heart doesn't sink, it stands on high alert. She could swing by any second.

Nora and Toros don't seem to know we're here, at least I hope not. Now part of me really wants to duck under the table and hide, considering what happened last night.

But I won't, of course. I've faced worse, though I can't recall a time right now. Maybe I haven't faced worse, but it doesn't matter, I couldn't leave my parents hanging like that, having to deal with the fallout of my words. Time to go own up.

I step out of the booth, to my mom hissing, "Nazeli!" I could tell her not to worry, but that'll do nothing to ease her mind.

I approach Nora and Toros, who are sampling a gluten-free granola and seem to be finishing up their conversation, with final-sounding *thank-you*s.

I clear my throat, and to my combination relief-terror, Nora turns around. No going back now. "Uh, parev, Degeen Nora," I say, using "Ms." in front of her name to feign some semblance of respect. She doesn't look horrified to see me, so that's a start.

Then Toros turns and he rolls his eyes. I tell myself to stay strong. "Baron Toros," I say, dipping my head slightly.

"Parev, Nazeli," Nora says in a much more clipped voice than I'm used to. It's not mean, maybe hurt, though.

I look straight at Nora and begin, "I wanted to deeply apologize for what you heard and saw yesterday. I never meant to say that about your food. It was incredibly rude of me, and it was horrible that you and everyone had to watch that clip. Also, I know you may not believe it, but I didn't laugh like that, they added in my laugh later." I glance at Toros, too, and switch between them, hoping they understand how much I mean my words. "I've been enjoying getting to know you, especially our relay race. I mean it when I say I'm rooting for us all. I want one of our brands to win PakCon Superstars."

Nora smiles and sighs, then pats my arm. "Shnorhagalem, Nazeli," she says, thanking me. Toros seems to have softened a bit when I mentioned the relay race and one of us winning.

Playing off that, I look at Toros and say, "We've made it this far, I bet one of us goes all the way."

I glance around surreptitiously, hoping Vanya might be making her way back here, if she's here at all, and that I might catch the back of her sun-kissed curls. No such luck, though.

Toros grunts.

"Much unfortunately," Nora starts, "your family is more like to win than us."

"Nora," Toros starts.

She shakes her head. "I could see the face of that judge, when she taste our pretend hot dog. I was so ashame."

Toros says, with great offense, "She has no taste."

She waves him off. "Perhaps it time for us to face fact, like I said to Vanya yesterday."

My heart trembles at the mention of her, at the conversation I imagine she and Nora had yesterday, based on my televised criticisms of their food. But then Nora's words swing at me again—she . . . agrees?

Nora looks at me. Shy, suddenly. "I have been meaning to try . . . your family's food."

She's spotted our booth, and my heart freezes. It feels weirdly intimate for them to visit our booth and sample our food, if that's indeed what they're going to do. Like now we're being judged for real, and it feels unfair, after what I said about their cooking, for them to taste my parents' sarma. Still, I'm curious about where this is going.

Mom and Bab, who had been whispering between themselves, instantly cease speaking. Bab nods at the Simonians. Mom is as still as a spaghetti straw you could snap in half.

Nora glances at the sarma halves in small white cups. "May I try, if that is okay?"

It's clear neither of them are going to say anything, so I reply, "Of course. Sarma? We also have lavash, manti," I say, pointing to the samples as if she doesn't know exactly what they are. "And falafel, though it looks like we ran out here and I'm not sure if we have more in the cooler."

"Thank you," Nora says, reaching for a sarma. "We don't have booth this year, decided to do only conferences."

I wonder if it was the cost, if business is so bad they couldn't rent the booth space. Toros glances around him as if he's waiting for someone else, but it feels more like a way to not have to speak to my parents.

The halved sarma is small, but still Nora bites off the end instead of popping the whole thing in her mouth. I can feel my mom mentally rolling her eyes.

Nora lets out a sharp moan of delight. "Superb," she says. Toros grunts. Then, motioning to the table, she asks, "Could I? Have 'nother?"

"Sure thing," I say, knowing Mom is secretly proud of herself right now and not thinking about how few samples we have left.

Nora finishes her other half and tosses the cup in the can near our table. My parents have busied themselves tidying up our booth, but I catch each of them sneaking glances toward Nora and Toros.

Nora plunks the sarma into Toros's mouth. It's a sweet marital moment, the kind I don't believe I've ever witnessed between my parents. They're more the "show love through acts" type of people. And that's fine, but I did always want the kind of relationship that could stay playful for decades. My throat tightens, thinking about how I fantasized Vanya and I could have that.

"This is just—" Toros says, in between a bite. Then he stops speaking, chews. He lets out an unfettered "Mmm," and then comprehension dawns that he's complimented the food of his nemesis.

Nora says softly, "I see now, what everyone says about the food from Hera's kitchen."

The fact that our brand is called *Hagop's* Fine Armenian Foods and Nora just called out the sarma as being my mom's invention (which it is)—I don't know, it means a lot to me to hear that acknowledgment. I can only imagine how Mom—

There's a shrug from my side, where Mom is standing, and she's reddening, fast.

Nora strides up to our booth. "Sometimes, Hera, I think the past would be better if we had decide to make one company together. Bring best of our talents together."

Mom is quiet, which only happens when she is truly so taken aback she doesn't have a response. Then at last she says, "Well, the past is in past." But not with malice, like she might have done earlier this trip. It comes out quietly, resignedly.

Toros and Bab are silent, and I can feel Bab is itching to say something but doesn't. Then Nora elbows Toros, a subtle movement I'm not sure I even saw, and he says, "The sarma, it was good."

My mom nods. "Thank you, Toros."

No one says anything again, so I poke Dad in the back. "Yes, thank you. Hera excellent cook."

And it is like the world has shifted. These tiny concessions are the first sign of repair, and yesterday I would have been tearing up at the prospect of Vanya's and my families making up. But today there is no "Vanya and me," so while it is nice to patch up a feud, I am not feeling as thrilled about it as I would have been just a day ago.

I give everyone a beat in case anyone takes this opportunity to continue to be vulnerable. Nothing comes up—unsurprising from a group of adults raised in our repressed culture—so I ask, "Is, uh, Vanya around?"

Nora shakes her head. "She's back in the room, preparing for this next competition."

Avoiding me, possibly. That shakes me up. If our parents can finally say something nice to each other after two decades, there's got to be hope for Vanya and me.

Chapter Twenty-Five

There's a new room waiting for us for the final stage of the competition, and somehow that makes me nervous. I like to be fully prepared. Now I'm assessing the layout of the room, the acoustics, where the judges will be sitting, where I should be directing my remarks. I want to visualize it all ahead of time.

The room is smaller than before, darker, with a stage set up and truly unfortunate late nineties–looking carpeting throughout. There are chairs arranged as if for an audience, and there are only fifty or so of us here, so it's easy to see that the Simonians haven't arrived yet.

I'm sitting in between Mom and Bab, who are checking their phones and talking over my person about what Veranoush said on Facebook today, how amot that she overshares about her job and that one coworker she cannot stand. Still, I think they appreciate her for giving them a weekly soap opera to look forward to.

Then the doors open, and I don't bother to hide my curiosity— I turn my body all the way around to see who it is. It's them . . .

it's her. Vanya looks hotter than ever, wearing *heels*, which I haven't seen her don all weekend, and a plaid miniskirt. Lord help me. This is her revenge outfit. And she's got the face to match, a painted smile with an underpinning of rage.

She's leading her parents, and my heart clenches when she chooses the row right in front of us. She plants herself down, sitting directly in front of me. Her curls are being crushed by the back of the chair. She doesn't say a word, but her parents say timid hellos to mine, and I wave back.

Benny's all-too-familiar voice resounds. "Welcome to our final competition. Finalists, congratulations, you've gotten this far."

"But only one of you can go home with the top prize," Stephanie adds, beaming, as if this is a good thing.

Benny continues, "We'll call on each brand one by one, and you need to send a single representative to the stage to answer our mystery question. You'll have one minute to answer. Please, folks, let's try to keep it under a minute."

I cringe at his patronizing tone but also semi-agree that I don't want to be sitting here listening to representatives speaking ad nauseum about their brands. There could be a lot to learn from them, so my ears are ready for that, but one minute is a pretty good limit.

As promised, Benny and Stephanie call up brands, where they are asked questions about their company's values and superpower, and one weird question from Melody about what color their brand's aura is. Even as I hope we don't get a question like that, I find myself forming the answer. For every question asked, I come up with my own answer, preparing for the real thing.

Then Stephanie announces, "Next up, Hagop's Fine Armenian Foods."

I absolutely can do this; product marketing is in my blood. Or at least, the last six years of my blood. And I've been nailing every answer in my head. But I also hope Vanya will pick up on the apology in my words and that they'll make any difference in how she feels about me.

I step up to the stage, and the lights are warmer than I'd expected, the audience darker than I thought. I can hardly see my parents or Vanya.

Benny says, "Please state your name."

"Nazeli Gregorian."

"Naz—um—Nazuli. We all got a preview of how you feel about your competitors—"

I interrupt. "That was taken out of context—"

Benny smiles with a tinge of annoyance. "It's okay, we like hardball players out here. So, our question to you, miss, is, what makes your brand special?"

Oh. Yes. A layup of a question if there ever was one. I could answer this in my sleep.

I don't bother taking a deep breath; I launch right in.

"Hagop's Fine Armenian Foods is a taste of tradition, of survival, of holding on to home. It's first a family company. My parents came to San Francisco with a suitcase each, so few material possessions, but behind them years and years of fighting for the right to exist. Our food carries our people's heritage and persistence. One taste of our sarma will take you back centuries to historic Armenia in the 1800s, when this recipe was passed down from my great-great-grandparents. But that's the thing about Hagop's Fine Armenian Foods: It may have my father's name on it, but it also has the word Armenian. The brand is more than just our family, the Gregorians; it's representative of all Armenians."

I squint briefly into the audience, where I remember Vanya sitting, and hope my eyes are connecting directly with hers. They could be connecting with the obsequious pasta sauce girl for all I can tell under these lights, but I hope Vanya can at least feel my intent is toward her.

I continue, "There is nothing more important for our people than unity. And when there are rifts, there is nothing more important than acknowledging your wrongs and apologizing, so I'm sorry." My voice cracks slightly on *I'm sorry*, so I clear my throat. "We haven't ever been able to count on outsiders, so we have to count on one another. And I hope, I truly hope, we can find a way back together."

The judges are staring at me; the health food judge has one eyebrow raised. I should probably—"Um, thank you."

I nod my head as if I'm in sixth grade again finishing up my Armenian poetry recitation (I came in third, for the record). Once I'm out of the lights, I home right in on the audience, and my heart leaps up because Vanya is looking at me, and she doesn't seem mad. Maybe it worked, my speech? She turns away abruptly the second I notice her. Or maybe not.

My dad pats me on the shoulder, and Mom leans in close. "Very good," she says, which is a major compliment from her. Bab says, "So articulate, my daughter."

Benny then says, "Up next we have the representative from the Green Falafel. You know the drill, please make your way to the stage."

I'm about to sit behind Vanya right as she stands, rigid and less loose than normal. Uh-oh.

As she takes the stage, her teeth appear clenched, and she has her thumb aggressively hooked into the belt loop of her miniskirt. She states her name before they even ask her.

"Thank you, Vanya," says Stephanie. "Our question is, how do you differentiate yourself from your competitors?"

I roll my eyes and thank Asdvatz Baba that the lights are dim in here so that cameras can't catch it. PakCon Superstars and their ridiculous drama agenda, again.

"I'm so glad you asked, Stephanie," Vanya says with a poison smile. "The food from my homeland can often be stodgy, stuck in tradition, unwilling to innovate. But not the Green Falafel. We're committed to bringing Armenian food to the masses in a palatable—pun intended"—she smirks so genuinely that I feel the shards of my heart cracking off—"type of way. The Green Falafel takes what's great about Armenian Lebanese food and gives it a modern, fresh spin. Because you can't always rely on other Armenians to prop you up, we have to be realistic and have a broad appeal. Which, luckily, we do!"

She actually winks at the judges. So the question of whether or not my speech helped stir any good feeling between us? That's a hard no.

She swishes back to her seat and sits down in a self-congratulatory manner.

I can't concentrate on a word of the rest of the speeches. Even when someone onstage says something funny and gets the crowd laughing, I don't hear it. I would love for us to win, and my answer was good, but losing Vanya because of such hurtful things I said? I can't believe I could be so stupid. I actually thought my speech would mean something to her. Instead, it seems to have set her off on a new level of anger. My gut feels scorched, blackened and gray, flaking off in pieces.

A round of clapping that feels more final wakes me to the scene, where Benny and Stephanie have taken the stage.

"Thank you, everyone, for your impassioned statements. The judges will now convene and score your responses from today and all your performances so far. Don't forget to leave a sample of your packaged food at the table by the door on your way out. We'll see you back here in an hour to announce the winner!"

The contestants slowly stand and begin to filter out, and I wonder how any of us are going to function for the next sixty minutes.

Vanya weaves her way quickly through the crowd and rushes out with purpose, which I can only guess is to avoid me. Clearly, she doesn't want to talk to me and my speech had zero impact on her. I feel myself giving up. I hate giving up, but at this point, I am all out of ideas.

Chapter Twenty-Six

There's another digital banner for the occasion, this one reading **PakCon Superstars: Winner Announcement.**

The committee has invited all participants back to view the ceremony, and about half of the eliminated teams are seated in here. I don't blame the others for not showing. With the rise in audience members, it's tougher for me to keep an eye on Vanya, which is the only thing I feel like doing. I want my family to win, of course, but it's still a one-in-twenty-five chance. Vanya and her parents are about ten rows in front of us, but my eyes are fixed on the back of her curls, how they swish as she turns from one parent to the other. I wonder what she's saying. She appears looser now, less angry than before. If I could catch her after the ceremony—

Benny and Stephanie take the stage, and Benny, as usual, speaks first. "It's only been a few days, but it feels like weeks, hasn't it, folks?"

"Sure does, my arches are killing me." Stephanie winces as she gracefully lifts her foot behind her.

Benny chuckles and begins to thank everyone once again for their time in a way that only he can make a touch condescending. I bite my thumb's cuticle, then immediately pull it away. I've been trying to break the habit for years, and it does *not* look good in a tense meeting to be chewing on your fingers. But then I put it back, 'cause this isn't a boardroom, and it's dark in here, and sometimes you gotta release your anxiety the way you want to.

Benny stares out at us meaningfully. "And the winner," he says, his voice slowing, deepening with importance, "which, as we don't need to remind you all, is a spot in our Super Bowl commercial, where your food will be featured along with a one-liner from your spokesperson—"

Come on. It's not just me—the crowd seems to collectively hold their breaths, like, "we all know the deal, tell us already."

"A very special brand that caught our eye early on for its connection to culture and tradition."

My pulse races, because holy—can it be us? I didn't actually have hope, I mean, I always wished, but didn't think it would be possible. But my speech, it was all about culture and tradition. Could we have clinched it? With Mom's peerless cooking and our inventiveness with the flatbread, and maybe even my speech . . . I turn to Bab, and his eyes are wide; we're on the same wavelength. We might need to prepare ourselves to walk up to the podium and—

"Audrey and Leo from Tossed Sauce!" Benny shouts into the mic.

The applause is clipped, polite to the point of severity, leaving plenty of room for everyone to hear Audrey's shrieks as she strangles her partner's neck in a hug.

Of course. Culture and tradition. Of Italy. What a brave and novel decision by the judges.

Bab sags beside me, while Mom straightens and clucks her tongue. "This is usual, the type of person they pick. Amot eerentz," she says, delivering shame upon them.

I can't believe for a second I thought we had a shot. My face gets hot, thinking about Benny coaching me like he was giving me preferential treatment, when all he was hoping for was a sound bite. They never had any interest in us as winners, just pieces for their reality drama.

As Audrey fixes her hair and poses for photos while accepting her award, some of the crowd already stands to leave. No reason to stay. Toros appears in the aisle, striding purposefully toward Benny.

Oh no. The Green Falafel. They needed this win, like Vanya said, and I wonder what's going to become of their business now. I can't see her among the crowd; she must still be sitting. I imagine her consoling Nora, who might be pretending to be strong now, but is obviously crushed.

Unable to help myself, I shoot out of my seat and trail Toros. I wonder if he's going to demand a recount or what.

He taps Benny on the shoulder in what I would not call a gentle manner. Benny, jabbering away with Big Mike, spins to face Toros. His eyes narrow. In a head-to-head between the two, I don't know whom I'd put my money on. Maybe Benny.

He seems a little younger and 'roided out, while Toros's muscle seems more natural.

I'm close by now, only a few people between us, so I easily blend into the crowd and don't seem like the eavesdropper I am.

"Where's our money?" Toros demands.

God, right, Benny has the $20,000 we won from the relay.

"Aw, damn, I have it but not on me. Why don't you come by tomorrow and I'll give it to you?"

"We leaving tomorrow."

"So are we all, we can make it work."

"Benny, I being serious here."

"Listen, by tomorrow I'll have two ten grand checks so you won't even have to see that other guy and split it with him. How's that sound? Meet me in the lobby by the Cafe-a-Go-Go around nine?"

I can't believe, at this point, after all he's put us through *and* considering Bab's name is the name of our brand, Benny still doesn't know my dad's name.

Toros nods once. "Fine. But we got your info. The Armenian mafia be on you if you bail."

Benny holds up his hands and waves. "I swear I will be there. Now if you don't mind—" He turns back to Big Mike, who is fawning over Audrey and her eager smiles at having won the Super Bowl jackpot.

Seeing a chance, I pop myself into Benny's view before he can get invested in his new conversation. "Me too. I'll be there at nine."

"Yep, yep," he says, barely making eye contact before turning fully away.

Toros grunts in annoyance as he stalks away, but turns toward me as if wanting to share in the annoyance. I'll take it.

"That guy," I mutter, both irked by Benny and thinking Toros would like that opener.

"What you kids all say? Douchebag?"

"Definitely," I say with a nod.

He almost shoulders into some of the remaining crowd. "At least we get something out of this."

"Sorry," I say. "I know winning would have meant so much to you."

"What we can do," he replies, futility in his heavy voice. "Benny better have that money tomorrow."

"If he doesn't, I'll be sure to lodge a formal complaint."

"I be sure to do a lot more than that," he growls.

I almost want to smile. Then Vanya is in front of us, and when she sees me, she flips around. An obvious "do not fucking talk to me" if I ever saw one. Still . . .

"Uh, Vanya, can we talk?"

She deigns to face me. "I'd rather not." Her voice comes out raw, less of the ice-cold performance than her speech earlier.

But Nora is there, looming shyly into the conversation. "Vanya jan, maybe it be good idea?"

I want to throw a parade in Nora's honor. Gentle meddling mom, platinum award.

Vanya huffs, her eyes rolling so far back I can see only whites. "Fine."

She stalks off, and I chase after her. I really don't care how pathetic it might look. I was in the wrong here, and I will grovel. She might be giving me this chance incredibly reluctantly, but I can take that and spin it into gold, I know it.

She stops in the hallway, by an alcove with a side table and a springtime flower arrangement plunked on top. It would almost be romantic, stealing away with her among the cornflowers and freesia and wild greens—this has to be one of the prettiest spaces of McCormick Place, this tiny spot you could easily walk past—if she didn't hate me right now.

"I'm sorry we—you—didn't win. I hope, um, I hope what I said didn't play into the judges' opinions at—"

"No," she says, tracing a finger along the bottom of the vase. "You were right anyway."

"What? No—" I implore, knitting my eyebrows together.

"You were. Our food was always decent, but something was missing. Then we cut corners and—well, I told you the rest. I know I was an asshole about your speech, but you were right, and I wish I wasn't so pissed at you, because it was a beautiful speech."

Two feelings clash in me. One, she is pissed at me. I mean, everything about her body language and her speech told me that, but it's another thing altogether to hear someone say it to your face, to confirm it. But also, she's telling me I'm right and that my words were beautiful. The hope alarm is ringing hard. If I don't do something astronomically stupid, I could bring her back to me.

"Thank you," I whisper. Then, when she doesn't say anything, her eyes continually fixed on the bottom of the vase, I add, "I'm still sorry."

She shakes her head. "It's fine. Opened my eyes to our whole situation anyway. In traffic we're like two hours apart, our parents hate one another, we've got different goals. And even though you're apologizing, I saw it—you're ruthless when you need to be. Makes sense, for your job and all."

I touch her hand, the one near the vase, and she looks up. But there's no desire in her face, no hope on her part that this could work. Still, I have to try. "That's not a part of me I like."

She pulls her hand away slowly. "I had high hopes for us. This is crushing me, too. Anyway, that's it. Please, Nazeli, we're done."

And she's off with surprising speed, a "please don't follow me" walk.

I'm left with the flowers, their beauty and hopefulness mocking me. *Well, you'll be dead in a couple of days*, I think.

After we collect our check tomorrow, it'll be time to go home.

Then I feel my phone buzz. It's a text from Jamie that reads, We need to talk.

Chapter Twenty-Seven

Still in the hallway, still stinging from Vanya's goodbye, I speed-dial Jamie. Stress vines up and down my body as my phone rings and I wait for her to pick up. Did I forget something? Or send a weird email last night? No, in fact, I didn't send her anything. I suppose that could be the problem, but it's Saturday, so there's time before our Monday meeting.

She picks up. "Ellie, finally getting a hold of you."

Her words make it sound like someone has *died*. Shit, did those lunges finally get the better of Jack? I knew overexercising is bad for you.

"What's up?" I say, not bothering to hide the worry in my voice.

She sighs. "I'm at a breaking point with you here, Ellie. It's been a trying couple of days while you've been out of town."

Breaking point? This is worse than her usual frustration. The stripes in the carpet, so rigid before, appear to sway. "Oh, but—"

She interrupts me, her voice sharpened steel. "There's nothing more important than Operation Wolf, and while you assured me you'd be constantly available, I haven't found that to be true. I was hoping for some deliverables this morning, but I received nothing."

Every word of hers is worse and worse, pricking me with her bitterness and disapproval. Shit. I knew I should have sucked it up and worked last night. Jamie taking the night off didn't mean I could take the night off. Time to apologize. "I have—"

It's like she doesn't even hear me. "So I'm asking you." And here she pauses with an awful silence, and my stomach twists in anticipation of her question. "Do you really want this?"

Am I . . . am I really about to be fired this time? It feels like it. The striped carpet has edged into focus. I realize I've barely moved since Vanya left me, and it feels unfair that so much should happen in this stupid spot of a conference hall. There's no hope for Vanya and me, we didn't win Superstars, but I cannot, cannot lose this job.

I fix my voice into evenness. "You're right, I haven't been as available as I thought. A week like this will never happen again, I can promise you that. I'm all in, Jamie, seriously. I'm this close to finishing, and I'll deliver everything to you in a couple hours. There's nothing more important to me than this. Nothing."

As I say that, a lump rises in my throat. The words are only true because I don't have anything else.

There's a short pause where I hold my breath. Then Jamie speaks. "Okay. Send me those deliverables. Your words are there, but I need action."

"Of course. I'm on it."

She hangs up, and I'm left feeling anxious, like I need to go jump on the work now, but I can't escape this hollow feeling. A nagging sensation. But I push it away, because I have to hang on to my job, at least—it's the only thing I haven't failed. Yet.

Chapter Twenty-Eight

*A*fter a full evening of work and going back and forth with Jamie, I've nearly finished. Just waiting for her to okay a couple of new slides. I did it, but I'm not feeling triumphant. That'll be judged at the Monday meeting.

It's 9:00 a.m., and I'm at Cafe-a-Go-Go, like Benny requested. I've already checked out of the hotel, ruefully, having stared at the desk, the bed, the prints against the window, memories of a short time ago when everything was going perfectly.

Benny is there, sitting at a table drinking a venti from Starbucks, which is not the most polite thing to do at a rival coffee shop, but it's also what I've come to expect. Plus, if the café's drinks are anything like the food, he sort of has a point.

It's two minutes after nine, though I bet I've preceded Toros.

"Hey," I say, not sitting, and enjoying towering over Benny.

"Ah hey, great," he says. "Take a seat if you like. No need to worry, your frenemies already picked up their check."

My face twists into a frown, I can't help it. "Really."

"Super eager for that check. I swear the guy was here since eight."

I bet he doesn't know Toros's name, either.

Part of me was hoping for one last shot with Vanya, that I might see her this morning. Now, I'm not sure when I ever will see her again. As she so clearly reminded me, with traffic, we live almost two hours apart. Our Armenian social circles haven't overlapped since we were kids, and they aren't due to. So that moment by the flowers, the resigned look on her face, that was it. That was the last time I'd see her.

Benny reaches into his coat pocket. He hands me the check, and I try to ignore the warmth of the paper, which had been tucked close to his chest. "For your troubles," he says.

"Our troubles?"

"We put you through a lot. I know that. But you helped us out a ton with our new reality show proposal. We're putting together a pitch to some of the networks and streamers and needed some sample footage. You guys certainly provided. So anyway, this was the least we could do."

The sharp knives, the large garlic cloves, the small-sized chicken. They helped us win. They wanted us to fight over the check and pay us off in the end.

"I don't believe we agreed to that in the paperwork."

Benny nods serenely. "You did. It's all covered under the use of the footage. Don't worry, it's not like you'll be on the actual show. Unless you want to, of course. If it gets picked up, we'll extend an invitation."

Snakes, to use my dad's word. I hate being played like this, especially when it comes to paperwork. I should have been more meticulous. Still, as diligent as I am at my work, there's a reason I didn't go into law, fulfilling every Armenian parent's dream.

"How generous."

"I mean it. There's money to be made, fame, appearing on our show."

"Well, thanks, I don't think that's going to happen. I have a real job anyway."

"What do you mean? Your family business isn't your real job?"

"No. And in fact, I've been balancing it with this conference and competition all week. I work in tech, at a company that does performance review software. I'm—a marketing director."

I don't know why I lie, exactly, except that the director position seems in the bag now, and maybe I want to puff myself up around Benny. I'm someone, too, you know.

He purses his lips. "That's wild. I would have thought this was your jam for sure. Every time you talked about your family's food, you were so enthusiastic, you crushed it. Not only that, your guys' food was some of the best, if not the best. You would have won if not for—" He stops himself. "Well, never mind."

I'm not sure how to take all this in. We were the best, but didn't win. The compliment is nice and all, but something sinister is itching at the edges of his words. I wonder if it has anything to do with the way Benny looked at Audrey at the styling competition, like they knew each other. I decide to take the chance.

"Since you and Audrey's families go way back."

His face twists in alarm. "How'd you know about that?"

God, I was right. So, the insiders won after all. Even a cooking competition out in Chicago operates that way. Fantastic.

I shrug. "I work in tech. Fear us."

I smile inwardly, thinking how I did the complete opposite of running hard data; I just went off intuition.

"But that's not why," he says. "Their sauce, it's gonna be the new hot thing, they've got their finger on the pulse. I mean, you've seen their jars."

It's true. Their branding is fresh. I groan, thinking about our stuffy logo.

Benny continues, "Anyway, you should really think about switching. Join your parents' company."

Why, in this late hour, does he continue to compliment me? He clearly doesn't want or need anything more from me, so I have to suppose he means it. And it is tempting. These past few days, anything having to do with the competition or my parents' brand, I wanted to do first. I loved diving in. And everything having to do with my actual job felt like a chore. But still. I've worked so hard to get to where I am at Abilify. I can't just throw that away.

"Right" is all I say.

He stands to leave. "Well, do what you want. I've gotta head out."

"Me too." I turn and walk away first. Not wishing him luck. Not saying thank you.

I WHEEL MY suitcase up to my parents' room and remember the Simonians are just a few doors down. When I step off the elevator, my heart hitches, hoping I'll get to see Vanya. The hallway is bare, though.

In my parents' room, I offer them the check.

"At least we get something out of this whole business," my father says, folding it neatly into his Bible-sized wallet. His tone is regretful, like we never should have entered it to begin with, and I'm not sure what I can do to convince him we got so close. If I shared what Benny told me, he'd dismiss it as Benny sucking up to a younger woman.

"We can get new oven and refrigerator, too," my mom replies, a lot less cheerful about this prospect than I'd imagine she'd be. Normally she'd be listing off the finest brand names, googling the specifics, and bragging to her friends, in that order.

The weekend wasn't a loss for my parents—they did have that Ned Richardson meeting, the one I missed. And he told them he'd follow up.

"What about Ned Richardson? Did you hear from him yet?" Bab stands and packs his toiletry bag into his suitcase.

"We have not heard," Mom says.

"Oh." I can't think of anything else to say. The glow of hope that at least my parents had secured a follow-up meeting is snuffed out.

I help them pack and tidy up the room mostly in silence. We're on the same flight home, a huge relief to my mom and reassurance that I'm not abandoning the family.

Once we're nearly finished, I prop open the door, hoping I might catch some bit of Vanya and her family. And oh my God—what if we're on the same flight? What if Vanya and I are accidentally seated next to each other? I couldn't get a seat next to my parents, so what if, out of the one hundred or so seats on the plane, Vanya is seated next to me? Fate will bring us together, I can feel it. It's going to happen.

And part one of that fate is happening now. Toros and Nora shuffle out of the room with their knockoff Louis Vuitton luggage, and then there's Vanya, with her stuffed-to-the-brim olive weekender bag slung over her shoulder. She doesn't look so good, though. Haggard, hunched, and I can't tell if it's the weight of the bag or her general posture. God, how do *I* look? Why didn't I put in more effort this morning?

She sees me and gives the tiniest, most heartbreaking sigh.

"Hi, Vanya," I say, my breath hitching. "Parev, Nora, Toros. Heading to the airport?"

"Ayo, Nazeli jan," Nora replies with a kind smile.

I turn to my parents. "Maybe we should all get a van together? Save some money?"

It'll be hard for my parents to resist such an offer; there's no rip-off like the cab to the airport, and they would be delighted to share the cost, usually, with anyone but their mortal enemies. But something has changed between them. My parents, upon seeing the Simonians, no longer clench their jaws and scrunch their shoulders. They seem fairly relaxed. Maybe resigned.

"Maybe," my mother says, her tone genuinely unsure.

"What time is your flight?" I ask them.

"It is at noontime," Nora replies. I appreciate her volunteering information like this, but I keep hoping Vanya will respond. She's become suddenly fascinated by a cuticle on her pinkie.

Noon. That's when our flight is, too. I knew it; we're on the same flight, and this is just the beginning. Luck is on our side, and it's going to steer Vanya and me together, because we belong together.

"You guys flying into San Jose, too?" Toros asks, confused.

"No," my father responds. "Es Eff Oh," he intones, as if needing to spell it out slowly.

"We flying out of, uh, what the airport called. Halfway?" Nora asks Toros.

"Halfway . . ." he ponders.

"Midway," Vanya says, with a hard period at the end of her sentence. She's looked up, but only to her parents, not to us, not to me.

With that one word, the hope of our romantic airplane reconciliation is obliterated. We're flying out of O'Hare, one of the largest airports in the country, so I assumed of course they would, too. They aren't, though, so what does it matter what I thought moments ago.

Then it strikes me. This is my last moment to say something to Vanya. Not on some fanciful plane ride—now.

"Vanya, can I talk to you—"

But the second I say her name, she speaks up. "Forgot something in the room," she says, and dashes toward the door with her key card out. I step toward her, but then she's inside, and I am outside, with both sets of our parents staring at me. Even Toros has pity in his eyes.

I cough. "Well, it can wait. We better head out." No one's buying my nonchalance, but I had to say something.

I lead the charge, saying a polite goodbye to Toros and Nora, telling them it was nice to meet them, not stopping for their reactions.

Bab, who is trailing me with his squeaky ten-year-old luggage, stops. "Nora, it was nice to see you, as it always is. And . . ." He draws himself up. "Toros, it was pleasure being in competition with such worthy adversary."

Toros steps forward, and I can't read his face, but he sticks out his hand to my dad. "You not such a bad guy after all, Hagop. Maybe you come over some time for kef night."

"Maybe I do," Bab says. Then he pauses and adds, "If you're still interested in joining church board, perhaps I put in a good word?"

Toros smiles a genuine, megawatt smile and extends his hand again. They both heartily shake.

Mom steps up. "Why the men have all the fun? Nora, perhaps I see you at the Great Mall Neiman Marcus outlet some time. I be there next Sunday, at one p.m. Would be nice to get more opinion."

Nora has literal tears in her eyes. "I absolutely love Neiman Marcus outlet. Thank you, Hera jan."

And she reaches forward and gives my mom a quick hug, which Mom receives, her eyes wide at first, and then melting into kindness.

I really wish they had figured all this out fifteen years ago. They could have bolstered each other's businesses, given help and advice in each of their domains. Hagop's Fine Armenian Foods and the Green Falafel would have been better for it.

And maybe Vanya and I would have met sooner, not within the context of our parents hating each other, but being allies, and not with the backdrop of a stressful competition and too many Chicago Fizzes.

But that didn't happen. Instead, I'm first to reach the elevator and step inside when the doors open.

Chapter Twenty-Nine

On Monday, my eyes are fixed on the presentation screen in the Platypus room as I deliver my conclusion slide. Everything was done, right in the nick of time, with Jamie complaining that I wasn't available during takeoff and landing, but damn it, it was done.

"Any questions that haven't been covered so far?" I ask the business development VP of Zarek's, staring into his teleconference box with a confident smile.

"Honestly, we don't normally do this—"

I hold my breath. This is the conclusion of Operation Wolf, and the entire key team at Abilify presented their slides, ending with mine. His voice is so tough to read; there's reservation and hesitancy in it, and I'm so sure we're about to lose it all. The many hours of work put in the last few months, not to mention the last few days, juggling PakCon and Jamie's constant directives. For nothing. I only wish I could have been more present in Chicago. Maybe I could have had even more time with

Vanya, when she still liked me. When she was still talking to me. I try not to let my face fall.

"But I can tell you that we're ready to sign. I'm the key decision-maker here, and I'm all in. Let's seal this. We'll get legal to review the terms you sent over."

Holy—oh my God. We did it, we actually did it. This partnership is going to take Abilify's name to a whole new level. My shares, too. Three years vested. Only one more to reap them all in.

The room erupts in the quietest show of triumph I've ever seen. Jack flies out of his chair and begins doing celebratory burpees off-screen, Reid turns his hand into a fist and gives a small pump, and Jamie's face bursts into red relief. Kyle (whom I have not spoken to since I left his "I miss you" text hanging, and haven't seen until we walked into this room an hour ago) turns his mouth into an O, before he clamps his hand over it. Several people give tiny silent claps. We are still on video, after all.

Reid and Jack wrap up the rest of the call with the Zarek's people, while I stop sharing my screen and watch Slack blow up with congratulatory messages in our #operation_wolf channel. Once we hang up with Zarek's, some of the cheers turn audible, and Jack does a high five lap around the room.

Among the ovations, Jamie leans toward me and asks if I can meet her downstairs in ten. She seems pleased.

Everyone slowly filters out, except Kyle, who has been taking his sweet time putting his things together. I hang back, too.

Once the door shuts, he steps over to my side and sinks into the chair beside me.

"Terrific work today," he says, smiling wide. I rarely see him smile like that.

"Thank you," I say. "Kyle, we need to talk about—"

"I know." He shakes his head. "I was a dick. I was wrong. Seeing you today, you're so . . . strong. Impressive." Then, under the table, he takes my hand in his. His feels hard, bony.

I pull mine away.

"That's nice of you to say, but this isn't what I want. You were squirreling me away for months for your Friday night booty calls and—"

He shakes his head with fury. "I can change. I'm nervous about the work thing, you know, what people would think of us together."

I squint at him. "What *would* people think of us together?"

"I'm more senior than you—"

"But on a completely different team—we're lateral. Plus, you're probably not going to be more senior than me for long."

He pauses briefly with another smile, and he seems genuinely happy that I'm going to be getting a promotion. That's what it took for him to want to be with me? He says, "It doesn't matter now. Give me some time, and I'll be ready."

I stand and shut my laptop with quiet intent. "You're not listening to me. I don't want this. I don't want you." I gather my items in my arms and stride toward the exit. "Thanks, though, I did kick ass today."

And I allow the door to shut behind me.

* * *

I'M BACK IN Dingo with Jamie, which is the spot we had our last tête-à-tête. She has her pink notebook and pen set on the table, but they're closed. The smile hasn't left her face.

"We nailed it. This is going to be a huge win for our team. And . . ." She looks at me importantly. "I have some good news for you."

"Oh yeah?" I say, and I cannot believe how I can't bring myself to feel more excited about Jamie's uncharacteristically fantastic mood and the delivery of good news.

"I'd like to offer you the director of product marketing position in two more quarterly cycles. Upon review by the CMO, of course, but I'll be going to bat for you."

This is what I wanted. Sort of. She's not offering it to me this quarter, and possibly not even the next if the CMO nixes it. Normally, I'd be jumping up and down at this concession, because it's been said out loud now: Director most likely will be mine.

But here in the Dingo room, glass all around us, efficient yet chic gray carpet at my feet, a treasure trove of Mac products out in the main floor with my coworkers buzzing around, I realize, I don't want to be here. Even if she had offered me the director position right now. I mean, if she had done that, I probably should have taken it for a while, enjoyed the bump in salary, and then quit, but that's not the case.

"Thanks, Jamie."

Before I can elaborate, Jamie pipes up. "Good for you, I see you took our talk about emotions to heart. It's okay to show some positive emotions, but reining them in like you are right now, very admirable. Very Reid."

I want to do something dramatic in response, like give my two weeks' notice—God, how sweet that would be—but I can't do that to my team. I need to make sure they're prepared for my departure. Plus, they need one last review cycle with glowing appraisals and setups for promotions. Besides, what's itching at me, gnawing at my mind—the new yet very familiar thing I'm dying to do next—I need to check if it's even possible.

After Jamie offers me some details on what's to come, Operation Wolf–wise, I head into the oversized fridge / phone booth. I have two calls to make.

One is to my college friend Anna, who has published two children's books and is a finalist for a picture book award.

The second is to my parents. I'm coming home for dinner tomorrow night, but first, I need to finish what I started.

Chapter Thirty

Three Months Later

"*C*hecking in about the delivery date of the new labels. USPS seems to have it under 'pending,' but I remember you said you shipped them last Friday."

The vendor promised the new labels by today, and I'm so nervous that this first big project under my belt isn't going to come together.

"Oh no, that's strange. We did ship 'em off last Friday. Let me see if there's any other information I can see on my end. Can you hold?"

I tell my vendor contact that'd be fine, and get switched to the elevator music du jour, a sensuous, New Agey ballad.

Then there's a loud one-two knock at the door.

"Just a second," I yell, making my way from the back office, through the kitchens, to the front door. I open it to the familiar sight of the industrial side of San Francisco—delivery trucks, car mechanics, power lines. But no one is there.

Then I look at my feet, and there's a large box, shipped by USPS. Oh my God, this is it. With the phone squeezed under my ear, I heft the box onto a counter. I put the phone on speaker so I can let the rep know that we received the package whenever she comes back on, so there's hold music blasting through the kitchen.

"Mom, Bab, come look," I say.

Mom is squatting by the oven, and Bab is shelving a row of filo dough into the fridge.

"One moment, I need to check the sarmas," Mom says, pulling a giant pot out of the oven in her mittened hands.

I grab a knife and strip open the box, remove the giant paper receipt, and there, beneath it, is the most beautiful sight. I pull out the first sticker, the one for sarmas, and set it on the counter. Bab sidles up to me, followed by Mom.

The label reads HERA'S KITCHEN in a modern font. Our new logo, ready to be slapped on all our new containers. The lavash sleeves are inside, too, and I pull one out and marvel at how updated everything appears. So stylish and fresh, but with a nod to the past with traditional Armenian symbolism around the letters.

Before I told my parents I wanted to quit Abilify to join them full-time, I spent all night finishing and perfecting my slides for Ned Richardson, then shot him an email with a PDF teaser of my proposition. The preview must have done the job, because he agreed to a meeting where I pitched our brand and why we needed to be in his grocery stores, and he agreed to think on things further.

When my parents heard what I had done with Ned, and then when I told them I wanted to join the family business, they were a lot more receptive to updating the logo. And strangely, it was Bab's idea to name it Hera's Kitchen. "It been my name long enough. Hera's cooking is soul of the food, it is now her time to shine."

Mom shifts her weight next to me, and I see her head down-turned, her eyes red and watering. Oh God, Mom's crying always sets me off, and I feel the hot tears forming.

"Is very nice. Thank you, Hagop. Thank you, Nazeli."

I give her a hug, and I feel thankful. I missed food; I missed creating and working with my hands. I'm thankful for my time at Abilify, and mostly thankful that I can apply what I learned to bring Armenian food to the masses, instead of . . . performance review software.

I'm thankful and happy about everything, most of the time. Except when thoughts of Vanya flit into my mind, which they do often. Very often. Bab did go to Toros's kef night and spent the next day with a hangover swearing that being a fun guy simply isn't for him, and Mom did meet up with Nora and showed off the Badgley Mischka dress she snagged at 90 percent off. But neither mentioned Vanya. I asked and they said she didn't come up.

It doesn't seem like they're going to be hanging out with the Simonians all the time—after all, we do live far away—but it was such a promising start that I thought Vanya might follow suit, with everyone else feeling that spirit of forgiveness.

When I sent my writing friend Vanya's way, I did finally hear from her. A text that read, Thank you for introducing me to Anna. That was really kind of you.

But she didn't add any questions or follow-up. I told her no problem, I was happy to do it, and asked her how she was. And she's ghosted me ever since. I try to maintain some dignity and haven't texted her after that. Though I desperately wanted to when I saw a new bar in town was serving frosés. I wanted to tell her I quit my job, that I'm working with my parents, and I'm curious to see how their company is doing, how she is doing. But I can't.

Back in the kitchen, my parents and I decide that after we finish up, we'll go out to a celebratory dinner. With the True Foods Grocer contract signed, things are going better than ever for Hagop's—I mean, Hera's Kitchen. We might even be able to expand to a larger, more modern kitchen if things continue this way. But for now, a fancy dinner sounds pretty nice.

Chapter Thirty-One

The following day, I'm back in the office preparing for our new logo launch—of course I have a full launch plan. Hera's Kitchen now exists on social media, and the website is no longer hosted on GeoCities (just kidding, but they were using a netscape.net email). I've been through two rebrandings at Abilify and got to use my experience for our family business. Honestly, it's pretty exciting to own every part of it and know that my parents trust me now. And it couldn't have happened without PakCon Superstars. My heart sinks slightly at the thought of the conference.

There's a knock at the door, short and confident, and I wonder if it's USPS again. I thought we got enough labels, but maybe Mom bought more cross statues from Armenia to match the three we already have in this small office.

I open the door. It's—it's Vanya. I don't—how does she know to come here? Is she here for me? Is she looking for my parents?

"Hello is customary," she says, the tiniest smile forming.

"Hi—hello, Vanya."

"Hi, Nazeli."

She looks resplendent in a short navy blue dress with a daisy print, perfect for the warm weather we always have in September. And contributing to the effect is that she seems . . . happy. A complete change from the last time I saw her in the hotel hallway in Chicago.

"Are you here to see, uh, my parents?"

She cocks her head in mock confusion, and the tiny smile is growing. "Why would I be here to see them?"

"Because we haven't talked in months—and how did you know I was here anyway?"

She nods. "Both valid. Want to take a walk? I saw a mini–food truck park that way. I could use caffeine in some form."

Talk, say something. Words are entirely failing me; it's been so long and Vanya is here and she's not pissed at me? She wants to get a coffee with me?

"My bag," I start. "Uh, let me get my bag."

She chuckles.

I stride past the kitchen, hoping to avoid questions from my parents.

"Nazeli?" Mom asks, a strong nosiness to her tone. "Who that you're talking to?"

Her mom-tuition never fails.

I grab my bag. "Explain later, I'll be back soon. Going on a short walk."

"It dangerous out there. Pay extra attention when crossing streets, people drive like crazy here."

I assure her I will, and join Vanya outside.

The door shuts behind us, and we begin to walk. Everything outside has taken on a hazy quality, and it's not the smog. I want to keep it all blurry because I feel hope rearing its optimistic head and I want to shut that up. If everything stays muddied, it won't hurt as much if I'm let down.

"So," I say. "What's new?"

"A lot, actually."

"Oh yeah? Like what?"

Like not hating me anymore, perhaps?

"After you put me in touch with Anna, I was still . . . bristled by our last interactions, so I didn't properly thank you. But man, chatting with her completely changed things for me."

"Really?"

"I found community—did you know there's this whole massive writers' community on Twitter?"

"I didn't, but that doesn't surprise me; it is the text platform, and writers like that kind of thing, I hear."

Glad that got a smirk out of her.

"I've met so many people, heard about picture book writing contests, have other writers looking over my work, and I'm looking over theirs, too. It feels like the mist has been lifted over so many of my problems. Anyway, I love it, and I really owe Anna a lot. You too."

"Oh . . ."

We reach the food trucks. This is not the upscale food truck scene that most techies flock to—these are simply adorned (if at all) and greasier, and there's nothing fusion about them. One of their mottoes is "Tastes better than it looks!"

This whole part of San Francisco, in fact, is not for the techie crowd. The closest it gets is that the rideshare companies stick their mechanics services out here, but the office workers never have to step beyond their comfort zone. It's on the outskirts, a seemingly forgotten area unless you visit during the week and see how lively it is. There's street traffic from all the construction, discount furniture, mechanics, recycling centers, etc. All the things I thought I was—and the thought is shameful— better than. What I was trying to escape.

But I had my slice of tech, I learned what I needed to learn, and felt how useless it was to work yourself to the bone for the end goal of pushing employee-policing products into the world. And for the founders' and board's ultimate gain.

My quitting was completely incomprehensible to Jamie. She laughed at first. Just like that VC who laughed at Bab at the swim team social all those years ago. Must be a joke, very funny, Ellie. I told her I was serious, that my time in Chicago helped me realize a new life direction for myself. Again, she didn't buy it, and asked if one of the big five was courting me with a ridiculous compensation package. That Abilify couldn't match it dollarwise, of course, but they'd try their best and give me more stock. It was thrilling to turn that down, to tell her nope, I was going to go work for Hagop's Fine Armenian Foods (we hadn't decided on the name change yet). I thanked her for all she taught me, and then said, "And by the way, I absolutely despise the gym and I like how I look. But you can go ahead and have fun there."

Then I left.

Now, I steer Vanya toward a coffee and doughnuts truck that's pretty good. She orders a coffee with room for milk and sugar, and I order a maple doughnut. It's ten, so it's not busy with the lunch rush yet, and there are plenty of seats open. We sit at the white plastic table and chairs.

Vanya sips her coffee. "We shut down the Green Falafel."

I set my doughnut on the table. "What? Oh no, Vanya, I'm so sorry."

She shrugs. "No, it's okay, it's really okay."

I read her face; it's none of the pain I saw those last days in Chicago. "If you say so. I mean, your parents, too? They're all right?"

"Definitely. They've focused all their energy on our new venture. Through Dad's network, he heard about this cheap commercial property in Foster City, and you'll never guess what they're going to open now. Or maybe you will."

Remembering our conversation by the lake, I ask tentatively, "Is it . . . pizza?"

"So smart."

I blush unabashedly at the compliment.

She continues, "Yep. We're opening up a pizza parlor with Mediterranean flair, and hookahs and whatnot on the weekends." As she speaks, her face lights up vividly. "There's an awesome outdoor space for the hookahs and some reasonably volumed music."

It warms me, seeing her happy like this, seeing her dream being realized. "All those Friday night pizza experiments paid off."

She stares at me. "You remember it was Friday nights?"

I pick up my doughnut again. "I feel like I remember every last detail from Chicago."

Then I take a large bite, hoping to not have to elaborate.

Vanya's not smiling anymore. "Benny told Dad about their plans for the reality show. I guess they—I guess he set you up, too, with that video. That's what you were trying to tell me."

My mouth is still full, so I give the tiniest shrug.

She continues, "I was still so hurt by what you said, because it was true. I knew we'd have to shut down when we came back here, and it was so painful, and it was tied to you, too. Hearing it from someone I started to care so much about—"

Hope is flaring up, but I tamp it back down. She's telling me that she *cared* about me, past tense. I take another bite out of caution.

"I guess I turned you into a villain, which was completely unfair. I see that now. And then I was too embarrassed to reach out—it was just easier to think of you as a bad person I shouldn't have contact with. But you connected me with Anna, and then Mom told me you joined your parents' business."

"Your mom knew?"

"Well, yeah. Your mom's consulting on our recipes. She agreed to, anyway. I don't think they've met up yet."

What? My mom working *with* the Simonians?

Her face falls when she sees my reaction. "They didn't tell you?"

"They failed to mention it."

She takes a quick sip of her coffee as if hiding behind the cup. "Shoot. Sorry to ruin the surprise."

I give a small smile. "It's okay, now I have something to yell at my parents about for once." I make an expression of mock anguish. "You didn't care to tell your only daughter?"

Vanya nods. "We learn from the best."

I set down my half-eaten doughnut. "Can I ask why you came here?"

She takes a deep inhale. "I wanted to say I'm sorry and that if you were willing, I'd . . . like to try again?"

Hope is blossoming, unfurling fast and kaleidoscopically bright. "Yes, of course. There's nothing I want more. You are—" I hesitate, praying it's not too much to say. "You're the one thing that's been missing. Everything's been going so well, except I miss you."

She reaches over and clutches my hand, her soft fingers in mine. "I miss you, too."

Then, she says, "Your fingers are sticky."

I pull my hand away, wiping it furiously on a napkin. "Can't help but humiliate myself."

"Not at all, never said I didn't like it."

I smile at her, and can't believe this is happening. Vanya, here, wanting a fresh start.

We pause a moment, taking each other in. Then she gets this new look on her face, a little bit of excitement, and something else I can't quite read. "I mentioned Benny earlier—I'm guessing you haven't seen the latest D-list celebrity gossip today?"

I shake my head. "I haven't been online much today. Benny's in the news?"

Vanya smirks, that trademark side smile of hers I adore. Then I realize the expression she has: schadenfreude. "Oh yeah, he is. The Food and Beverage Packagers of America Association—you know, the one that puts on PakCon and has the Super Bowl ad—they found out he was using PakCon Superstars as a way to get his new reality show going, so they investigated the Superstars challenges. They interviewed us, actually. I'm guessing they interviewed you, too?"

I'm shocked. Benny's behavior actually being looked into? The Simonians giving their story? "No," I say. "They didn't. Guess they were doing a quick job?"

Vanya confirms, "It wasn't very in-depth or formal, just a phone call, so maybe they got what they needed."

"That makes sense." I quiet so she can continue. I'm dying to know where this goes.

Vanya is still energized. "So the article said that the association found so much cheating and general unethical behavior that they dropped the winner—that pasta sauce, whatever it was called—and not only fired Benny but are suing him, too. They pulled their Super Bowl ad and are blaming Benny for it. I don't want to be too gleeful about someone getting into legal trouble, but . . ."

"He kind of deserves it," I finish. "It's comforting to know that he didn't get away with using us—all of us, not just your and my families—nonstop for three days."

"Exactly," Vanya punctuates. "Sometimes there are consequences. When I read the article this morning, well, I had already made plans in my head to visit you, but that just made me want to come here all the more. Like a sign. 'Don't chicken out, Vanya, get in that car and go.'"

I scoot closer to her, and our knees are touching. "I'm glad you did. Though it must have taken you forever. At least there's no traffic at this hour."

"That's the only part I didn't mention yet."

"What?"

"My parents sold our house, moved to Foster City by the restaurant. And I actually got a place of my own. A tiny studio right next to downtown San Mateo."

Why am I tearing up at this? This makes such a huge difference—we are so much closer to each other, and I am so proud of her for getting her own place. It's tough, breaking away from your Armenian family, but it seemed like she really wanted to.

"That's such awesome news. I'm so happy for you."

She leans into me, and I love feeling the press of her body. She whispers, "I'm happy for us."

I feel radiant, giddiness pulsing off me. This is it, it's truly happening. Another chance.

"Me too."

AT THE DOOR to our kitchen, after making plans to see each other Friday night, Vanya steps close. That mischievous smile is back.

I pull my head toward hers, like the time on the Chicago

rooftop, then lean in and kiss her. I hold the back of her neck, feeling her curls between my fingers, and she kisses me back with such insistency. I remind myself this is just the beginning.

After, she begins to say goodbye, but I ask if she wants to come in and see the premises.

"Are you sure?"

I nod. "I am so sure."

No more hiding. This time, I'm doing everything right.

I push open the door, and Mom and Bab are hard at work (making me feel only slightly guilty for my extremely pleasurable break and the cloud I'm walking in on). Bab spots us first and pushes his glasses down for a better look.

"Oh, welcome."

Mom spins around. "Nazeli, eench—" she begins to ask a forever unformed question before spotting Vanya. "Parev, Vanya jan."

"Parev, Tantig Hera, Keri Hagop."

So polite, using *auntie* and *uncle* to address them. My heart contracts with joy because my parents don't seem appalled by this.

"Mom," I say. "I heard the Simonians are opening a new restaurant in Foster City. Can you believe it?"

Mom laughs uneasily. "Oh yes, I think I hear of this."

I smile at her. "Mm-hmm."

Bab says, "Tell Toros I thank him for the kef night invitation, but my liver bids me not go. I will, however, be happy to join you for grand opening of your restaurant, Vanya jan."

"Merci, Baron Hagop, I'll be sure to tell him."

I stand a little straighter. "Vanya and I are going to hang out Friday night. Just wanted to let you know."

Bab waves his hand like he doesn't actually need to know. Mom says, "Lav, janig. Amen pani mech parik muh ga."

That's when my eyes start to water. Vanya must see it, because she takes and squeezes my hand. *In everything there is a blessing.* It might not be much, but it's a start.

"Very true, Mom," I say.

Vanya nods at my parents, and I walk her out.

Outside, I say, "Not a bad start, huh?"

"You kidding me? For our parents, that's practically an invitation to the altar."

I whip out my phone. "I'll call my mom's cousin's daughter-in-law, the wedding planner, and let her know."

"Fantastic, but I insist on peonies, okay?"

I nod. "June wedding it is, not cliché at all."

"Pride month themed? With rainbow cupcakes, obviously."

I laugh and gather her in my arms. She's smiling broadly, maybe the happiest I have ever seen her.

She says, "Can it be possible, to have everything you wanted? I feel like I don't deserve it. Like the other shoe has to drop."

"No," I say, and kiss her on the cheek. "It is possible. You, me—*we* deserve good things. Today, we created our own."

She kisses me then, and I know we will continue forging our paths to happiness, together.

Acknowledgments

A big thank-you to my agent, Katelyn Detweiler, for your enthusiasm and believing in this story in my moments of uncertainty. I am so glad to have you steering this ship, and so grateful for your encouragement and the many confidence boosts!

Sam Farkas, thank you so much for your amazing subrights work. Thank you to Denise Page and Sophia Seidner, and the whole team at Jill Grinberg. What a pleasure to work with you!

The team at Berkley, you are all rock stars! Thank you so much to Angela Kim and Cindy Hwang, who said yes to this book, much to my surprise, and then gave such excellent direction in shepherding the story toward its ultimate direction. Thank you for all you do behind the scenes, too. It's so appreciated.

Thank you so much to Kaila Mundell-Hill for your publicity prowess. Thank you to Elisha Katz, marketing maven, for all you do to share my books with the world!

Thank you also to Megha Jain, Christine Legon, Catherine Degenaro, Sammy Rice, Heather Haase, Emma Tamayo, and Angelina Krahn for your eagle-eyed attention to *Lavash*!

As for the cover team: Sarah Madden and Katie Anderson, thank you for your lush, gorgeous illustrations and cover design. And to Diahann Sturge-Campbell for the beautiful interior, thank you.

Thank you so much to Gillian Green and Chloe Davis for making my UK dreams come true. I've been so grateful for your great efforts in getting my books seen, and I'm so glad we get to work together. I am tickled every time I see my book in a European bookstore. Thank you for that!

My earliest draft readers, Elizabeth Reed and Natalie Budeša, a huge thank-you to you. Without you I could never have written *Lavash* on time and with as much happiness as I did. You kept me on track, gave such useful, fun feedback, and helped make my book better. Many, many thanks, my dear friends!

To Kate Minassian, thank you for your early read and feedback on *Lavash*. You had excellent insights that I took to heart. Also, thank you for pointing out no one would be wearing velvet in Chicago in June. ;)

Thank you to Tiara Blue for your generous championship of my writing. You've made my day, time after time, and I am thankful for you, my friend.

To Robert Nazar Arjoyan for being there through the editing process and providing much-needed motivation. Thank you for always steering me back to the words.

Elyse Moretti Forbes, first, thank you for all the early Chicago ideas for *Lavash*. You really helped the events in this book take form. My dear friend, thank you for the anytime, anywhere chat sessions, and your empathy, encouragement, and always being here for me. <3

Thank you so much to Jess Sutanto for being around through my gripes and always finding the most positive (and most hilarious) spin on things. You're the best!

A hundred thank-yous would not be enough to the Berkletes. This group of Berkley writers is an absolute gem. Such kind, helpful, hilarious folks all in one place. Thank you for always being there.

Thank you to my fellow writer friends Courtney Kae, Jenny L. Howe, Dahlia Adler, Elle Gonzalez Rose, Lisa Lin, Brent Love, and Astrid Kamalyan for your kindness, empathy, and love. Stars, all of you!

Thank you to all the readers and reviewers who took the time to shout about *Sorry, Bro*, and most especially Samantha Nicole, Jaqueline, Jordi B, and Decklededgess, who have made me absolutely squeal with glee at your words.

Thank you to the dedicated booksellers who have done so much for *Sorry, Bro* and have supported my authorship. Special shout-outs to Abril Bookstore, Book Passage, Christopher's Books (Hi, Jackson and Tee!), Books Inc., East Bay Booksellers, and BookShop West Portal for all you do.

Thank you to the organizations that have brought this story to their audiences, particularly Litquake, IALA, and GALAS. I am so grateful for you.

Marina T., it's been an honor having you by my side. I'm amazed by all you do for the queer Armenian community and wanted to thank you for supporting my writing so boldly.

Mari Manoogian, you've been so generous with your promotion of *Sorry, Bro*. I am so thankful for your championship of it and of Armenian causes!

JP Der Boghossian, a class act, thank you for all you've done for *Sorry, Bro* and for your work with the Queer Armenian Library.

Thank you so much to Vivian Manning-Schaffel, Lara Vanian-Green, Amy Kazandjian, and Chris Bohjalian for your generosity and kindness in promoting my work. I wanted to let you know how appreciative I am of you Armenian superstars!

For everyone who read *Lavash at First Sight* early, and posted early reviews: a thousand thank-yous would not suffice. You are so appreciated.

My family, thank you for all your love and support, and for always checking in about the book. Your excitement and pride mean the world to me.

Thank you to Yuri for your kindness about my writing and for all you do for our family. We adore you and appreciate you.

To Tamara, thank you for reading my draft and as always, for your astute eye with editing. I'm so glad you laughed at the places you did. Once again, you're the person I think of when I think about the audience for my writing. Thank you for being the best sister ever.

To Ryan, thank you for our year in Chicago, which fueled all the setting love for this book. Thank you for giving me the space and the ability to write. Without you, it could never happen, and I am so appreciative of you.

Thank you, D, for turning me into a better writer by your

mere presence, and all the moments of unfettered joy. Thank you, V, for keeping me company in my stomach while I wrote, and giving me the very clear deadline that I wrote toward. Seeing you two together makes my days brighter.

Finally, thank you to anyone who picked up and read *Sorry, Bro* or *Lavash at First Sight* and took the time to share your enjoyment of the book. It still feels like a dream that my books sharing Armenian culture are available to anyone wandering a bookstore, and every time I see your photos, posts, and DMs, it comes true all over again. Thank you so much.

Author photo by Clouds Inside Photography

Taleen Voskuni is an Armenian-American writer who grew up in the Bay Area diaspora. She graduated from UC Berkeley with a BA in English and currently lives in San Francisco, working in tech. Her first novel, *Sorry, Bro*, received starred reviews from *Kirkus Reviews* and *Booklist*, was named an Amazon Editors' Pick, and was favorably reviewed in the *New York Times*. *Lavash at First Sight* is her second published novel. Other than a newfound obsession with writing rom-coms, she spends her free time cultivating her kids, her garden, and her dark chocolate addiction.

VISIT TALEEN VOSKUNI ONLINE

TaleenVoskuni.com

🐦 TaleenVoskuni

📷 TaleenAuthor

Ready to find
your next great read?

Let us help.

Visit prh.com/nextread

Penguin
Random
House